Accidental Babies

By

Michael Wojciechowski

PART I – SEVENTEEN YEARS EARLIER

CHAPTER 1

The soft hum of the elevator's ascent was the only sound that penetrated the sealed cage. Lexi took her compact from her purse and checked her reflection. Normally, she wouldn't feel nervous. She'd done hundreds of bachelor parties, and like any job, it now had its own routine and commonality. She no longer experienced anxiety-stricken bouts of trepidation or apprehension. Taking her clothes off for the wonderment of inebriated men had become as second nature to her as breathing. But tonight was different. It was different because Nichole was with her.

Lexi pocketed her compact and studied her friend. Nichole chewed at her fingernails, tearing them free with her teeth and then spitting the fragments onto the elevator floor. The overcoat Lexi loaned Nichole dwarfed her, like a blanket thrown haphazardly over a work of art, a nearly naked work of art. She selected her own ensemble from the plethora of barely-there outfits Lexi had acquired in the two years since she had started stripping. The selection process made Nichole giddy—clothes did that to Nichole. She tried on a dozen lingerie varieties before finally settling on a black lace number outfitted with a garter belt and bra that accentuated her relatively small breasts. Her excitement was contagious and appeared to be genuine and that was why Lexi agreed to let her come. Her excitement dissipated the closer the elevator brought them to the hotel's suite, which housed the reality of the situation they were about to enter. Lexi now regretted letting Nichole come along.

*****

It all started with a forgotten flash drive. After arriving at work and searching unsuccessfully for several minutes through her desk, workbag, and car, Nichole suddenly remembered she'd left it plugged into her desktop at home. She needed it today. Of all the days she needed it, today was the most important. It had updated charts, graphs and data for the fiscal year. Numbers in the red and more in the black, with projected earnings and expenses analyzed to warrant larger returns. She told her boss yesterday she would have the data on his desk no later than eleven o'clock today. It was a quarter after nine. If she hurried, she could make it back in time.

She didn't recognize the car parked in the driveway. It couldn't be Leroy's because he didn't own a car. It could be a friend's, but Leroy didn't have many friends. Sure, he *knew* a lot of people, but they wouldn't consider him a friend. No one really liked Leroy. Nichole didn't even really like him, she just put up with him because she was used to him.

It wasn't always like it was. Leroy once was more than an out-of-work failed poker prodigy. He used to work construction. He started the day after he graduated high school making $12 an hour. By the end of the year, he was making $15, by the end of the next, he was making $20. Most days he logged overtime. When he and his brother got their own apartment just outside of Las Vegas, Leroy was twenty-years-old. His living costs were minimal, he had no debt, and he claimed close to fifteen thousand in the bank. For his twenty-first birthday, he and some friends found a fifty-dollar buy-in poker game in the old part of Vegas. He called, checked, bluffed and remained stoically optimistic throughout. He left twelve hours later with two thousand more than when he started. He was hooked.

He almost worked hard enough to sustain his gambling habit. Early on, when he primarily played with friends and other known acquaintances, he was modestly successful. He never broke the bank, but he never lost his shirt either. A six-hour poker night with friends usually netted him a couple hundred dollars. Sometimes more, rarely less. His hubris took him to more exotic locations, calling on weak hands and bluffing on weaker ones. The pots got bigger and his losses became more frequent. He burned through his savings and became a pawnshop regular, hocking his valuables while negotiating the re-sale value of outdated video games and counterfeit jewelry.

When he started owing too many people too much money, some of those people came to his apartment with baseball bats. Leroy wasn't home, but his brother was. He took the physical beating, and then Leroy took the verbal one upon his return. His brother moved out amidst promises never to speak to Leroy again unless he got some help. Leroy didn't seek help because he didn't feel he had a problem—at least not a gambling one.

Show me a loser and I'll show you why he thinks he isn't.

His brother's absence, however, did present the problem of a rent bill he couldn't pay on his own. That's when he asked Nichole to move in to help supplement his income. She was young enough to think the suggestion was just a prerequisite to a marriage proposal that would soon follow. Did she want to marry him? Why not? It's what people did, even if more than half failed at it. Nichole and Leroy wouldn't be like the failures. Nichole was convinced their love was exceptional, just like them.

Show me a failure and I'll show you why they think they're not.

At the time, Nichole didn't know about the bookies, the underground poker games, and a mounting debt that was approaching six figures. All she knew was Leroy wanted her to be a more permanent fixture in his life. She loved him so it was an easy decision. She packed her things.

Leroy possibly could have kept his secrets secret if it weren't for the accident. The construction scaffolding wasn't secure, and he fell twenty feet. He broke his back and lost his source of income. The interest owed to the wrong people started to mount. They staked out his apartment and waited for him to return from the hospital. His first night home, some men arrived demanding money. Leroy pleaded with them, saying he deserved an extension since he no longer had a job. They gave him until the end of the month.

Leroy explained to Nichole that it wasn't *his* debts, but rather his brother's, the men were after. He convinced her the reason his brother had moved out in the first place was to escape with the money he owed. Nichole believed Leroy because she wanted to believe him. She offered to help. She used her savings and borrowed the rest from her parents. She started working overtime to help pay off the debts. She was twenty and working eighty-hour weeks.

It was Lexi who convinced Nichole that Leroy was playing her. Lexi came from a family of addicts, so she easily recognized the signs. Nichole didn't believe her at first. Believing her meant invalidating her own choices. Ignorance is the vice of the foolish. One night, at Lexi's insistence, they followed Leroy to what Nichole thought was a midnight janitorial shift at an office supply store. "It's not much, but it will get us to the end of each month," Leroy said about his new job.

When Lexi and Nichole pulled into a residence's driveway instead of an opened parking lot, Nichole knew what Lexi already suspected. They entered the shady house, got past the guard (thanks to some playful flirting on Lexi's part) and spotted Leroy in the corner staring at a pair of pocket aces his pocket kings couldn't beat. Nichole yelled "asshole" across the room and saw herself out.

She could have left him, and threatened to do so every time he stumbled home drunk after blowing a week's wages—her wages—at a poker game, but her threats never blossomed beyond threats. Nichole was too passive to change the course of her life. As much as people like to pretend otherwise, all they really want in life is a routine, no matter how lifeless. They want to wake up, go to work, and know what's waiting for them when they come home every night. What's more, they like to complain about how their life hasn't materialized into anything more than weekend Costco visits, generic social events, and the occasional obligatory family gathering. The complaining is one of the more satisfying features of the monotony. A jilted spouse's anger doesn't come from the knowledge of their lover's infidelity. What's so upsetting is the disturbance of the comfortable life. Leroy was part of Nichole's routine. She was too afraid to disrupt that. If she didn't have her routine, she became vulnerable to life's mysteries. Mysteries were for the young-at-heart and Europeans. She'd already given him two years of her life. To walk away now would be like cashing in an investment before it had time to mature.

*****

She opened the front door quietly and found the living room empty. Leroy usually spent the mornings on the sofa playing interactive videogames with other unemployed men from all parts of the country. Men yelling at other men while they shot each other from the comfort of their own home. Violence in comfort: The American wet dream.

Nichole looked down the hall and noticed the bedroom door was closed. This wasn't necessarily unusual, but it wasn't common either. Save for the bathroom (and only when Nichole used it; Leroy didn't believe in modesty) doors were seldom closed in the apartment. Nichole crept down the hall and pushed open the bedroom door. Leroy stood in the center of the room, his back to her. He was naked. Her eyes rested momentarily on the long, smooth surgery scar that ran down the crevice of his back. Suddenly, a feminine white hand reached around and clutched Leroy's black ass. The woman gripped Leroy's flank from her knees, using it to thrust him deeper down her throat. Nichole couldn't help but wonder if her white skin had that much dissimilarity with Leroy's black body when she touched him.

She watched the act for nearly a minute, too numb to move and too deflated to react. Had she been surprised, she later thought, she would have acted in a more appropriate fashion. She would have screamed and cried and called Leroy names that he would have tried to repel with half-hearted excuses and hollow rebuttals. But Nichole didn't do any of that because she knew the man she had tried so hard to love over the past couple of years, was exactly the kind of man who would proposition another woman for a blowjob at ten o'clock on a Wednesday morning. Her denial kept her silent in the moment, and her hope that he would change kept her subjugated in the relationship. So she simply watched her boyfriend with indifferent eyes, willing herself to act, yet incapable of doing so.

Leroy looked down at the woman on her knees and held her hair back from her face so he could get a better view of her performance. He could tell she wasn't enjoying it, which made Leroy enjoy it more. For Leroy, there was something exciting about a woman doing something for him, or to him, that she didn't want to. It gave him a false sense of superiority. The woman leaned back, gasped for air, and spotted Nichole in the doorway. She screamed. Leroy turned around, nearly knocking the woman across the face with his erection. The woman scurried to the near corner of the room where she tried to hide behind a lamp.

"Aw fuck," Leroy said. He made no attempt to cover himself. In fact, he didn't attempt to do anything other than stand in full view of Nichole, his erection straight and stiff. If anything, he actually appeared annoyed that Nichole had interrupted them, as if *she* was the one in the wrong and the situation should embarrass her.

Nichole looked at Leroy and then at the girl. She had full hips, tired eyes and pockmarks littering her face. She looked old and haggard and more worn out than someone should at ten o'clock in the morning. Nichole tried to figure out what it said about her that Leroy would cheat with someone so repulsive. Nichole would never publically admit that she was more physically appealing than anyone else, but even a layman could see that Nichole was far superior than the miscreant currently nesting in the corner. Did Leroy prefer women with permanently bruised knees because they made their living on them, or was this just a one-time tryst in an attempt to curb an animal instinct? Nichole couldn't come to a consensus because, after all, it didn't warrant one.

"I forgot my flash drive," Nichole finally managed to say. Her voice was hollow and distant and didn't sound like her own.

"Flash drive?" Leroy asked. He dug his index finger into his belly button, retrieved a piece of lint and then flicked it to the ground. "What's a flash drive?"

Nichole traversed the room to the computer, stepping over Leroy's discarded pajama pants and the woman's black nylon bra, and pulled her flash drive from the monitor. She crossed back to the door, stopped, and faced Leroy. He had his finger jammed back into his belly button trying to pull more lint from the hole. He looked at Nichole, his eyes blank and detached.

"Aren't you at least going to say something?" she asked.

Leroy kept his finger in his belly button, looked at the woman in the corner, and then back at Nichole. "I didn't think you were coming home."

Nichole laughed. "That's the best you can come up with?"

Leroy paused and thought. "She means nothing to me, baby," he said. The girl in the corner didn't react, but it didn't stop Leroy from shooting her a threatening look in case she felt the need to interject something.

"So you're sleeping with someone who means nothing to you. Is that supposed to make me feel better?" Nichole asked.

"You never want to anymore so I have to get it from somewhere else."

"I never want to anymore?" Nichole said. "We did it two nights ago, Leroy!"

"Yeah, but—"

"Maybe we'd have a better sex life if I wasn't so goddamn tired from having to work so goddamn much to help pay your debts."

"I have needs, baby. I'm a man."

"Yeah? What kind of man are you?"

Leroy couldn't tell if Nichole's question was an insult or an actual inquiry. He stared at her dumbly.

Nichole shook her head and closed her fist tightly around her flash drive. It dug into her palm, reminding her that had she remembered it when she left for work, she wouldn't now be forced to play out this scene. She wasn't sure at the moment who she was more upset with: herself for forgetting the flash drive or Leroy for not coordinating his philandering better.

"How many times have you done this?" Nichole asked, as if the number depended on her decision to forgive him or not.

"This is the first."

"You're such a liar," the woman behind the lamp shrieked.

Nichole looked at the woman. "How many times?"

She lowered her eyes and whispered, "Every Wednesday for the past three months."

"He pays you?" she asked.

"Yeah," the woman said. "One-fifty for an hour."

Nichole gasped, doing the math quickly. She had to work over eight hours to make what Leroy was paying this woman for one.

Nichole sighed heavily and spotted the bedside clock. She was going to be late. She turned to exit the room, but stopped herself and turned back to Leroy. She walked up to him. He watched her approach, curious and mystified. She stood before him and looked down at his penis. It was still hard, but losing some of its stiffness. If she had the right tool, she would have lopped it off right there on the spot. Instead, she opened her hand and slapped him hard across the face. She turned and walked out.

When she returned to work, she faxed and copied all the pertinent data her boss requested and then left work early. She sat in her car but didn't know where to go. She didn't want to go back to the apartment because she was still mentally writing the script of what she wanted to say when she faced Leroy again. Shopping could usually lift her spirits, but it was best with Lexi, and she wouldn't be home for a couple hours. Also, shopping was a harsh reminder of how much money she didn't have. Nichole was already swimming in debt. Impulse purchases were something she had to abandon months ago. Another element of her life that Leroy had stolen.

It occurred to Nichole that dating Leroy was a lot like having a child. He was dependent, insensitive to her feelings, and lacked any financial stability. It had been seven months since Leroy last covered his half of the rent, and it had been longer since he ever covered anything else. Even last Valentine's Day when he surprised Nichole with a dinner reservation at an upscale restaurant, he still slid the check across the table at the dinner's conclusion, claiming he'd forgotten his wallet at home.

Across the parking lot, Nichole spotted the food truck as it pulled into its designated spot. The truck came every lunch hour and sold street tacos, two for three dollars. It was a father and son operation. The father was a widower who lost his wife to breast cancer five years earlier. He cashed out the insurance policy, quit his job, bought a truck and parked it in various business lots throughout the week and sold tacos to businessmen and women. People loved the food almost as much as they loved him. He was affable, charming, and carried with him just enough pain behind his eyes from his wife's death that the plastic tip jar he kept on the truck's sill often had to be emptied two or three times during any given lunch hour. His dream was to be a chef in a high-end restaurant, but his deceased wife's insurance policy only afforded him the luxury of a restaurant on wheels. Still, he loved what he did, and felt accomplished with the fruits of his labors.

His son joined the truck last year after graduating from high school. He had gray eyes, but Nichole noticed a hint of blue in them whenever he looked at her. She liked to think everyone else only saw gray, that he reserved the blue only for her because he saw something in her that no one else could see. One day, under his steel gaze, he asked her why she allowed herself to "live within limits."

"Limits?" she asked, handing him a five and telling him to keep the change. "What do you mean?"

"You're limitless, but you don't think you are," he answered.

Nichole stared back at him, trying to grasp what he meant, but not sure she fully understood. "I'm not following."

"You'll figure it out one day," he winked.

She wanted to talk to him longer, inquire further into his brazen observation, but the line behind her was fifteen people long. She ate her lunch on a patch of grass on the fringes of the parking lot and watched him work. He was certainly his father's son. His ability to interact and create lighthearted banter with the customers was a sight. *He* was a sight. His blue-gray eyes outfitted the rest of his body perfectly. He wore a white V-neck T-shirt that outlined the curve of his broad chest and shoulders, revealing just enough of what lay underneath without ruining the surprise if he were to shed the fabric. He was tall and handsome but not in a young, cocky way. More of a refined youthful exuberance. People gravitated to him without knowing exactly why, only that they wanted to be near him.

Later, as the lunch crowd dissipated, Nichole approached him.

"Remember me?" she asked.

"Of course," he said. "Nichole, right?"

"I never told you my name."

"You were wearing a name tag the first time I ever served you."

Nichole recalled the day. There was a training at her office and everyone was required to wear one of those "Hello, my name is…" nametags.

"That was over six months ago. You remember that?" Nichole asked.

"Some faces are worth remembering," he said. Nichole knew he was feeding her a line, but his delivery was so genuine it felt sincere.

"And who are you?" she asked.

"I'm Lance."

"Nice to meet you officially, Lance."

"You want me to explain what I meant earlier, huh?"

"How'd you know?"

"I understand women," he smiled.

Nichole laughed. "You understand women? No man can make that claim."

"I can."

"How old are you?"

"I'm old enough to know that if I were to ask you out, you would say no because you think I'm too young."

"How old is that?"

"Nineteen. I'll be twenty in two months."

"I just turned twenty-two," Nichole said.

"So is nineteen too young for twenty-two?"

Nichole pondered his question for a moment. She never really thought age mattered, but suddenly confronted with it, she had to admit that nineteen did seem too young. He couldn't even get into a bar, let alone buy her a drink.

"It's not your age," Nichole lied. "It's something else."

Lance smiled, but Nichole could sense her answer hurt a little. "I don't believe you," he said.

Nichole smiled weakly. "It's not *just* your age."

"Is it because I work out of a truck?"

"No."

"Part of it is my age. What's the other part?"

"I'm with someone."

"I figured as much," Lance said, "but you're not happy with him."

"How do you know that?"

"Because you're talking to me."

"I...," Nichole started, but couldn't say much else. Lance laughed and reached out and moved a strand of hair that had worked its way to the edge of Nichole's mouth. Nichole caught herself blushing under his touch.

"There's a lot of tension in your upper body," Lance explained. "You're twenty-two and already beginning to lean forward. It could be your job, but I doubt it. If you were tied to your job, you wouldn't spend your lunches talking to nineteen-year-olds. You'd spend them at your desk trying to get ahead."

Nichole scoffed but didn't verbally protest his claims. She didn't want to admit that he was actually on to something. "So what is it then? Why do I lean forward and have tension?"

"You know why, but you don't want to admit it," Lance smiled.

Nichole felt embarrassed by the accuracy of his observation and stood up straight. He fascinated her, and she suddenly felt her heart breaking from the harsh reality that Lance probably knew her better than Leroy did.

"What did you mean earlier?" Nicole asked. "About me being limitless."

Lance thought how best to answer. "This guy you're with that's older than me, when things don't work out, ask yourself if nineteen is still too young. If it isn't, maybe I'll explain what I meant."

"That's not fair."

"Neither is being nineteen when the girl you want is twenty-two, but that's the hand I was dealt."

"The guy I'm with," Nichole said, "He's a…good guy."

Lance leveled his eyes on Nichole. "You almost sound like you mean that."

"He is."

"Are you trying to convince me or yourself?"

Nichole tried to force a smile, but it wouldn't come. "I should probably get back to work."

"It was good talking to you, Nichole."

Nichole turned and returned to work. From the office window, she watched Lance and his father clean up and then drive away. That night she went home to Leroy, her twenty-six-year-old boyfriend, who could legally buy her a drink in a bar but never did because he couldn't afford it.

Nichole hadn't been back to Lance's truck since their exchange.

Now, as she sat in her car and watched him trade tacos for crumpled bills, it occurred to her that he was now twenty. *Was that old enough?* She thought. Did it matter that she was now closer to twenty-three than twenty-two? She flirted with the prospect of approaching the truck and telling Lance she no longer had a boyfriend and would he be willing to meet her somewhere in an hour so they could make love? Afterward, she would rest her head on his chest and listen as he explained what he meant earlier when he called her limitless. It would be a memory worth creating. She was certain he would agree if she gave the proposition, but she couldn't find the wherewithal to trek across the lot and make the offer official. She watched him for thirty more minutes and then started her car and drove to Lexi's.

*****

Nichole didn't plan on telling Lexi about Leroy's infidelity, but her friend sensed something was wrong the moment Nichole walked through her front door. Nichole broke down and told her about Leroy and the other woman. She spewed hot, angry sobs about how much she despised him and how much she couldn't believe he could do what he did. Lexi listened and repeated what she had been saying for the past two years: "You can do better, leave him." She'd recited the same litany for so long she didn't believe it would have much impact on Nichole, but this time, surprisingly, it appeared that Nichole finally heard her friend's advice. She nodded at every incendiary remark Lexi made about Leroy. She let her friend berate him, and found herself agreeing instead of offering half-hearted defenses.

"Can I stay with you until I find an apartment?" Nichole asked after her tears subsided.

"Of course. You can stay as long as you want."

In an attempt to mitigate Nichole's grief, Lexi suggested they order Chinese takeout and spend the night watching bad movies. Breakups dating as far back as junior high followed the same protocol. Nichole retrieved Lexi's mink comforter—a gift she had received from an out of town client who recently had found more reasons to book business trips to Vegas after Lexi entered his hotel room for the first time a year ago—and wrapped herself tightly in the lavish blanket to appropriately indulge in her own self-pity.

Then the phone rang.

Lexi looked at the glowing screen and sighed before answering. It was her boss and he needed her for the night. Some horny out-of-towners had seen her flyer on the Las Vegas Boulevard and wanted her services.

"It's kind of a bad night, Ray," Lexi whispered, turning away from Nichole.

"It's a bachelor party," Ray said. "I bet I could get them to pay double."

"I don't care if it's a bachelor party. Besides, if there's more than two guys I need an escort and there isn't anyone working tonight."

"Is that Ray?" Nichole asked.

Lexi nodded.

"I'll do it."

"What?" Lexi asked.

"You need an escort, right? I'll be your escort."

Lexi looked at her friend and told Ray she'd call him back.

Lexi was a stripper. She wasn't a dancer or an entertainer or an entrepreneur. She wasn't a struggling student just trying to pay her way through school. She tried to get by on those lies in the beginning but grew tired of the charade. She was a stripper. For five hundred dollars an hour, she came to your hotel or house and took her clothes off. If you wanted to touch, you paid more. If you wanted to do more than touch, you paid a lot more. Handlers even passed out her own smut flyer on the Las Vegas Boulevard featuring a picture of her with stars covering her nipples. She was indifferent to the work, and never seriously considered doing anything else because the money was too good and her morals were too loose.

Lexi started when she was twenty. She told herself she would only do it to make enough money to finance a trip to Europe. She earned enough for the trip in two weeks. She went to Europe for a month before returning to the states where she landed a cashier job at Whole Foods. Europe awoke something in her that became her life's pursuit. She made a goal to return to Greece before her twenty-fifth birthday, not as a tourist, but as a resident. She knew selling organic artichokes to shaggy men and shaggier women wouldn't get her to Europe by her appointed deadline. She needed money fast and without taxes, so she put in her two weeks and traded her cashier's apron for a sequined thong. In the beginning, when family or friends asked what she did for work, she spat out one of the aforementioned titles, but when Nichole inquired, she never received the generic euphemisms.

Nichole never judged Lexi for stripping. A part of Nichole often wondered what it would be like to do what Lexi did. She wanted to experience the power Lexi often claimed she possessed whenever she was naked in front of men. The things they would do at her command, the money they would part with, the helplessness they exhibited. It all excited Nichole, but she knew she could never lose her inhibitions enough to pursue it. But tonight was different. It was different because hours earlier she'd caught her boyfriend with another woman, and if Leroy were to ever learn that she accompanied Lexi to a bachelor party, he would be pissed. And Nichole knew that after all was said and done, in terms of relationships, the only thing that mattered was getting back at the person that hurt you.

The party was in the penthouse suite at the Bellagio. Ray negotiated twelve-hundred dollars for Lexi and five hundred for Nichole (tips not included) for ninety minutes. Ray completed the credit card transaction over the phone and told the buyer, "Make sure to have cash on hand when the ladies arrive. The more you give, the more they do. These are high-class girls. No singles. Tens, twenties, fifties, hundreds."

In the elevator, Lexi could sense the uneasiness setting in with Nichole. It was foolish of her to bring her along. She understood that stripping, for all its depravity, still required a special skill set. It was more than simply taking off your clothes and rubbing your body against inebriated men. It was an art that, when fully mastered, could leave the lady thousands of dollars richer for only a couple hours' work. Lexi was a master, which is why she should have known better than to let her best friend talk her into chaperoning.

"You don't need to do this," Lexi said.

"I know. I want to."

"Leroy isn't worth this."

"I'm not doing it for him."

"I know. You're doing it *to* him."

Nichole looked at her friend, ready to explain why she was wrong, but then fell silent. There was no use trying to pretend with Lexi.

"You need an escort, right?" Nichole said. "Nevada state law."

31

"Don't use the law as your reason. You should only be here if you want to be here. Don't do this to get back at Leroy and don't do it to help me."

Nichole shook her head. "I gave him two years of my life, Lexi," her voice trembled, but she quickly coughed and pushed the wave of emotion from her.

"I know. He's an asshole. But *you* chose to stay with him. You always knew what he was."

"I didn't know till I moved in."

"Yeah, but you never moved out."

Lexi's brutal honesty silenced Nichole. Her life was what she had made it. She didn't have to give two years of her life to Leroy. She chose to. If she needed a reason to leave, Leroy gave her plenty in the two years they were together. She wasn't a victim of Leroy's infidelity; she was a victim to her own passivity.

"Look," Lexi said, interrupting Nichole's thoughts, "by definition you're just the escort. You don't even need to take off your coat. Only do what you're comfortable with, and if you want to leave, just say so and we're out the door. Got it?"

"Yeah."

The elevator stopped. Lexi took one last glance at her friend, nodded, and then stepped into the hall with Nichole.

Muffled music filled the hallway and grew louder as Lexi and Nichole got closer to the suite. They stopped at the door. Lexi looked at Nichole, offering her one last chance to back out. Nichole took a deep breath and then nodded toward the door. Lexi pounded on the penthouse door; the music inside stopped. From inside, they could hear deep muffled voices followed by approaching footsteps. Nichole's heart raced, and then a man thrust opened the door. This was Arnold. He wore an expensive suit, black with white pinstripes, and a matching silk tie. He looked like a high-class criminal or the cunning villain in a bad comic book movie. He slicked his receding hair back and pasted it down on his scalp, exposing a shining forehead that glistened under the hotel's fluorescent lights. He held a glass of champagne in one hand and an unopened, overpriced cigar in the other. He was ripped straight from the Las Vegas bachelor party guidebook. He looked Lexi and Nichole up and down, like an art buyer contemplating a purchase. Their overcoats didn't reveal much, but Arnold still smiled after a moment and nodded to the ladies, pleased with what he saw.

"Right this way," Arnold said, stepping to the side so they could enter.

Arnold led the women into the suite where the other men awaited their arrival. Nichole gave the room a brief overview, before lowering her head and ducking behind Lexi.

There were five men total. All had been friends since childhood, save for Arnold. He was there because he had enough money to afford the penthouse, and he was delusional enough to pretend that his friends didn't use him because he had money. All the men were in their early twenties and all were born and raised in Oregon, except Arnold. He was thirty-seven and from New Jersey.

Marlon Brown stood behind the bar at the far end of the room. He noticed Nichole the moment she entered. He liked how she looked a bit clumsy in her five-inch heels. He liked the way she had her dark hair pulled back to better show her delicate bone structure and the way her blue eyes quickly surveyed the room and then fell to the ground because there was obviously nothing worth looking at, including Marlon. She simply didn't fit the scene; Marlon was drawn to her immediately.

Because of her coy demeanor, Marlon didn't think Nichole noticed any of the men, especially himself. Sure, she quickly appraised the room, but he assumed she ducked behind her friend too quickly to take stock of anyone or anything. The truth was Marlon was the first thing Nichole noticed when she entered. His hypnotic stare forced her to quickly avert her eyes and lower her head. She sensed he caught her looking and she blushed under his gaze and crept further behind Lexi. She stole another furtive glance in his direction and found him smiling back at her. A knowing smile, an inviting smile. She awkwardly raised her head and smiled back.

She liked looking at him. He didn't appear to be pretentious like the others. All but him wore designer suits or knock-offs. They had the all too common countenance of tourists that came to Vegas to get drunk, get laid (hopefully), and then return home and brag about that time they went to Vegas to get drunk and laid. Marlon's appearance was more authentic. He wore a simple button-down shirt and jeans that showed enough of his body to entice a woman without showing too much of it to turn her off. His hair wasn't standing stiff from too much mousse or plastered flat to his scalp to help cover impending bald spots. It was just natural because he was natural. He was what most women would want in a man in his early twenties: handsome, sensible, and if his proximity in the room was any indication, he knew how to make a drink.

The men immediately assessed Nichole and Lexi as they stood in the center of the room. Lexi stood rigid and ready, comfortable in the climate and basking in the spotlight. She liked being judged because she knew men liked what they saw when they looked at her. She appraised the men with a more discerning eye than they did her. She surveyed each one and determined instantly the short man sitting at the bar with the nervous grin was the engaged bachelor. He had that look of excited curiosity that could only come from someone afraid his fiancé might find out what the next hour would bring. She also assumed, correctly, that Arnold was the man with the cash. The betrothed would get Lexi's attention initially, but Arnold would harness the majority of it. How ever much money was burning a hole in his pocket at the moment would be spilling out of her purse by the end of the night.

"So is anyone going to offer us a drink?" Lexi asked the room.

"What would you like?" Arnold asked. He casually placed his hand on the small of her back and led her toward the bar. Nichole followed. The bachelor scurried off, afraid of getting too close to the women he wanted badly to get close to.

"Vodka tonic. Two limes," Lexi said. She stood at the bar and watched as Marlon poured the drink, eyeing him conspicuously in case he thought of adding something to the mixture. Nichole took a seat at the bar across from Marlon and watched him work. He finished Lexi's drink and handed it to her. He then looked at Nichole and asked what she wanted. Nichole looked at Lexi, unsure what the proper Nevada escort drink was, but Lexi had turned away and was talking to one of the other men.

"Anything with Grey Goose," Nichole answered, trying to sound confident and failing.

Marlon mixed a Cape Cod and handed it to her. She took a sip. It went down smooth, too smooth, and she knew she wanted another one before she had even finished her first. Marlon watched her. She looked at him over the rim of the glass and blushed. Too nervous to think, she quickly downed the rest of her drink.

"Want another?" Marlon asked.

Nichole smiled and pushed the empty glass across the bar.

"So where's the lucky bachelor?" Lexi asked, even though she knew the answer. She placed her drink on the bar and winked at Nichole. Nichole smiled back.

"He's right over there," Arnold announced and pointed to the nervous guy in the corner. He perked up and smiled dumbly.

"What's your name?" Lexi asked.

"Brian," Brian mumbled.

"You're nervous. That's so cute," Lexi teased. The men laughed stupidly and Brian blushed. "Can we get some music in here?"

Arnold went to the stereo. Music filled the room and Lexi danced her way to Brian as her trench coat fell to the floor, and the men, save for Marlon, cheered when they saw her flawless figure fighting to be free from the taut fabric of her dominatrix outfit.

Nichole swallowed her drink, turned back to Marlon, and handed him her empty glass. Marlon refilled it casually.

"So what's your name?" Nichole yelled over the music.

"Marlon."

"Marlon what?"

"Brown."

"Marlon Brown?" Nichole repeated. "That's suspiciously close to Marlon Brando. Do you know who Marlon Brando is?"

"Yeah," Marlon smiled. "My mom's favorite movie is *On the Waterfront.* That's where she got my name."

"You're kidding."

"I'm not."

"Well, it could always be worse. Be grateful she wasn't a…Orson Wells fan."

Nichole laughed at her joke, but Marlon didn't react. He either didn't think it was funny, or he was a huge Orson Wells fan and thought her joke was in bad taste. To hide her embarrassment,

Nichole finished her drink and slid her empty glass toward Marlon. He quickly refilled it and pushed it back across the bar to her.

"Are you trying to get me drunk?"

"No. I was designated the bartender. If you hand me an empty glass, it's my job to fill it. I'll stop filling as soon as you stop drinking."

"You should have one with me."

Marlon nodded and poured himself a shot. Nichole reached across the bar and took the vodka bottle from him. To her left, she took two shot glasses from the rack and poured two additional shots.

"You need to catch up," she said.

Marlon smiled and raised the first shot to Nichole. He swallowed it in one gulp and winced at the burning.

"Two more," Nichole said, tapping the extra shots with the tip of the vodka bottle.

Marlon took the two remaining shots. "Now it's your turn," he said.

Nichole swallowed her drink and slammed the glass down on the bar. Marlon laughed and poured each of them another.

A sudden cheer erupted in the room. Marlon and Nichole turned to find Brian's face buried between Lexi's breasts. She held his head in her cleavage and poured champagne down her chest. Lexi leaned back and let Brain lick the drink from her nipples. His three friends looked on jealously, giving each other high fives and clapping to the beat of the music. Arnold tossed a hundred at Lexi. It fluttered to her feet. She bent over to retrieve it, giving the men a glimpse of her backside. They cheered and Arnold threw another hundred. Nichole laughed and turned back to Marlon.

"I'm not a stripper, you know?" Nichole said.

"You're not?"

"No."

"So what are you?"

"I'm a bookkeeper. For a marketing firm."

"Sure you are."

"I mean it."

"Then why are you here?" Marlon asked. He raised his newly refilled shot to Nichole before swallowing it in one gulp. Nichole followed suit. The alcohol was setting in. She knew it was dangerous to get drunk in a foreign environment, but she was having too much fun to care. Besides, sobriety made her think about Leroy. She didn't want to think about Leroy. She wanted to think of Marlon. The way he smiled with his eyes. Cold, strong, and somehow innocent all at once. Sobriety wasn't needed at the moment. She pushed her empty glass across the bar so he could refill it.

"Nevada state law requires all dancers have a chaperone if the party has more than three people," Nichole explained.

"So you're just the chaperone?" Marlon asked.

"I'm just the chaperone."

"Then what do you have on under that trench coat?"

Nichole laughed. "You got me." She took a step back from the bar, looked over both her shoulders and then hurriedly opened her trench coat for Marlon to see. She was only on display for a second, but Marlon didn't need much more to appreciate what was under her coat. She quickly closed the coat, proud of her newfound bravery, and stepped back to the bar.

"I'm *really* not a stripper, though," she said. "I came here because I caught my boyfriend cheating on me today."

"I don't understand."

"I'm here for revenge."

"How is this revenge?"

"It will piss him off."

"Sounds like a healthy relationship."

"There is no relationship now. It's over."

"Of course it is."

"You don't believe me?"

"I don't know you."

"You know more about me than I know about you."

"Is that a violation of the stripper code?"

"I'm not a stripper!" Nichole yelled.

"Sure, you're not," Marlon winked at her.

"Does your wife know you're here?"

"I don't have a wife."

"Does your girlfriend?"

"I don't have one of those either."

"So you're not a cheater?"

"Is going to a bachelor party cheating?"

"Depends on who you ask."

"I'm asking you."

"Depends on what you do at the party."

"What if you spend the night talking to a stripper that isn't a stripper?"

"Are you talking to her to be nice or do you have a hidden agenda?"

"A hidden agenda?"

"Yeah."

"What would that be?"

"I don't know. Maybe you want to see what I have on under this coat."

"You just showed me. Remember?"

Nichole laughed. "Did you like what you saw?"

"I was…impressed."

"I like talking to you. Do you like talking to me?"

Marlon smiled. "Immensely."

The urge struck Nichole to leap across the bar and kiss Marlon passionately. *Immensely.* So much impact with one word. The drunken euphoria took hold of Nichole. The room spun. The music pulsated. Nichole fought to resist what the alcohol promoted. She wanted Marlon. She wanted to feel him on her. His breath, his body, him.

Arnold came up behind Nichole, draped his arm around her and moved with the music. He put his empty glass on the bar and told Marlon to make him a screwdriver. Marlon did as instructed, annoyed with the interruption.

"Hey, man, are you going to talk to her all night?" Arnold asked over the music. His words were slurred, his greased back hair flayed about, disarrayed thanks to Lexi. "She's on the clock."

"She's not a stripper," Marlon said. If Arnold wasn't so drunk, he would have sensed the frustration in Marlon's response.

"Then what is she?" Arnold asked.

"She's just a chaperone." Marlon smiled at Nichole. She smiled back, touched that Marlon corroborated her story.

Arnold looked at Nichole and then pulled a wad of bills from his jacket. "Well, chaperone, do you want to make some money?"

Nichole appraised the money and then looked at Marlon, as if for permission. Marlon offered a hurt smile, one that asked her not to do it, and then quickly took a drink to mask his unfounded concern. Nichole snatched the money from Arnold, finished her drink and then stepped away from the bar and removed her coat. Arnold raised his drink and cheered. The other men looked in the direction of the outburst and joined Arnold's celebration when they saw Nichole, nearly nude, dancing. She made her way toward Lexi, finding rhythm with her best friend and keeping her eyes on Marlon the entire time.

CHAPTER 2

The room was completely dark. Lexi slowly pushed open the door and a slice of light fell on Nichole and Marlon. Both were sleeping. Marlon on his stomach, Nichole on her back. He was shirtless but still wore his boxers and a lone sock. Nichole's naked breasts rose slowly in cadence with her breathing. Lexi crept to the bed and gently shook her friend awake. Nichole opened her eyes and moaned, before turning on her side so she could fall back to sleep. Lexi shook her harder and gently slapped her back to consciousness. Nichole forced her eyes opened and looked at her friend. She stared at her for a moment. Soft snoring suddenly cut into the silence of the room. Nichole turned and saw Marlon lying next to her.

"Oh, shit," she gasped.

"Get your stuff," Lexi whispered. "We need to get out of here."

"Did I sleep with him?"

"Looks that way?"

"Did I...have sex with him?"

"I have no idea."

Nichole sat up. The expensive bed sheet slipped from her body and fell in a pool on the bed. She looked down at her unsupported breasts. *Shit!* She lifted the sheet. Her sequined thong was still in place. Seeing the sparkling thong in its proper place gave Nichole a sense of comfort. It glistened like a beacon of false affirmation. A faux diamond chastity belt. She looked back at Marlon and noticed his underwear was still in place. This elevated her comfort. Something on his underwear caught her eye. She leaned closer and recognized a squirrel holding two nuts printed on the boxer shorts. She couldn't decide if his adolescent garment choice was endearing or upsetting.

"I don't think we had sex," Nichole whispered. "I would remember that, right? I don't remember anything and we both still have our underwear on."

"I'm sure you didn't. Come on, get up," Lexi instructed. She helped Nichole to her feet, but the movement was too much; she bent over and vomited on the floor.

"Okay," Lexi said. "That's okay. Get it all out."

They both looked at Marlon. He didn't move. Nichole stood up and wiped her mouth, nearly falling over at the effort, but Lexi steadied her.

"Here," Lexi said, grabbing Marlon's shirt from a nearby chair, "wear this."

Nichole slipped the shirt over her head. She spotted her shoes a few feet away and started toward them. She took a step and felt something hard with her foot. She leaned down and picked up Marlon's wallet. She opened the billfold and found his driver's license. She read his name: Marlon Brown. "Huh," Nichole mumbled. "His name really is Marlon Brown. From Oregon."

Lexi grabbed the wallet and opened the money slot. She reached in and took the bills. Nichole watched her incredulously.

"You're robbing him?"

"We've been here about three hours longer than they paid for." Nichole started to protest, but then Lexi split the wad of cash in half and handed it to Nichole. Nichole stared at the money, trying to decide if it was wrong to take it.

"Baby, we really need to go," Lexi said. She kneeled down and retrieved Nichole's shoes. She thought to help her into them but figured she could navigate her friend out of the suite more easily barefooted. She took Nichole by the hand and led her out of the room. Nichole clutched the money and followed her friend.

The other men were in the suite's main room, all passed out and sleeping soundly. Liquor bottles and other party paraphernalia littered the suite. Lexi and Nichole weaved themselves through the chaos, only stopping to recover Nichole's overcoat, and then slipped out the door. They scurried down the hall and into the hotel's elevator.

Neither said anything as the elevator began descending the fifty floors to the hotel's lobby. Lexi stole furtive glances at Nichole, trying to gauge if she was okay. Nichole knew she was being watched, but she had nothing to say, not because she was upset or distraught, but simply because she was hung over and still hadn't fully processed exactly what had happened, or may have happened, at the party.

The elevator stopped at the twentieth floor. The doors opened and two men stood stupidly outside the cage waiting to enter. They looked at Lexi and Nichole, nodded and then shuffled inside. The one closest to the door pushed the button for the nineteenth floor. Lexi scoffed and shook her head, bothered that they couldn't use the stairs to go down one floor. The elevator descended one floor and reopened.

Lexi looked at Nichole and noticed her chin was quivering. She quickly crossed to her friend. One of the men glanced over their shoulder at Lexi and Nichole as he stepped into the hallway. He thought to say something, but couldn't think of anything worth saying. The doors closed behind him.

"I don't even know what happened," Nichole said, choking on the words.

"It was my mistake. I shouldn't have brought you."

"Did I...sleep with him? Do you think I did?"

"I don't think so. Neither of you were naked, but I didn't see you go into the bedroom with him. Once I realized you were gone, I went in after you. It couldn't have been more than ten minutes. By the time I got there, you were already passed out. I tried waking you, but you were out cold, so I stayed till the morning."

"What about the others?"

"What do you mean?"

"What did you do about them?"

"They didn't touch you. I made sure of that. I slipped something into their drinks and they all passed out."

"Slipped something into their drinks?" Nichole repeated incredulously.

"Yeah. You can never be too careful."

Nichole began to cry. She was touched by the precautions Lexi had taken for her and remorseful for behaving so shamelessly after having begged Lexi to let her come. Her sobbing was light and suppressed, but Lexi knew this was just a precursor of what was on the horizon. She took Nichole into her arms and held her friend tight as the sobs increased and the regret heightened.

CHAPTER 3

Leroy was waiting on Lexi's porch. Twelve empty beer bottles and a pack's worth of cigarette filters littered her walkway. It was six o'clock in the morning.

Lexi pulled into her driveway. Leroy staggered to his feet when he saw them arrive. He wore his Michael Jordan replica jersey. He always donned his Michael Jordan replica jersey when he needed to make things right. It made him feel stronger in some unexplainable way. Athletes have that effect on people, especially people whose happiness is contingent on how well their favorite athletes and sports teams perform. Leroy's life only ever seemed worth living when his favorite franchises had good seasons.

"Shit," Lexi said. "What's he doing here?"

Nichole was reclined in the passenger seat. She propped herself up and spotted Leroy standing on the porch.

"Do you think he's been here all night?" Nichole asked. Lexi couldn't tell if the question was asked out of concern, annoyance, or just plain curiosity.

"I don't know. It looks like he's been drinking, though." As if on cue, Leroy took a step from the porch and stumbled from the effort. He caught himself and clumsily made his way toward the car. Lexi grabbed her purse and retrieved her stun gun. Nichole spotted the gun and thought to protest, but stopped herself; she understood Leroy's temper. If he knew she'd spent the night in a hotel with a stranger, they would need more than a stun gun. Nichole nodded to Lexi, ready to face Leroy. They stepped out of the car.

"What are you doing here, Leroy?" Lexi asked. She kept her stun gun at her side, concealed but ready.

"I want to talk to Nichole," Leroy slurred.

"I could have you arrested for trespassing," Lexi said.

"I never went in your house."

"You're on my property."

"I just want to talk to Nichole."

"I don't have anything to say to you," Nichole said, stepping out from behind Lexi.

"Baby, please come home. I've been thinking about you all night."

Nichole shook her head and started for the house, but Leroy cut her off and gave her a slight push. Lexi clutched her stun gun and came up behind Nichole. As Nichole staggered backward, her overcoat briefly came opened. Leroy caught a glimpse of her lingerie underneath.

"Why are you dressed like that?" Leroy asked. He grabbed at the fold of Nichole's overcoat. Nichole slapped his hand away.

"Let me by, Leroy," Nichole demanded.

"You work a street corner or something last night?" he asked. He took a step toward her and reached for the coat, but she turned away from him.

"Don't touch me."

"What are you wearing?" he asked.

"Nothing. It's none of your business."

Leroy looked to Lexi, half expecting her to offer an explanation for Nichole's apparel. She silently scorned Nichole for throwing Marlon's shirt out her car window as they drove away from the hotel. But upon further reflection, maybe her intuition compelled her to do it. Who knows how Leroy would have reacted if Nichole was still wearing it.

"Baby, please…" he said.

"Let me by, Leroy."

"Not until you talk to me."

"She doesn't want to talk to you," Lexi said.

"This doesn't concern you, Lexi," Leroy said.

Lexi tightened her grip on the stun gun and took a step toward Leroy. Nichole put her hand on Lexi's shoulder and slightly shook her head. Lexi gave a slight protest but relented and stepped back.

"Nichole, come home," Leroy said, lowering his voice in a failed attempt to sound more sincere.

"I'm staying here."

"You live with me."

"Not anymore."

"Baby, please."

"You only want her back so she'll pay your rent," Lexi said. Leroy shot her a look, but Lexi didn't flinch. He looked back at Nichole and softened his eyes.

"Nichole, that woman…she means nothing to me."

"Is that supposed to make me feel better?"

"It was a mistake. I won't make it again."

"You only feel bad because you got caught and you're broke," Nichole said.

Lexi laughed, proud to hear Nichole admit the things she had been trying to show her for so long. Nichole's assertiveness was new to Leroy. In the past, a stern command or a blatant insult from him could always silence her into submission. Her newfound confidence was foreign to him.

"You need to leave, Leroy," Nichole said.

"I love you, baby," Leroy whimpered. Nichole let the word hang in the air for a moment. *Love.* Leroy said it, but did he mean it? Did he know this was the first time he had ever used it with Nichole? He said it so theatrically, that Nichole sensed it was just a last-ditch effort to reclaim her.

She hated how the word sounded coming from Leroy. It suddenly lost all meaning. Leroy had robbed it of any substance it once had. His remorse was an act. One he had perfected. All freeloaders used the same template to stop someone from leaving. Nichole's anger boiled over and suddenly, without warning, she slapped him hard across the face.

It was an impulse that surprised her almost as much as it surprised Leroy. Lexi's mouth fell open and hung opened stupidly. Leroy rubbed his cheek in disbelief. If he wasn't sober before, he was now. Lexi suddenly burst into laughter, stunned and amused by the scene. Her derisive cackle catapulted Leroy back to reality. The ridicule Lexi enjoyed at Leroy's expense lit a flame in him. Any more fabricated attempts to show his sorrow fled. He stepped toward Nichole, raised his arm to strike, but Lexi plunged the stun gun into his chest. He fell to the ground, convulsing. Lexi stepped over Leroy and started for her house. Nichole stood and watched him for a moment, and then followed Lexi into her house, locking the door behind her.

CHAPTER 4

Marlon entered the coffee shop and his eyes instinctively darted to the table in the corner. She was there, like always, reading a book. Marlon craned his head to read the title. It was partly obscured by her hand, a hand he noted, that wasn't weighed down with a wedding ring, but he recognized the book was *Cold Mountain.* Last week it was *The Fountainhead.* Marlon had read both. They had so much in common.

She had a refined, simple beauty. She appeared elegant without being pretentious. Inviting but not suffocating. People often looked twice at her, once to see her and then back to really notice her and take in the finer details they may have missed the first time. Her steely blue eyes entrapped, yet somehow made you feel liberated. Her lips were themselves a disheartening contradiction. What did a man want more, to feel them on his or force them upwards into a smile that, when directed to you, suddenly gave your life purpose? She was inspiring. More than one previous lover had written bad poetry for her hoping she wouldn't recognize the trite similes that peppered their prose. She was the reason consumers still allowed themselves to be tricked into believing love wasn't some fabricated illusion perpetuated by Hollywood to steal the average sucker's dollar.

Marlon stepped in line at an angle where he could continue stealing glances at her from over his shoulder, hoping to catch her looking at him as he looked at her. She didn't though. She hadn't so much as glanced at him in the two months since Marlon had first noticed her. She was completely oblivious to anything outside whatever book she read. If she would just look at him, he could approach her. He needed her to look at him though, as if her acknowledgment would somehow grant him permission to enter her world. But she never looked up, and so Marlon never dared advance. He was fearful about interrupting her reading. She intimidated him, but he couldn't explain why. And even though they had never shared a word between them, he was drawn to her immensely.

He ordered his coffee and then stood to the side of the counter and waited. He was more visible to her now, but her eyes stayed locked in her book. She was killing him, and she didn't even know it. After a moment, the barista called Marlon's name. He stepped to the counter and took his coffee. He turned and looked again at the woman; she still read. Marlon started for the door slowly, reducing his gait to give her a longer timeframe to notice him. He kept his eyes on her, urging her to look up. He inched closer to the door, but she still didn't stir, and then finally, right as he put his hand on the door, she looked up and offered a knowing smile. Marlon smiled back dumbly, but his momentum was too great. He pushed through the door and exited the shop.

The door slammed shut. Marlon stood outside, cursing himself for not stopping when she looked at him. To go back in now would look ridiculous. What would he say? What line would he use? He thought of this moment every day, but his introduction always started inside the coffee house, with some insight into literature. To return now would look desperate, a sign that he was *waiting* for this moment. He paced outside for a minute and then, before he could give too much thought to what he was doing, he rushed back through the door.

She was waiting for him. She had neatly closed her book and placed it on the table. She sat upright with her hands in her lap, anticipating Marlon's return. Marlon looked at her, but couldn't find anything to say, so he said nothing.

"I saw you pacing outside," she said. "What's causing you so much anxiety?"

"I was looking for the right line."

"To use on me?"

"Yeah."

"What did you come up with?"

"How's the book?"

"'How's the book'? That's the best you could do?"

"Yeah. Under the circumstances."

"It's beautiful," she said. "Have you read it?"

"Yeah. A couple times."

"Does he die? Inman?"

"Do you really want to know?"

"Would you really tell me?"

"If you really wanted to know."

"I get the feeling you would tell me anything," she said, smiling.

"You're probably right."

Marlon wanted to take the empty seat across from her but didn't want to appear too forward. He shuffled his feet and waited for her to say something else.

"What's your name?" she asked.

"Marlon."

"Like the fish?"

"No, like the actor," he explained. "My mom was a huge Brando fan. What's your name?"

"Karen. My mom wasn't a fan of anything."

"Karen is a…beautiful name," Marlon said unconvincingly.

Karen laughed. "No. Karen isn't a beautiful name. It's just a common one."

"Well, you're…beautiful," Marlon mumbled awkwardly.

Karen laughed harder. "Are you always this awkward?"

"No. Just right now. This may be the most awkward I've ever been in my life."

"Why?"

"I've practiced this moment in my head for two months, but it's not going how I envisioned it."

"How did you envision it?"

"You'd look at me from across the room and our eyes meet. I'd approach, and as I made my way over, you would push the chair out with your foot. I would sit and—"

Karen pushed the chair across from her out with her foot, knocking Marlon in the groin. He winced and doubled over.

"Oh, shit," Karen gasped.

"What did you do that for?"

"I was trying to play out your fantasy."

Marlon stood up straight, took a deep breath, and tucked the chair back under the table. "Try again."

Karen placed her foot on the chair. Marlon took a precautionary step back. Karen laughed and gently slid the chair out with her foot. "Why don't you sit down," she said seductively.

Marlon nodded and sat down. He suddenly felt more confident sitting across from Karen rather than standing awkwardly in front of her on full display.

"So, Karen," Marlon said, "what do you do?"

"I'm in marketing. What about you?"

"I'm a high school English teacher."

"Isn't it against an English teacher's credo to tell someone how a book ends?"

"I don't have any credos," Marlon smiled.

"Where do you teach?" Karen asked.

"Zion High."

"That's just up the street, isn't it?"

"Yeah."

"Why haven't I seen you around?"

"I moved here a couple months ago," Marlon said.

"Where are you from?"

"Oregon."

"How do you like Utah?"

"It's nice. A little sheltered, but nice. Are you from around here?"

"Grew up in Kansas. Came out here for college, graduated last spring and decided to stay."

"What did you study?"

"Business."

Marlon checked his watch. He was running late. He hated that he was running late. "Look, I have to go, but I was wondering…"

"Yeah?"

"Would you maybe…if you weren't busy this weekend…," Marlon stammered.

"Why is this so hard for you, Marlon?" Karen asked, touched that she could elicit so much nervousness from someone.

"I don't know," Marlon answered.

"Is this the first time you've ever asked out a girl?" Karen teased.

"No."

"So then what's the problem?"

"I guess it's the first time I've been afraid the woman would say no."

"Why would you think I would say no?"

"That seems to be a common theme in life."

"What?"

"To not get what you want."

"Somehow I get the feeling you always get what you want."

"I was thinking the same thing about you," Marlon said. "Until now I've never really wanted something."

"I'd love to go out with you." Karen took a pen from her purse and scribbled her phone number and address on a napkin.

"How about tomorrow?" Karen asked handing the napkin to Marlon.

"Tomorrow is perfect."

CHAPTER 5

For the second night in a row, Nichole's retching woke Lexi. She looked at her bedside clock, 1:34. A.M. Yesterday Nichole blamed her sickness on bad sushi. Lexi was suspicious but kept silent. They lived in Las Vegas, hundreds of miles from the nearest ocean, so bad sushi wasn't completely out of the question. But two nights in a row? Lexi wasn't buying it. She got out of bed and made her way to the bathroom.

She found Nichole on her knees huddled over the toilet bowl. Another bout of vomit took hold of her, and she started heaving. Lexi stood over Nichole and held her hair back. After Nichole finished vomiting, she sat back against the bathroom wall and moaned. Lexi flushed the toilet. She took a washcloth from a nearby shelf, doused it with cold water and handed it to her friend. She felt Nichole's face. It didn't feel warm. Nichole exhaled deeply, dabbing the washcloth on her forehead and neck.

"I don't think it's food poisoning," Lexi said.

"What else could it be?" Nichole asked.

Lexi opened her medicine cabinet and retrieved a box of pregnancy tests. She unwrapped one, and turned back to Nichole.

"I'm not pregnant," Nichole said.

"Have you taken a test?"

Nichole shrugged and mumbled something that Lexi couldn't understand.

"Use your words," Lexi said.

"I'm not pregnant."

"Prove it."

Lexi held out her hands and pulled Nichole to her feet. "Why do you have pregnancy tests anyway?" Nichole asked.

"For nights like these."

"That's…weird."

"Have you ever taken one before?" Lexi asked.

"Yeah."

Lexi turned to leave, but Nichole grabbed her by the elbow.

"Stay," Nichole said.

Lexi looked at her friend and understood. She sat on the edge of the bathtub.

Nichole pulled down her pants and sat on the toilet with the test. She stared dejectedly at the wall while she urinated on the stick. She finished and placed the test on the sink and sat on the edge of the tub next to Lexi.

"You didn't wash your hands," Lexi said. It was her attempt at a joke, but it fell flat. Nichole appreciated the effort even if she wasn't in the mood. She took Lexi's hand and held it tightly.

"How long does it take?" Nichole asked.

"Just a few minutes."

"When was the last time you were with Leroy?"

"The night before I left."

"Do you always take your pill?"

"I'm not on the pill."

"How come?"

"I can't afford it."

"So what—"

"We use condoms."

"Always?"

"Lexi, I may be stupid, but I'm not dumb."

"I have no idea what that means."

"I don't either, actually. I saw it on a bumper sticker and have always wanted to say it."

They sat silently for the next few minutes. Nichole put her head on Lexi's shoulder. From where she sat, Lexi thought she could see two pink lines forming on the test strip, but she couldn't be sure.

"I think it's probably ready," Lexi said. "Get up"

"I don't need to get up. I can see it from here."

"What does it say?"

"It says…," but Nichole couldn't finish her thought. The words got caught in her throat and then she started crying.

CHAPTER 6

Because he had only lived in Utah for a couple months, Marlon
wasn't very familiar with the state's dining options. He said as
much when he called Karen to get directions to her apartment. He
told her he would pay for their second date if she chose the
restaurant for their first. She asked how he was so certain she would
agree to a second date. "We have to have a second if we're going to
have a third," he answered. It was a stupid line, and Karen felt a
slight twinge of embarrassment for having set herself up for the
delivery, but she couldn't help but laugh anyway. Marlon was silly;
she liked a little silliness.

She picked a casual brewpub in the heart of the city. The
hostess sat them outside on the patio. The chairs were wrought iron
contraptions that offered little lumbar support but boasted a
rusticated elegance. The tabletop was an antique door lacquered and
stained cherry with dismantled bike frames holding the surface
upright. Nailed to the building's brick walls were all sorts of
knickknacks (an old blackboard, an antique watering can, a rusted

thrasher). Flowerbeds lined the patio, but wooden sticks with beer bottle caps glued to the tips emerged from the soil in place of flowers. Everything that served a purpose at one time served a different one now.

A light breeze tickled Karen's skin. The gentle wind sent subtle waves of Karen's perfume toward Marlon. It made him want to be closer to her. It was unseasonably warm for fall, so Karen wore a sleeveless summer dress. She looked beautiful to Marlon, like a reason to live.

"So…who is Marlon Brown?" Karen asked after the waitress dropped off their drinks.

"He's a lowly paid high school English teacher."

"That's what you do," Karen retorted. "That's not who you are."

"Oh," Marlon smiled. "You want a more…existential answer?"

"Do you have one?"

"Not off the top of my head, but I could invent one."

"Okay," Karen said, leaning forward, "Let's hear it."

Marlon thought for a moment. "He's a paradox."

"How so?"

"His tastes. They're…subtlety contradictory."

"Does that include his taste in women?"

"Especially in women," Marlon smiled.

"Now you really have my attention. Describe for me your perfect woman."

Marlon thought for a moment. "She has to be genuine without being condescending, honest without being abrasive. She needs to maintain an inviting presence but can't seem overly eager to be wanted or even needed. Beautiful some of the time and sexy the rest. She needs to work on her own terms, be independent but want me because I love her in spite of, and because of, her imperfections."

Karen appraised Marlon, stared into his eyes and saw something in them that she couldn't define and wasn't sure she wanted to. She liked him, and she assumed this is what kept her entranced; she couldn't remember the last time she really liked a guy. They were too generic, as if their main function was simply to disappoint. Maybe Marlon was the exception.

"Where does one find a woman like that?" Karen asked.

"Coffee shops, maybe," Marlon said. Karen smiled, absorbing the compliment.

"So…who is Karen Bowden?" Marlon asked after a moment.

"Just a simple country girl from Kansas."

"You're not simple."

"How do you know?"

"You read too much to be simple."

"Maybe that's why I read. My life is so simple I need to live vicariously in the complicated."

"Having a simple life and being simple are not the same thing," Marlon countered.

"I can agree with that," Karen said. Marlon waited for her to offer more, but she seemed content to let the conversation end there.

"So that's all I get?" Marlon asked. "A simple country girl from Kansas?"

"For now," Karen said and looked at Marlon over the rim of her glass as she took another drink.

Marlon sat back and stared at Karen. She was genuine without being condescending, honest without being abrasive. She maintained an inviting presence without appearing overly eager to be wanted or even needed. She worked under her own terms. She was subtlety contradictory. Marlon liked her a lot.

"Telling me something about you that you don't want me to know," she said.

"Why would I do that?"

"Because you're trying to impress me."

Marlon grinned. "Don't flatter yourself."

"You're not trying to impress me?"

"Supposing I was, why would I tell you something I don't want you to know? Wouldn't that defeat the purpose?"

"It's our first date," Karen said. "We could sit here and go through the checklist of what we do, where we grew up, how many brothers and sisters we have, our favorite book, movie, TV show, and all that other boring stuff, or we could skip that and get straight to the stuff we're ashamed of. The stuff that, if we make it, we would have to disclose anyway. Let's put it all on the table now so there aren't any surprises later."

Marlon looked at Karen and processed her pitch. He was intrigued.

"Okay," he said. "You go first."

"Okay," Karen said. She thought for a moment, trying to recall something worthy of her requirements. "When I was sixteen I stole a pair of jeans from the mall."

"That's not so bad."

"It was a total waste. They didn't even fit."

"So what did you do with them?"

"I returned them to the store. I said they were a birthday gift from my mom and they didn't fit. I didn't have a receipt, obviously, so they gave me store credit."

"That's…clever."

Karen smiled. "Now you go."

"Okay," Marlon said, thinking. "When I was eleven I cut the head off of my sister's favorite Barbie and flushed it down the toilet."

Karen laughed. "What did she say?"

She started crying so I blamed it on the neighbor."

Karen smiled and shook her head. "You're the stereotypical older brother, huh?"

"Something like that."

"Tell me another."

"You said one thing," Marlon argued.

"Come on. Isn't this more fun than learning my sign?"

"Okay, but you go first again."

Karen thought for a moment and then said, "I was a drug dealer for nine days."

"Only nine, huh?" he asked.

"Yeah."

"Too bad. I heard somewhere you get a promotion after ten."

"What kind of promotions do drug dealers get?"

"Better street corners," he said. "What happened?"

"My boyfriend was a dealer," Karen explained. "I didn't know. He went out of town for two weeks and some people came looking for him. I found his stash in a drawer. I was about two thousand dollars short for my tuition, so I sold what I found and moved out before he got home. I left a note on the fridge, and I never heard from him again."

"Never heard from him again?" Marlon asked. "Was he killed by the people who were looking for him?"

"I have no idea."

"What?"

"I'm kidding," Karen said. "I saw him about three months later on campus. He was walking through a parking lot. He didn't see me." Karen paused and took another sip from her wine. "Okay, it's your turn. Make it a good one. Something really embarrassing."

Marlon thought for a moment and then said, "My first wet dream was to Peggy Bundy."

Karen laughed. "From *Married with Children?*"

"Yep," Marlon said.

"You seem to be more proud than embarrassed."

"I'm embarrassed. I'm just pretending like I'm not so it isn't made into a thing."

"Wow," Karen said. "How am I supposed to top that?" She thought for a moment. "I was a stripper for a night," she said.

"A drug dealer for nine days and a stripper for one? What other part-time work have you had?"

"Just those two," Karen blushed. "Tuition again. I worked one night and made $400."

"You seem proud. Is that some kind of a record?"

"I'm not proud of it," Karen said, turning serious. "It was a low point in my life."

"How come?"

"Oh, just your typical twenty-year-old quarter-life crisis."

Neither spoke for a minute, and then Marlon said, "Last month I was robbed by a stripper."

"You were robbed by a stripper?" Karen repeated.

"Yeah."

"She have a gun hidden in her G-string?"

"It was a friend's bachelor party. Another friend, well more like an acquaintance, booked a suite on the strip and called one of those smut fliers. Two strippers came. I had too much to drink and passed out next to one of the girls and when I woke up my wallet was empty."

"You passed out next to her?" Karen asked. "Is that the nice way of saying you slept with her?"

Marlon opened his mouth to offer a rebuttal and then closed it and looked away.

"You did?" Karen asked, laughing.

"No," Marlon fumbled, "well, I don't…I don't think I slept with her."

"You don't *think* you did?"

"I'm pretty sure…I didn't."

"You don't sound sure."

"I didn't." Marlon sounded surer of himself now.

"I don't know that I believe you," Karen teased.

"We were drunk," Marlon explained. "We passed out, and when I woke up she was gone. My underwear was still on. So unless she dressed me afterward, I'm pretty sure we didn't sleep together."

"So is that a regular thing you do? Pass out next to strippers at bachelor parties?"

"I do it about as often as you work as a stripper."

"I needed tuition money. What's your excuse?"

"I...I don't have one," Marlon said, lowering his head.

Marlon thought to explain the connection he had made with the stripper (that wasn't a stripper), hoping it somewhat justified why he passed out next to her. He thought of telling her how he tried, unsuccessfully, to track her down in the silly hope that he could take her to dinner and continue the conversation they were having before they were interrupted. His friends derided him for pursuing her. They derided him more vigorously when he told them they didn't hear the conversation he was having with her before Arnold interrupted, and if they had, they would know that she was probably thinking of him the same way he was thinking of her. He knew how ridiculous he sounded. He wasn't the first man to think a stripper liked him for more than just the contents of his wallet. However, he refused to believe that their connection was less than what it appeared to be. There was a connection. He felt it; he needed to know if she felt it, too. He flew home two days later and spent every day thinking of her until he accepted a teaching position in Utah and saw Karen sitting alone in the first coffee shop he entered.

The waitress arrived and dropped off their food. Karen plucked a shrimp from her pasta and ate it, savoring the taste.

"What would people do with all their free time if they didn't eat or drink?" she asked.

"What do you mean?"

"Think about it," Karen explained, "if you take eating and drinking out of life, if we didn't need to eat and drink to live, what would people do? It's the only reason people ever get together. 'Hey, wanna go grab something to eat?' 'Can I buy you a drink?' 'Would you like to get a cup of coffee?' Our lives are consumed by the task."

"I've never looked at it that way."

"Pretend we didn't need to eat dinner. What would we have done tonight? Where would you have taken me?"

"I don't know. Bowling?"

"Oh, god. Really? Bowling?"

"You don't like bowling?"

"No."

"Why?"

"Because I'm not fifty and I don't like the smell of mass processed nacho cheese."

"Mini golf?"

"Mini golf is worse than bowling."

"Tell me something you *do* like," Marlon said.

"I like originality. I like...an honest moment."

"What do you mean...an honest moment?"

Karen studied Marlon for a moment and then returned to her food. "Nothing. Forget about it."

"No," Marlon argued. "Don't be one of those people."

"What people?"

"The people who bring something up just to say they don't want to talk about it."

"I hate those people," Karen smiled.

"Then don't be one."

"Okay. I'll give this a try." Karen put her fork down and leaned forward. "An honest moment. It's like…like…do you ever feel like everyone is just running around as fast as they can because they're so afraid that if they slow down they might actually…feel something?"

Marlon stared at Karen for a long time before answering: "I know exactly what you mean."

"Yeah?"

"Yeah."

"Prove it," Karen said. "Give me an honest moment. Show me that you're capable of feeling something."

Marlon studied her for a moment and then put down his fork. He leaned in closer and lowered his voice. "It's been my experience in life that most people feel the same emotions, but we're too afraid to act on them or even voice them, so we spend a lot of our lives feeling alone."

Karen thought for a moment. "I'm not sure I'm following."

"Have you ever wanted something so badly that your body ached for it? Have you ever hurt so deeply that you embraced the pain just so you could prove to yourself that you still had the capacity to feel? Have you ever been so…blissfully happy that you wished you could pause your life, or so miserable you wished you could end it?"

"Sure," Karen said softly.

"Those are all universal moments, feelings. We all have them, but we pretend we don't."

"How are you so sure we all have them?"

"Because we spend our lives experiencing them with other people, fictional people. It's why you go to the coffee shop and read books. It's why I teach English instead of…gym. It's why we watch TV and go to the movies. We're too afraid to reveal what we're feeling so we allow others to do it for us. It's safer that way. We're less exposed." Marlon paused, but could read in Karen's expression she wanted him to continue. "Sometimes we're so afraid of an honest, revealing moment that we'll take a pill just to escape them. Life's easier when you're numb. It's less…fragile."

Marlon looked at Karen, stared at her, to see if she made the connection with what he said. She looked back at him, touched and even to some degree, smitten.

"How was that?" Marlon asked.

"It was perfect."

CHAPTER 7

Lexi kept her car running. If Nichole suddenly changed her mind, Lexi wanted the quickest possible getaway. She didn't want to leave her best friend's happiness hanging in the balance because of a flooded engine or some other unforeseeable car issue. She knew Nichole wouldn't change her mind, though. She stuck around for two years when she wasn't pregnant. Now that she was, she would never leave Leroy.

Lexi pitied her friend. She worked with women like Nichole. Women who would need to take days off so their unsightly bruises could heal. Women who thought they needed a man in order to be complete, and who rationalized that being a man sometimes justified losing their temper. When Lexi offered this observation to Nichole, she replied that Leroy had never been physical with her. Lexi scoffed and told her not all bruises are visible. Now Lexi felt like a mother seeing her child off to fight in a war that was happening, like most wars, under the pretext of freedom, but was nothing more than a series of misunderstandings that now needed to be resolved with the lives of those who had nothing to do with the initial conflict. Nichole was entering a battle that would last the rest of her life against an opponent who had no business even being at the negotiation table. Leroy was the worst type of man: weak, who felt strong by preying on the weaker.

"Are you mad?" Nichole asked.

"No, I'm not mad," Lexi answered. "I just don't know why he has to know."

"He's the father. That's why."

"So?"

"So that gives him the right to know," Nichole said brusquely. She was tired of explaining it to Lexi.

"You have other options, Nic."

Nichole lowered her head. "I couldn't do that," she mumbled.

"That's not what I meant," Lexi said. "You could raise it alone. I would even help you. You could still stay with me. You could stay as long as you need."

"What do you know about raising a kid?"

"About as much as you and a hell of a lot more than Leroy."

"You're going back to Europe, Lexi. You don't want to raise this kid."

"When did you become this weak person who couldn't do anything on her own?" Lexi asked. "You're better than this stereotype."

Nichole stared out the window. "I'm not better than anything."

Outside, Nichole spotted a newly married couple pushing a child in a stroller. They arrived at their car where the mother unbuckled the screaming child and then carried her, kicking and screaming, to her car seat. She buckled the girl in the seat and quickly slammed the door to try and flush out the child's crying. It had never occurred to Nichole how much buckling children required. The mother returned to her husband and watched his struggle breaking down the stroller. His wife yelled something to him, but Nichole couldn't make out exactly what it was. Her mannerisms and tone indicated it had something to do with his inability to complete a task as simple as collapsing a stroller. She pushed her husband aside so she could show him how to do it properly. Even with the expert at the helm, the stroller refused to collapse. The husband started laughing. His wife punched him hard on the arm. Nichole looked away, unable to confront the reality that was on the cusp of being hers.

"Nichole, you don't need to do this," Lexi said. "I can drive away right now and you never have to see him again."

"Leroy's the father," Nichole said.

"You keep saying that like it means something. How is raising it with him going to be easier than raising it alone? How are you going to be able to afford his life along with your child's?"

"I'm not going to pay his debts anymore."

Lexi scoffed. "What you say and what you do are never the same anymore."

"What the hell does that mean?"

"You know exactly what it means, Nic."

Nichole sighed heavily and lowered her head. "Maybe this baby will change him. Maybe now he'll...he'll be...better."

"Leroy's life isn't yours to fix, Nichole."

Nichole put her hand on the door. "I'm going in there to tell Leroy he's the father. I love you, Lexi, but if you're not here after I tell him, I'll understand." And with that Nichole pushed open the door and walked quickly toward the café. Lexi unclipped her seatbelt to go after her friend but stopped herself before opening her door. Leroy's life wasn't Nichole's to fix, just as it wasn't Lexi's responsibility to fix Nichole's.

Nichole entered the café and scanned the place looking for Leroy. She heard him in the back corner of the restaurant yelling at the TV mounted in the corner. He wore his Larry Bird replica jersey. *Sportscenter* was on, and the highlights often caused outbursts from Leroy that triggered the other patrons to shoot threatening looks in his direction. No one ever took their threats further than a crooked stare, though. Leroy was too big and too black to provoke any real protests in regards to his animated outbursts. Nichole lowered her head and started toward him. She arrived at his booth and sat down across from him. Leroy knew she was there, but he didn't acknowledge her. She wasn't worth missing the Celtic's coverage even if he had seen them earlier. Nichole waited stubbornly yet sat passively, listlessly. She often found herself ignored in favor of sports' highlights. Leroy only ever gave Nichole attention during the three-minute commercial breaks. This was what she was about to sign up for. For life.

Sportscenter cut to commercial and Leroy, following protocol, looked at Nichole. She looked defeated and tired. He relished in her haggardness. He felt her appearance manifested that she made a mistake breaking up with him.

"You look old, Nic." Leroy said.

Nichole shifted in her seat and scanned the restaurant. An elderly man sat at the bar staring at Nichole. Nichole read something in his eyes she couldn't quite define. Remorse? Pity? She couldn't tell exactly what his expression revealed, only that it wasn't complimentary. His old eyes angered her. If he knew her situation, he would understand why she was here giving the father of her child another second chance. He didn't know her though, so he couldn't judge. Nichole sneered at the old man and looked back at Leroy.

"You haven't seen me in over a month and the first thing you say is I look old?" Nichole asked. She looked at the bar to see if the man overheard her defend herself. He hadn't. Nichole sank lower in her seat.

"It's just…you're usually so beautiful, you know?" Leroy explained. "It hurts me to see you like this. Like you're in pain or something. You never looked this…run-down when you were with me."

Nichole lifted her head and looked past Leroy and out to the parking lot. Lexi was gone. If she hadn't already left, Nichole would have stood up and marched out of Leroy's life for good. She would have left, and Leroy would never learn about the pregnancy. She would have walked out and never looked back and raised the child on her own, and when it asked who the father was, Nichole would have answered "Just some guy from my past." But Lexi wasn't in the parking lot any longer, so Nichole couldn't walk out. She was alone. Abandoned so unceremoniously like all people who liked to play the victim to their own circumstances. Everyone was always abandoning Nichole. Everyone but Leroy. He was always there. He was the only one who didn't leave her. He would make a good father. He had to, and Nichole believed if she kept telling herself this, it would come true. Forget about Lexi and everyone else. She didn't need them. She only needed Leroy and their baby. Together they could start a family, and if they stayed together, they could avoid the other pitfalls that plagued so many other couples.

Outside, she noticed the married couple from earlier had successfully collapsed the stroller. The husband loaded it into the back of the car and then kissed his wife affectionately. They both mouthed something to the other. Nichole couldn't hear what they said, but she guessed it was an apology followed with a heartfelt, 'I love you.' It was a beautiful moment, even if Nichole fabricated it to fit her narrative. She smiled weakly and looked back at Leroy.

"Leroy, I'm pregnant." It was out before Nichole even realized she had said it. She didn't really say it, but rather mumbled it as one long consecutive string of words. *LeroyI'mpregnant.* After she said it, and she knew she couldn't take it back, she closed her eyes and waited for the blowback. But it didn't come. She opened her eyes. Leroy was watching the television again.

"Did you hear what I just said?" Nichole asked. Leroy looked at her.

"No. I was…," he trailed off, his eyes fixed on the television.

"I'm pregnant."

She said it loud enough and clear enough this time for the other customers to hear. Some shifted in their seats to see from whence the confession came. The old man at the bar stared at Nichole for a beat and then scoffed and shook his head. Nichole shot him a look, but it went undetected. She hated the man for being too afraid to vocalize his distaste for Nichole, and she hated him more for turning away before she could defend herself with her steely-eyed reprimand. She looked away from the man and back at Leroy. He stared at her with awed wonderment.

"No, shit," he whispered, bringing life to his thoughts. "So it worked?"

"So what worked?"

Leroy still stared at Nichole, but his eyes were blank, distant. He looked at her without seeing her. "What worked, Leroy?" she asked again.

Leroy returned from his reverie and blinked away his thoughts. "Huh?"

"You just said 'it worked.' What worked?"

"Ah, nothing."

"You're lying," Nichole said.

"Forget it, baby. It's not important now."

"What's not important now?" Nichole said, raising her voice.

"Nothing," Leroy said, lowering his voice. "I was just thinking of...of ...something...," he trailed off.

"Don't lie to me!" Nichole said and slammed her fist on the table. Leroy jumped in his seat. The manager, who'd been watching the scene unfold from behind the bar, made his way to their table. Nichole saw him coming and lowered her head hoping that the gesture would be enough to convince him she didn't need a public scolding. It wasn't.

"You're disturbing the other customers," the manager said. "If you can't keep it down, you're going to have to leave."

Nichole looked at Leroy, expecting him to stand up for her, but he just sat silently, letting Nichole absorb the embarrassment of the moment.

"I'm sorry…we…we'll keep it down," Nichole said.

The manager shifted his gaze from Nichole to Leroy and shook his head. He then turned and walked back behind the counter.

"So are you moving back in now?" Leroy asked, keeping his voice low.

"I don't…know." Nichole whispered. God, she was tired.

"I think you should. We should do this thing together."

"You mean you want to be involved?" Nichole asked hopefully.

"Yeah. Of course."

Nichole sighed heavily. "Leroy, I need to know that you're going to be there for this child."

"Yeah, baby, sure. Yeah, I'll be there."

"I'm…I'm…," Nichole faltered. Leroy knew she was on the threshold of tears. He got out from his side of the booth and sat next to her. He put his arm around her. His arm felt nice. It was supportive and protective. She liked that he took the initiative to comfort her. It was a good sign.

"I'm really scared, Leroy," Nichole said. "I don't think I can do this alone. I need to know that you're done with that other woman."

"I swear, baby."

"You can't sleep around anymore."

"I won't."

She was crying now. Leroy held her tight and Nichole sobbed into his chest. He stroked her hair and told her everything would be all right. And it felt so good to be held that tightly that she actually believed him.

CHAPTER 8

Karen sat at her usual table reading a magazine. Marlon entered and took the seat across from her. Her latest book, *The Mysterious Stranger*, sat abandoned on the table next to the sugar caddy. Marlon craned his head and read the cover of the magazine.

"You traded Twain for a *Cosmopolitan* magazine?"

"It was on the table," Karen said, still reading. "Someone left it."

Marlon picked up Karen's coffee and took a sip. She didn't protest. He liked that he could sip her coffee without any resistance. It felt intimate and familiar. He put the cup back on the table and watched her, wondering when she would stop reading and pay him attention. He might as well have been invisible. He started tapping his finger on the table and ostentatiously cleared his throat. Karen smiled. She wasn't reading any longer but pretended just to keep Marlon waiting.

"So…what has you so interested?" Marlon finally asked.

Karen lowered the magazine. "How many dates do you think people go on before they sleep together?"

Marlon thought for a moment. "Seven."

"Three," Karen answered.

"Well, that's not fair. We've been out six times and I haven't even touched a breast," Marlon said.

"What about last night when you accidentally on purpose grazed it as you reached across me to open the door?"

"You caught that, huh?"

"It was pretty obvious."

"I get a pass though because it occurred during an act of chivalry."

"Chivalry isn't dead, huh?" Karen mocked.

"Not in this relationship."

Marlon smiled and took another sip from Karen's coffee before handing it back to her. She took her offered coffee and sipped it. The exchange seemed so common, like an old married couple familiar with each other's mannerisms and idiosyncrasies.

"Can I ask you something?" Karen said, turning serious.

"Sure."

"This," Karen said, holding up the magazine, "says that more than half of people kiss on the first date. Ninety percent kiss on the second." Karen looked at Marlon in anticipation of an answer, but Marlon wasn't sure that a question had been asked.

"We didn't kiss till our third," Karen said, frustrated that Marlon wasn't picking up on what she was trying to say. "And it was just a peck on the mouth. We didn't really kiss until our fourth."

"So?"

"So what took you so long to try and kiss me?"

"Are we really taking relationship advice from a *Cosmo* magazine?"

"I'm just trying to understand why we fall into the ten percent and not the ninety."

"Isn't it a good thing to be part of the minority? It makes us exceptional, doesn't it?"

"I don't know. Does it?"

Marlon sipped her coffee again. Karen wasn't sure if he was stalling or just really liked her coffee.

"It's because I respect you," Marlon said.

"What do you mean?"

"Do you like me?"

"Yeah."

"Would you like me as much had I tried to kiss you after just one date?"

Karen thought for a moment. "Fair enough. What about the second?"

"I didn't kiss you on the second because I wanted you to wonder why I didn't kiss you on the second."

"That makes…no sense," Karen said, her frustration growing.

"Look, if it's a question of attraction…," Marlon began but stopped when it was evident his answers were hurting more than helping. She wasn't getting his point. He leaned forward and leveled his eyes on her.

"Since I've been coming here, I've watched you sit at this table, by yourself, reading. You've read *The Fountainhead, The Poisonwood Bible,* and *Cold Mountain.* I know this because I've watched you. There are three coffee shops on my way to work and I've come to this one for the past two months waiting for the day that you would look up from one of your books and acknowledge I exist."

"Why didn't you just come up to me?"

"I didn't dare."

"Why?"

"Because you were, and are, the most beautiful woman I have ever seen."

Karen stared at Marlon, touched. Marlon stared back, not averting his eyes so that Karen knew he meant what he said.

"I was frightened by you," Marlon continued. "I was worried that I would say the wrong thing. I'm still frightened by you, but in a good way. The way that makes me constantly try to better myself. I haven't been forward with you physically because I don't want you to think I'm just another guy looking to get laid. You've been out with those types of guys a hundred times. I don't want to be in their category. Yeah, we've been on six dates, and yeah, we haven't made love, but those six dates have meant more to me than any night

I could have spent with some girl who has nothing more to offer than pop culture insights and butterfly tattoos." Marlon paused and leaned closer to Karen. "I would love to make love to you, Karen. I think about it all the time. I ache for the day when we can feel each other."

Karen was speechless, hypnotized by Marlon's words. "What would it be like?" she asked.

"What?"

"Making love to me."

"It would be…transcendental."

"You can do better than that," Karen answered.

Marlon thought for a moment. Karen liked testing him, asking for more when most would settle for what was already offered. Marlon stood and stepped to the side of the table and kneeled down in front of Karen. He undid two buttons on his shirt and reached for Karen's hand. He took her hand, put it inside his shirt, and placed her palm against his chest. He looked at Karen and she stared back at him, unsure what he was doing, but not resisting whatever it was.

106

"Do you feel that?" he asked.

Karen shifted her focus from Marlon to her hand. At first, she felt nothing, and then suddenly, beneath her palm, she felt Marlon's heart beating. It was more than beating; it was racing.

"Yeah, I can feel it," Karen said. "Why is it beating so hard?"

"That's what you do to me."

"What do you mean?"

"You bring me to life."

Marlon pressed her hand harder against his chest. His heart beat faster. "When we make love," Marlon said, looking squarely into Karen's eyes, "You'll feel this too."

Karen stared at Marlon, touched. She bit her lower lip and whispered, "Let's go back to my place."

CHAPTER 9

Nichole was late. She couldn't find her purse and keys, and her frustration grew with every place she searched that didn't yield her things. She asked Leroy if he had seen them, but he didn't hear her over his videogame gunfire. He sat on the sofa, shirtless, engaged in an epic battle with some other shirtless guy in another state attempting to give his life purpose by killing computer-generated soldiers. They both wore the standard-issued soldier headset so they could communicate in monosyllabic grunts and obscenities with each other.

Nichole emerged from the bedroom and asked Leroy if he had seen her purse. Leroy ignored her. He killed a soldier on the screen, and then yelled at the TV, letting the video game graphic know who was whose bitch.

"Leroy, have you seen my purse?" Nichole asked, raising her voice. Leroy kept his focus on the game, so Nichole crossed to the TV and turned it off.

"Hey," Leroy cried. "What the hell?"

"I can't find my purse or keys. Help me find them."

Leroy dropped his controller and pulled off his headset. He placed his hands on his knees and pushed himself to his feet. He sighed loudly, annoyed that he had to get off the sofa. He stretched and brought his arms over his head, before dropping them to scratch his crotch. Nichole watched him, mysteriously hypnotized by his animal-like disposition. Once Leroy had his situation situated, he started toward the bedroom. He returned a minute later holding Nichole's purse. Nichole took her purse and rifled through its contents until she found her keys.

"Why did you have it?"

"I needed it last night," Leroy said. He plopped back down on the sofa.

"What for?"

Leroy grabbed the remote and switched on the TV.

Nichole stepped in front of the TV. "Why did you have my purse last night?"

"I needed your credit card," he mumbled. He craned his head trying to steal glances at the Celtic highlights playing behind Nichole.

Nichole turned and switched off the TV. "What did you use my credit card for?" she demanded.

"Nothing."

"Did you use it to pay off a gambling debt?"

"No."

"Then what did you need it for?"

"Nothing. Shit."

"Leroy, I'm not fucking around," Nichole yelled. "You promised me—"

"It's a surprise."

"What?" Nichole asked, confused. "What are you talking about?"

"It's a surprise."

"What is? What's a surprise?"

"I can't tell you. It will ruin the surprise," Leroy explained.

Nichole sighed. "Leroy, I don't have time for this. What's the surprise? Am I going to get my credit card statement and see that I paid for something you can't afford?"

"I just wanted to do something nice for you is all."

"What, Leroy? What is it?"

"Baby—"

"No, Leroy. Tell me!"

Leroy lowered his head and sighed. "It's in the top drawer," he said, pointing into the kitchen.

Nichole walked into the kitchen and pulled open the top drawer. A ring box slid to the base of the drawer. Nichole looked at it for a moment and then grabbed the box and opened it. It was an engagement ring, half karat, cheap. The sight of the ring sickened Nichole. She couldn't surmise if it was the ring or just a bout of common sense, but it hadn't occurred to her until that moment how much she didn't want to marry Leroy. The ring was a concrete manifestation of all that she didn't want and the harsh reality of all that she had. She stormed back into the living room.

"What is this?" she asked, holding the ring out to Leroy.

"It's for you, baby."

"What are you talking about?"

"Now we can get married."

"You stole my credit card so you could buy me an engagement ring? Don't you see how wrong that is?"

"No."

"It's my credit card, Leroy! It's my money."

"Your money is my money, right?"

Nichole clutched the ring box in her hand so tightly she almost caved in the top. She looked at her watch. She didn't have time for this. She took a deep breath and asked for the receipt.

"Receipt?" Leroy asked. "What for?"

"I'm taking it back."

"What are you talking about? Taking it back?"

"You don't steal from me to buy me a ring, and this is not how you fucking propose."

"Well, this isn't how I wanted to fucking propose!" Leroy yelled back. "But you wouldn't get off my ass about where your purse was so I had to tell you."

"What are you talking about?"

"I was going to ask you tonight at the UNLV game."

"UNLV game?" Nichole repeated, incredulously. "You were going to propose at a football game?"

Leroy laughed. "It's basketball season. Football is over."

"Goddamn it, Leroy! That's not the point."

"Why are you so pissed? I did a nice thing. I thought you'd be excited."

"You can't really be this dense, can you?"

"What you mean?"

Nichole ran a frustrated hand through her hair. "I don't have time for this. I'm already late for work. Just give me the receipt."

"I don't have no receipt," Leroy said.

"Why?"

"The guy I bought it from, he don't really give receipts."

"You used my credit card at a place that doesn't even give receipts?"

"It's our credit card."

"No, Leroy, it's not. It's mine. I'm the one that works, not you. It's my money. Do you understand? There is no us. I'm not marrying you under these conditions."

"We're having a baby together, Nic? What do you think? I'm not going to marry the mother of my baby?"

"Yeah," Nichole said, starting for the door. "That's exactly what I think. If you want to marry me, then get a job and buy me a ring. Show me that you're worth marrying."

Nichole opened the door and slammed it shut on her exit. Leroy sat on the sofa for a moment and then picked up the videogame controller and reapplied his headset.

CHAPTER 10

Marlon beat Karen to the coffee shop. He sat at their usual table and waited. Every time the door opened, he perked up, anticipating her arrival. And every time she didn't walk through the door, he became a little more deflated. He checked his phone. No message. He checked his watch. She was now thirty minutes late. He gave the coffee shop one more overview to make certain she wasn't sitting at another table. She wasn't. He stood and left.

When he pulled into her driveway, she was sitting on her porch as if expecting him. She sensed his arrival but kept her eyes fixed on the cracked concrete laid out in the walkway to her front door. Marlon got out of his car and started toward her. He stopped at the foot of the steps and waited for her to look up at him, to acknowledge his presence, but she wouldn't.

"I thought we were meeting at the coffee shop," Marlon said.

Karen trembled. Marlon crouched down and took her chin in his hand and forced her to look at him. "Hey, what is it?"

Karen stared back at Marlon with hollow eyes. "It's in the bathroom."

Marlon looked at Karen for a moment longer and then stood and entered her apartment. He took the hall to the bedroom, passed through it and into the master bathroom. He switched on the light. He wasn't sure what he expected to find, and as the bathroom came into focus, he didn't notice anything out of the ordinary. Various toiletries were scattered about the sink. Two towels hung side by side on the towel rack. (The far one Marlon had used two nights ago when he stayed over.) Karen's bathroom scale sat on the floor next to the heater vent. The shower curtain was pulled closed. He pulled the curtain back, but it revealed nothing other than standard shower paraphernalia. He turned back around and started for the door when he noticed the pregnancy test on the counter. He had overlooked it earlier, thinking it was a toothbrush or some other innocuous bathroom item. He picked it up and looked at the two solid pink lines that traversed the white window of the applicator. He stared at the test for a long time. His eyes shifted from the lines to the description of what they meant. Two pink lines: pregnant.

Marlon thought back to the afternoon they first had sex. "Do you have a condom?" he asked, working on the top button of Karen's jeans. "I have an IUD," she answered, pulling his shirt off. Marlon didn't think to ask how long ago her IUD had been inserted, and Karen didn't think to tell him it was well over five years ago. She was just a teenager when her mother checked her out of school and drove her to the doctor insisting she get outfitted with some form of contraception. Furthermore, Karen didn't pay any attention to the stats the doctor recited about the longevity of the device. It had proven successful thus far, so why fix something that didn't appear to be broken?

Marlon put the test back on the counter and sat down on the edge of the tub. He tried to process his feelings, but he couldn't define what he felt. He always knew he wanted to be a father, so the prospect of being one didn't particularly frighten him. He obviously didn't think he would find himself guilty of making the same sexual indiscretions that so many other irresponsible couples made before him. He now found himself reciting to his future child what so many other parents tell their children when they get older: *you weren't a mistake; you were a surprise.* Life was nothing more than one placated explanation after another. Decisions needed to be justified and courses re-routed to lies that served as truths.

Marlon got to his feet and looked at the test one more time, not sure if he wanted the results to have somehow changed in the sixty seconds since he last looked at it. The two lines still stood starkly pink against the dense white plastic. He stood over the trash and almost dropped the test into the cylinder, but paused, thinking maybe this was something he should save. He put the test back on the counter and went outside. Karen was gone.

CHAPTER 11

Marlon sat at his desk grading papers when someone knocked on his classroom door. He looked up and saw Karen standing in the window. He hadn't seen her in six days. He'd tried calling, but she wouldn't answer. Text messages weren't acknowledged. He stopped by her place, but she pretended not to be home. He went to his car, retrieved a book, and waited on her porch and read. She glanced out the window and then quickly hid behind the curtains when Marlon caught her watching him. He read for an hour, tried the bell again, and then left.

Now that she wanted to see him, Marlon thought to extend the same treatment to her that she had given him for the past six days. He briefly returned to his stack of papers and pretended to read over them, but it was a futile gesture. He wanted to talk to Karen, so he figured he had better stop with the charade before she turned around and left. He stood and went the door.

"Hi," she said, keeping her eyes on the ground. "Is it a bad time?"

"No. I'm on my break. Come in."

Marlon held the door open and Karen entered. It had only been six days since Marlon last saw her, but she looked like a completely different person. Her body appeared emaciated and fragile. Her warm complexion had turned sallow and riddled with new lines about her eyes and mouth. She looked wounded and afraid. It broke Marlon's heart to see her.

"Have a seat," Marlon said, pointing to a nearby desk.

Karen sat in the desk and Marlon sat down next to her. Neither spoke. The clicking of the second hand from the clock above Marlon's door penetrated the silence. Marlon, hypnotized by the clicking, bobbed his head in rhythm with the clock's second hand and waited for Karen to speak. He felt that by putting up with her avoidance of him for the past week, it was his right to embrace the silence for as long as he wanted.

"How have you been?" Karen finally asked.

"Fine."

Silence again.

"Anything new?" Karen asked.

"Evidently, I'm going to be a father."

Karen wasn't sure if Marlon meant this as a joke, or some offhanded comment about her dysfunctional birth control.

"Why have you been ignoring me?" Marlon asked.

Karen stayed silent for a beat and then simply answered: "I'm sorry."

"You're sorry?" Marlon asked incredulously. "That's it?"

"I don't know what else to say."

"It's been six days."

"I know."

"What's going on?"

Karen bit her fingernails. "I don't know how to deal with surprises."

"So you don't deal with them at all?"

"I didn't know what to do," Karen explained. "I still don't."

"You talk to me. You let me be involved. That's what you do."

"Okay, so we talk and then what? What are we going to do?"

"What do you mean?"

"I mean…Jesus, Marlon, I'm pregnant. I don't know what to do."

"We…explore our options."

"And what are our options, Marlon? I don't want a baby. I don't want to be your typical Utah mom pushing a stroller in her early twenties."

"There's nothing typical about you," Marlon said.

"That's not the point."

"What is the point then, Karen? Help me understand."

Karen rubbed her eyes for a long time. "I feel so…trapped. I want to live my life and achieve my goals. A baby puts a halt to that. I don't know that I have what it takes to be a mother. I'm too selfish."

Marlon looked at her, bewildered. She felt his eyes on her and lowered her head.

"What are you saying?" Marlon asked. "Do you want to…abort it?"

Karen trembled slightly. "I don't know. I won't lie and say I haven't thought about it, but…"

"But what?"

"I don't know if I could actually go through with that."

"Then we have it."

"I don't know if I want that either."

"Then what? Adoption?"

Karen turned to Marlon, her eyes wide. This is what she wanted. Marlon understood and looked away. After a moment he said, "I don't know if I could do that."

"What do you mean?"

"The thought of my child…out there with someone else, another family…I just…I don't think I could do it."

"It's the best option, Marlon. I couldn't go through with an abortion and I'm not ready to drop my life and be a mom. Someone out there wants a baby and I could give it to them. This is the best choice for me and the baby."

"Well, what about me?" Marlon asked. "Don't I have any say in this?"

"What do you want?"

"I want the baby."

"Marlon…"

"What if I took it?"

"How would that work?"

"Just what I said. I'll take it…er…him or her…whatever…and raise it. You won't have to be involved at all. I would do it all on my own."

Karen never suspected Marlon would want the child. She always thought it was the woman's duty to want children. She'd been conditioned to believe no man really wanted children. They just kind of fell into fatherhood the same way an accountant falls into accounting. She often thought something was wrong with *her* when friends and family members arrived at social events with their children in tow. Everyone doted and fawned over them while Karen kept a safe distance. She didn't laugh at their innocence or adore their recklessness. She never asked if she could hold her friends' babies, and if one were suddenly thrust into her arms, it always seemed to explode in a series of angry sobs, as if it knew Lexi didn't want it. Sure, some babies were cute, but that was not reason enough to have a child. Children were loud and messy and fickle.

They were expensive and only appreciative if they got what they wanted. Motherhood was a life Karen never thought she wanted. But now that it was on the precipice of happening, could she change her mind? Could Marlon awaken the maternal instinct in her that had been dormant her entire life? A part of her wanted to believe he could, if only to feel a little more normal.

"And where would that leave us?" Karen asked.

"What do you mean?"

"I mean if you took it, then what? Are we done? I couldn't just hand over the baby and go back to what we were."

Marlon narrowed his eyes, trying to figure out what exactly Karen wanted. "Do you want to go back to what we were?"

"Is that possible?"

"What were we exactly?"

"We were…," Karen began but didn't know how to finish her thought. They had never officially put a stamp on their relationship. "We're…together, right? A couple?"

"Are you asking me or telling me?"

"I thought that's what we were."

"I assumed that since you've been ignoring me and you just said you don't want to have our child that we were probably over."

Karen dropped her head and whispered, "I don't want that."

Marlon expelled a pent-up, frustrated laugh. He was at a loss. He stood and paced the room.

"You want me, but you don't want anything to do with me?"

"I want you," Karen said, raising her voice and exposing her eagerness to be heard. "I want us. I want what we have. I just don't...I can't...I'm not ready to be a mother. This changes what we were."

Marlon stopped and leaned down in front of Karen. "It doesn't have to."

Karen looked at Marlon and then looked away. He didn't understand what she was having such a hard time expressing. She couldn't fault him. What she wanted wasn't possible.

"I want this baby," Marlon said. "I would love for you to be involved. I would love to continue with us. This past month with you has been the best month of my life. I don't want to lose you. I know we can do this, Karen. We could do it together."

Karen lifted her eyes and stared back at Marlon. He reached across the desk and took her hands. His eyes pleaded for her to give him a chance.

"I'm so scared," Karen said, choking on the words.

"I know. I am too, but if I have faith in anything, it's us. Worse people have done this before."

Karen touched Marlon's cheek. He put his hand over hers and kissed her palm. "I don't want to lose you," she said.

"You don't have to."

"How can you be so sure?"

Understanding dawned on Marlon. He looked at Karen, recognizing what he could do to alleviate her fears. Having the baby frightened her, but the root of her fears stemmed from the certainty that Marlon would abandon her. She wanted a stronger a commitment. He smiled weakly, silently reprimanding himself for not seeing it sooner.

"Marry me," he said.

Karen's eyes widened. "What?"

"Marry me," Marlon repeated, keeping his eyes locked on Karen's so she knew he was serious. "I know there's still so much we don't know about each other, and this is completely insane, but...marry me."

"We don't...Marlon..."

"What?"

"I...I hardly know you," she protested weakly.

"I'm Marlon Brown. My parents named me after Marlon Brando. I'm a poorly paid high school English teacher. When I was a kid, I cut the head off of my sister's favorite Barbie and flushed it down the toilet. My first wet dream involved Peggy Bundy, and earlier this year a stripper robbed me." Marlon paused for a moment and then added: "I love you. Marry me."

Karen gasped and covered her mouth to keep from laughing or screaming or crying or all three. She didn't want to get married. She especially didn't want to get married in an effort to reconcile faulty birth control. She cared for Marlon deeply. She would even go as far as to admit she loved him. She certainly knew she enjoyed him enough to want to continue seeing him, and yes, it frightened her to think of having a baby alone and it frightened her more to think of losing Marlon when she felt so strongly for him. But marriage? She was only twenty-three. Life expectancy for an American woman hovered right around eighty. If she lived to be eighty, that would sentence her to fifty-seven years with the same man. A man whom she adored and admired, but what if that admiration wore off? Karen wasn't stupid. She knew more than half of marriages failed, and she knew that number increased drastically when the marriage occurred with young people. People grow apart when they grow up. There was nothing about her that made her exceptional, so why should she convince herself otherwise when it came to marriage? She was still a kid on many levels. Just an adolescent resisting adulthood who now needed to grow up quicker than she wanted.

She could count on one hand how many happily married people she knew. She would have to include her toes if she wanted to enumerate the opposite. She believed people got married under the packaged pretenses of bad Julia Roberts' movies and worse Bruno Mars' songs. Once real life factored into the equation, people realized the farce but often lost the fight in them to do anything about it. Marriage was submission. It was a war of attrition. It wasn't about being with the person you love; it's about finding someone you can tolerate. It's more of a cohabitation business arrangement with a bimonthly sexual clause. And those are the good marriages. The ones that stand the test of time simply because they're easier than the alternative.

In nine months Karen would give birth to a child. She wouldn't want the child to use her example as a justification to marry young when ill-equipped for the task. But what was the alternative? Let Marlon go? Possibly throw away a great guy because instead of submitting to him, she submitted to her own fears and insecurities? No, marriage wasn't submission; life was. And besides, if marriage was more of a business arrangement than a romantic notion, why shouldn't Karen cash in on the partnership? Marlon had good health insurance that could offset the cost of the child. In terms of tax purposes, marriage made sense. And maybe they could work. Maybe God—whoever He, She, or It was—put Marlon into Karen's life at this juncture to save her from a life of even worse decisions. Maybe Marlon was her savior instead of her jailer. If Karen was insightful enough to actually weigh the odds of marital success, maybe that did make her exceptional on some level. Isn't recognizing a problem the first step in solving it? Maybe her recognition of who she was and what she offered, could be enough to make a marriage work. The next fifty-seven years didn't have to take on the misery of a prison sentence. It could be a reprieve, an absolution. On their first date, she had asked Marlon for an honest moment and he had delivered. No other man had been able to give an answer so honest. He had coaxed her into bed with a beating heart that proved she gave his life...life. He knew how to touch her and where to touch her. How many people could say that about their partner? Maybe, just maybe, they could work.

Karen grappled with her thoughts and looked back at Marlon. He still waited patiently for an answer. She knew she needed to say something, but she wasn't sure what. If she had a rose, she would have stripped away the petals in the romantic gesture of letting a flower decide her fate. It made as much sense as anything else at the moment. Marlon waited, and Karen weighed the decision and suddenly pursed her lips slightly upward into a weak smile.

He loves me…He loves me not…He loves me…

She shrugged her shoulders and said, "Okay."

CHAPTER 12

Leroy pushed the shopping cart, and Nichole, her arm laced through his, walked to next him. They were having a good day. Leroy won a big hand at poker the night before and returned home with groceries. It was a first, both the winning hand and the groceries. Nichole interpreted it as a sign that Leroy understood he needed to contribute more if their relationship was going to work. Of course, when Nichole asked where he got the money, he lied and said he found a job pouring concrete. Nichole suspected his winnings came from poker (who pours cement until two in the morning?) but she didn't investigate. It was better to believe a comforting lie than face a harsh truth.

Nichole decided months ago to turn their extra bedroom into a nursery. It needed to be painted. During breakfast, Nichole asked Leroy if he wanted to go look at paint samples. She asked because involving the father in baby-related decisions seemed like the right thing to do. She offered it out of some unfounded obligation; she was surprised when Leroy said he would actually like to come. Maybe he really was changing.

"How about Michael?" Leroy asked. They were discussing baby names. Nichole processed the name. She couldn't find any real fault with it. It was common, but strong and most importantly to Nichole, the gender of the child would never be in question with a name like Michael. She didn't like ambiguity when it came names. Kelly, Shelby, Terry, Bailey, Pat. Those weren't names; they were riddles. She also liked that "Michael" wasn't overly "unique" to the point of being asinine. It wasn't a pathetic attempt at being original, thus sentencing her child to a life of explaining how their parents came up with a name that looked like someone sat on a keyboard and the result was absurdity disguised as uniqueness.

"I could get on board with Michael," Nichole said. "It's a strong name. A good name."

"Hell yeah, it's a good name," Leroy said. "Best baller ever."

"What?"

"Michael Jordan, baby. Best baller ever."

Nichole scoffed and untangled her arm from Leroy. She felt stupid for believing Leroy could suggest a name that wasn't from an athlete. Michael was still a good name; it just couldn't be the name of her child now that she understood the origin.

"I'm not naming my child after some basketball player," Nichole said.

"It's not just some basketball player. It's Michael Jordan. The best to ever play the game."

"I don't care. Michael is off the table."

"How about LeChole?"

"LeChole?" Nichole repeated. The name hurt her mouth. "What is LeChole?"

"It's Leroy and Nichole combined."

Nichole shook her head. People like Leroy were putting the people who created the Disneyland mouse ears and novelty license plate key chains out of work because no one could predict which names to stitch on the caps any longer. Did people realize that their attempts at being original just made them the same? Inventing stupid names has been around as long as stupid people.

"That's a horrible name," Nichole said.

"It's clever."

"No, it's not. It's whatever the exact opposite of clever is."

"It's original, baby."

"Originality and stupidity are not the same things, Leroy. I'm not naming my daughter LeChole."

"Of course not," Leroy said. "We're having a boy."

Nichole cringed. "You wanted to name a boy LeChole?" she asked incredulously.

"Yeah."

"That's even worse. Besides, you don't know that we're having a boy."

"Sure I do," Leroy said, puffing out his chest. "I have man cum."

Nichole blushed and looked to see if anyone overheard Leroy's comment. The nearest customers were twenty feet away enthralled with bathroom fixtures. Nichole quickened her step, trying to put more distance between her and Leroy.

"God, Leroy, we're in public. Don't talk that way."

Leroy laughed, proud of his masculine nature. He was about to offer more offensive musings when his phone vibrated. He pulled the phone from his pocket and flipped it open to read the text. Nichole stopped at the paint samples and studied the different colors. She pulled a yellow and blue sample and turned to Leroy.

"I think blue or yellow are our safest bets," Nichole said. "They're neutral colors."

Nichole waited for Leroy to acknowledge her, but he was too busy typing a text.

"Leroy," Nichole said, raising her voice. "Be present, okay?"

"Hang on, baby," Leroy said, still typing. "I'm trying to get into this poker game next week at Aaron's house."

"I thought you were done with poker," Nichole said.

Leroy looked up and silently cursed himself for his blunder. "I'm-I'm...not playing," he stammered. "I'm just...going to...it's not...I told them I can't play because I have to work."

Leroy could see that she didn't believe him, but like all liars, he wouldn't rescind the lie. Nichole looked past Leroy at a couple down the aisle standing at the mixing counter. They handed their paint sample to the worker and then looked each other, smiled and kissed. Nichole hated the couple immediately. Hated them, their happiness, and their stupid mutually selected paint. Nichole looked back at Leroy and handed him the paint samples.

"What are these?" Leroy asked.

"Yellow or blue?"

"What you mean yellow or blue? We can't paint the baby room yellow or blue. Those are Laker colors."

"They're neutral colors, Leroy."

"Neutral? What does that mean?"

"It could work for a boy or a girl."

"We ain't having no girl."

"Unless we do."

"Well, then why don't we just go and find out the sex?"

Nichole's hands shook. She was tired of having the same conversations. She had already decided she didn't want to know the child's gender before the birth. Leroy knew this. He put up a little resistance, but ultimately let Nichole have her way. It was important to her and he appeared to have accepted it. Maybe it was because he wasn't contributing financially at the time that he conceded the decision. Maybe he had other things on his mind like other women or pocket aces or a basketball score. Whatever leverage Nichole seemed to have earlier appeared to be slipping. She took a deep breath and collected herself.

"I want it to be a surprise," she said calmly.

"That's stupid," Leroy said.

"Not to me."

"I can't raise my kid in no Laker bedroom," Leroy said, dropping the paint samples. They fluttered to the floor. Nichole watched them fall and recognized the irony of her life in their slow descent. "I'm a Celtic fan," Leroy offered as a way of justifying his hatred for the paint samples.

"This isn't about sports, Leroy. It's about our child."

"Who will grow up a Celtic's fan," Leroy said.

"Don't you hear how pathetic you sound?" Nichole cried. "Your happiness is contingent on how well people you don't know, and never will know, can put a ball through a hoop. It's ridiculous."

139

"What are you talking about, Nic?"

"Us, Leroy!" Nichole screamed. "Our family." Customers and employees turned and looked at Leroy and Nichole. Leroy stepped to Nichole and lowered his voice.

"Hey, I'm here for you, right? I'm here for our baby, for our family. I'm picking out paint colors. I'm involved, just like you asked. What's the problem?"

"Sometimes your involvement makes things more difficult."

"What are you talking about?" Leroy asked.

"Just once I wish you made something easy."

"I'm making this really easy. No yellow or blue. What's not easy about that?"

Nichole opened her mouth to explain, but Leroy's phone buzzed again and he had his head down typing a text before Nichole could voice her thoughts. She stared at the top of Leroy's head and waited for him to look at her so he could see his affront wasn't going to be taken lying down. But he wouldn't stop typing, and Nichole was too tired to fight. She turned and started for the exit, passing the happy couple with their perfect color for whatever stupid room they were going to go home and paint. She offered a pleasant smile as she passed, which was received and reciprocated which made her hate them even more.

She pictured them at home, sheets covering the furniture and floors while they painted side by side. They would inevitably have their couples' paint fight where one of them "accidentally" gets paint on the other. To counter, the stained lover retaliates until paint in strewn about and they're suddenly tearing off each other's clothes in a moment of unadulterated sexual desire. They make mad love on paint-stained sheets and then lay naked and sweaty and happy in each other's arms and think of how goddamn perfect their life is and how great the fresh paint looks on their walls.

Nichole choked on the image, fighting back tears of a life that seemed to exist for everyone but herself. Leroy finished sending his text and looked up to find Nichole was already at her car.

CHAPTER 13

The townhome was a year old. Modest. Simple. The previous owner bought it brand new, met a girl about a week later, and moved in with her three months after that. He put the townhome on the market for the exact same price he purchased it. Marlon had a friend that was a realtor. He called and asked to meet for lunch. He told her about the baby and the proposal and how he and Karen now needed something small (but not too small), and basic (but not too basic). The realtor told him about the townhome. She gave him a tour, and Marlon returned the next day with Karen.

Marlon knew he wanted the home the moment he pulled into the driveway. It was clean, simple and practical—just like Marlon. His fear was that it might be *too* clean, simple and practical for Karen. It dawned on Marlon as he stood in the empty living room surveying the vaulted ceilings that he didn't really know that much about the woman he was marrying. Would she like the colors? The floor plan? The countertops in the kitchen? The carpet? The tile? Marlon loved it, but would Karen? He didn't know because he didn't know her, and yet he was engaged to her. They were going to have a baby. It was all so…sudden. Did sudden equate illogical? And if it did, were they doomed to fail? Marlon had always been pragmatic, but proposing to Karen wasn't pragmatic at all; it was the exact opposite of pragmatic. It was impulsive, and if other marriages were any indication, completely stupid.

Marlon looked at Karen and prayed that she loved the house, not because he loved it, but because at that moment, it seemed to represent so much more. What exactly? Marlon wasn't sure. But he felt that if she didn't approve, her refusal would somehow be indicative of the rest of their life. A precursor to a lifetime of disagreements and wrongful interpretations.

"So…what do you think?" Marlon asked, cautiously. They had been inside the house for over five minutes and Karen hadn't yet said a word.

She fixed her eyes on the canned lights shining down from the ceiling. Her eyes surveyed the room, working their way down the walls before settling on the floor. She was expressionless. Marlon sensed she didn't like it. He took a step toward her, ready to

143

recite his sales pitch, highlighting all the features and the economics of the home.

"The HOA fees are small," he said, "and the seller is asking for $10,000 less than what it's worth. He just wants to get rid of it without any haggling. Riley said if we lock in the interest rate today, we could get it at three and a quarter." He paused and then added: "It's a buyer's market." He cringed at his words. He sounded like a realtor. On the salesperson hierarchy, realtors resided just one notch above car salesmen.

It was evident Karen heard Marlon, but she gave him no reaction to what he said. Marlon inferred no reaction meant she wasn't on board.

"It's only two bedrooms," he continued "but we really only need two for now. We can turn the extra bedroom into a nursery."

Karen stared past Marlon at something on the far wall. Marlon followed her gaze, but couldn't tell what captured her attention. He turned back to her. She locked her eyes on him. He stared back at her and waited. Slowly, her lips turned upward into a beautiful, confused smile.

"I love it," she whispered.

Marlon went to her, picked her up, and spun her around. Karen screamed delightfully and waited for her world to halt before kissing Marlon on the mouth. His lips were soft, his breath sweet and inviting. He felt like she imagined someone should that you're going to marry. It felt good to allow herself the ecstasy of momentarily forgetting this moment was a result of neglectful decision-making.

"This is going to be our home," Marlon said. "This is where we will raise our child."

Karen shrieked and kissed Marlon again.

"What color should we paint the nursery?" Marlon asked.

"Any color you'd like."

CHAPTER 14

Nichole sat alone wrapped in Leroy's Boston Celtics blanket. Her eyes were blank and distant, staring at the far wall. A closed pizza box sat on the coffee table in front of her. It was after midnight. Leroy was supposed to be home at five with the week's groceries. At six, she found the condoms next to the opened safety pin. At seven, she thought about packing a suitcase. At eight, she packed one. By nine, she packed another and a duffle bag. By ten, she loaded the suitcases into the trunk of her car. She left the duffle bag resting by the door. She wanted Leroy to see it when he got home.

Shortly after one, she heard Leroy fumbling with his keys outside the door. She thought about getting off the sofa and opening the door for him, but she didn't want to extend the effort or the courtesy. From outside, she heard him drop the keys twice. It was a full minute before he finally managed to get inside.

He switched on the light and saw Nichole sitting on the sofa. She didn't move.

"What you sitting in the dark for?" Leroy asked, closing the door behind him.

"Where are the groceries, Leroy?" Nichole asked. She knew he didn't have the groceries. She knew he would lie. She wanted to hear him lie.

Leroy took a step into the living room and almost tripped over the duffle bag. He eyed it curiously. "Why's there a bag by the door?" He asked.

"Where are the groceries?"

"Shit, baby. I totally spaced it. I can get them in the morning."

"It is the morning," Nichole said. She still hadn't looked at him. She was lifeless save for the movement of her lips.

"Yeah, I guess it is," Leroy said.

"Where have you been?"

"Working."

"You're lying."

Leroy sighed heavily and sat down in the recliner. "Shit, baby, you wouldn't believe what happened tonight."

147

"I know exactly what happened," Nichole said, keeping her voice level. "You weren't working. You were playing poker."

"No, baby, I was working."

"Bullshit."

"I was. Honest."

"Why didn't you call?"

"My phone died."

"Where are the groceries?"

"I didn't...look, it's late and...let's just get in bed."

"I need to hear you admit that you weren't working. That you were playing poker."

"Okay, look," Leroy said, trying to figure out a story in his head. "I *was* working. My boss was supposed to give me a ride home. I told him I had to get groceries, but he had already paid in for this game—"

"You're so pathetic," Nichole said evenly.

"No, baby, listen," Leroy pleaded. "You won't believe what happened."

"You were up. A big hand came, a hand that only one other hand can beat. You went all in. Someone else went all in. And that someone else had the one hand that could beat your hand."

Leroy eyed Nichole suspiciously. "How'd you know that?"

"Because that's what always fucking happens, Leroy," she said. "All losers have the same loser story." She paused a minute and then added under her breath: "even me."

Nichole wanted to cry but willed herself not to. Leroy didn't deserve any more of her tears. She had the epiphany a few hours earlier. That moment of clarity that finally breaks through and shows you all the lies you've told yourself in the past won't ever manifest to truth. She was done with Leroy. Free of him like an addict taking a final drink because the alcohol no longer retained its hold.

Leroy sat on the edge of the recliner and tried to plead his case. "No, baby, this time it was different. I had him till the turn card and then that motherfu…," he leaned forward and opened the pizza box. He looked inside for a long time, not understanding what he was looking at.

"What the…what is this?" he asked.

Inside was a safety pin and a handful of unopened condoms. All the pizza was gone. Hours earlier Nichole had one slice and threw the rest away. Leroy loved pizza.

Confused, Leroy continued staring into the box. He didn't know what he was most upset about: that there wasn't any pizza, or that it appeared Nichole suspected he tampered with the condoms.

"What is this?" he asked.

"You tell me," Nichole said.

"Tell you what?" he said. "Why don't you tell me why you ate all the fucking pizza? I'm starving."

"I didn't eat it. I threw it out."

"What?"

"In the drawer next to your side of the bed, where you keep your condoms, I found that safety pin."

Leroy shifted in his seat. "So?"

"So I filled one of your condoms with water. It leaked. In about twenty different places the condom leaked."

"What do you mean, 'leaked'?"

"I mean there were tiny holes in the condom and water was leaking from them."

"So?"

"Remember that day in the coffee shop when I told you I was pregnant? After I told you, you said 'it worked.' Do you remember that?"

"I never said that," Leroy lied.

"Is this what worked, Leroy?" she asked, pointing at the pizza box.

"I don't…"

"Were you trying to get me pregnant? Did you purposely poke holes in the condoms? Is that what worked?"

"Poked holes? Shit. What are you talking about?"

"For the past year I kept threatening to leave. If I left, who would pay your rent? Who would buy your food? You figured if I got pregnant, I couldn't leave. You needed me to pay your bills so you knocked me up and then went out and fucked some other girl."

Leroy scoffed but didn't deny Nichole's accusations. His silence confirmed what Nichole already knew. She threw the blanket off from her and stood up. Leroy couldn't believe his eyes. She wore his Michael Jordan replica jersey. She turned to him, looking at him for the first time since he got home. Across the front of the jersey was a bright yellow paint streak.

"What the fuck did you do to my Jordan jersey?" Leroy cried.

Nichole walked to the door and picked up her duffle bag. "I painted the extra bedroom while you were out losing all our grocery money."

"You what?"

"Go Lakers."

Leroy bolted down the hall to the spare bedroom and switched on the light. Nichole waited long enough to hear him scream and then walked out the door with her bag. Leroy fell to the ground and stared hopelessly at the giant Los Angeles Laker logo that covered the wall.

CHAPTER 15

When Lexi saw Nichole's car in her driveway, she knew something was wrong. The car was parked diagonally, taking up most of Lexi's driveway. The interior light was on. Lexi parked at the curb, and cautiously approached Nichole's car, surveying for damage. She didn't spot any damage, just two suitcases on the back seat. She rushed inside.

Her house was dark. From down the hall, she could see her bedroom light shining dimly. She started toward it, calling Nichole's name as she went.

She found Nichole passed out on the floor with an empty vodka bottle next to her. Lexi put the bottle on her dresser and then leaned down and sat Nichole upright. She moaned at the effort. Lexi went into her bathroom and returned with a cold washcloth. She held it to Nichole's forehead and slightly slapped her friend until she opened her eyes.

"Nic. Hey, Nichole, what's wrong? What happened?"

Nichole squinted and held her hand over her eyes to flush out the bedroom light. She tried to focus on Lexi and the rest of her surroundings, but the effort was too exhausting. She opened her mouth, slurred something, but it was incoherent. She closed her eyes and tried to lie down again, but Lexi wouldn't let her. She slapped her again, this time harder, forcing her to stay awake.

"Nichole, what happened?"

Nichole stared at Lexi for half a minute and then started laughing deliriously. The laughing quickly turned to sobbing. She was drunk and hysterical.

"You're eight months pregnant," Lexi said, trying to make sense of the situation. "What are you drinking for?"

Nichole stopped crying. She lifted her hands so Lexi could look at them. They were trembling and her knuckles were red.

"I punched my baby," she sobbed.

"What?"

"I punched...I tried to hurt it and...," she covered her face with her hands and cried. Lexi took hold of Nichole's wrists and pulled her hands from her face.

"Stop it, Nichole! Stop it! What happened?"

"I can't have this baby," Nichole cried. "I don't want it."

"What happened? Did Leroy hurt you?"

"Leroy poked holes in his condoms."

"What?"

"He was trying to get me pregnant. He poked holes in his condoms without telling me. He wanted to trap me and I found out about it."

"Is that why you're here? Did you leave him?"

Nichole nodded. "I packed all my things. They're in my car."

"Okay," Lexi said, piecing together the night's events. "That's good. You can stay here."

"I can't have this baby, Lexi."

"Is that why you're drinking?"

Nichole nodded. "I don't know what else to do. It's too late for an abortion."

"Getting drunk isn't a solution, sweetie," Lexi said.

"I know." Nichole lowered her head. "I just didn't know what else…" she trailed off.

"This isn't the baby's fault, Nic. You can't be this irresponsible."

"I know. I'm just lost, Lex. I can't take care of a baby that's half Leroy's. I couldn't love it knowing that he was part of it."

"You don't know that."

"If I have this baby—his baby—he's going to be in my life forever, Lexi."

"He doesn't have to be. And if you don't want the baby, you don't have to keep it. You can still give it up for adoption."

"Adoption?" Nichole said. The word rolled off her tongue like a new discovery.

"Yeah. You find a nice family. Give the child to them. You don't ever have to see Leroy again if you don't want."

"Why would anyone want a baby I made with Leroy? Why would anyone want anything I helped create? People like me, people like Leroy, we shouldn't even be allowed to have kids."

Lexi didn't mean to laugh, but she couldn't help it. Nichole's pathetic tone lent itself to laughter, and the brutally honest observation that Leroy and her shouldn't be allowed to have kids was both painfully accurate and hilarious. Too bad, Lexi thought, that more people didn't recognize their own inadequacies when it came to reproducing.

"It's not funny, Lexi," Nichole said, but then she started laughing, too.

"I know it's not," Lexi said, trying to stifle her merriment. "I've just never seen you so…honest before."

Nichole stopped laughing and turned serious. "What am I going to do, Lexi? I'm trapped."

"No, you're not. You stick this out for one more month. Have the baby and if you don't want to keep it, you give it up for adoption. I'll help you. I'll help you in any way I can. But you can't drink again. No matter how bad things get, this can't happen again."

Nichole nodded and then fell into Lexi's arms. "I cursed my baby tonight," Nichole said. "I punched myself in the stomach and

cursed it. I told it I didn't want it, and I wanted it out of my body."
Nichole began to cry again. "I'm so sorry. I was stupid. I wasn't
thinking."

"It's okay," Lexi said.

"Do you think I hurt it?"

"We can go to the doctor tomorrow and check. We'll see if
anything is wrong, okay?"

"I was so stupid. I don't want to hurt it. I don't want to lose
it. I could be such a good mom. I have so much love to give."

"I know, sweetie," Lexi consoled. "I know. We'll go to the
doctor tomorrow."

"I painted the nursery Laker colors."

"What?"

"The extra bedroom at Leroy's. We turned it into a nursery.
I painted it Laker colors just to be mean. Yellow and blue."

Lexi released Nichole and held her at arms' length. "You
did?"

"Yeah."

"Why did you do that?"

"He's a Celtics fan. He hates the Lakers."

"No shit."

"Are you proud of me?"

Lexi studied her friend and smiled. She understood that at that moment, nothing mattered more to Nichole than Lexi's approval. It was hard for her not to laugh again.

"Yeah, I'm proud of you. I'm so proud of you."

Nichole smiled. "He screamed when he saw it."

"I bet he did," Lexi said. "Let's get you to bed." She helped Nichole to her feet and guided her to the bed. Lexi pulled back the comforter and Nichole got inside.

"I should have listened to you," Nichole said.

"About what?"

"Leroy."

"You're listening now."

"Yeah, and look at the mess I got myself into."

"It's nothing you can't get out of."

"One day I'm going to be a great mom."

"I know."

Nichole opened her mouth to say something else, but the thought escaped her, and before she could reclaim it, she closed her eyes and was softly snoring. Lexi pulled the comforter over Nichole and turned out the light as she exited the room.

CHAPTER 16

Moving boxes cluttered the living room. Old newspapers and bubble wrap used to protect glass and other valuables littered the floor and counter space. Movers carried in and randomly dropped furniture that did not yet have a permanent destination. The house seemed to have shrunk now that it was furnished; it seemed to have shrunk even more due to the haphazardness of the furniture's placement. Marlon hated the mess but knew it would subside once they got everything organized. At the moment, he was just enjoying the madness, knowing that this level of chaos was just part of the agreement of becoming a husband, father, and homeowner. It all felt so...adult.

Marlon stood in the corner over an opened box. He pulled a stack of books from the box and then turned to the bookcase in the corner to shelve the books. Karen was ten feet away shuffling through her own box. She sat in a chair under the burden of her six-month pregnant belly. They worked in comfortable silence. Lately, just each other's presence was enough to satiate the other; words didn't need to ruin their moments of contentment.

Karen stood to stretch and watched Marlon fastidiously rearrange his books on the shelf. After much debate, he'd decided to arrange his novels alphabetically by title. He entertained the idea of arranging them chronologically or by author's last name until ultimately settling on titles. Karen smiled, amused by his meticulous nature. It was Marlon's top priority to unpack his books. They were trophies to him. Stories read and collected to help shape him into the man he was. Karen loved that man, even if she didn't fully understand him.

She traversed the clutter and went to him, hugging him from behind, pressing herself into his back. Marlon felt her pressed up against him and smiled. Her hands settled on his chest; Marlon clasped his hands over hers, holding her against him. She turned her head and rested it between his shoulder blades, getting lost in his scent and the comfort of the moment. She stood silently for a minute, thinking of the choices that had brought her to where she was. As her mind wandered, a reoccurring thought racked her. Her body stiffened slightly, and she loosened her grip on Marlon.

"Do you ever think about God?" she asked after a minute.

"What do you mean?"

"I mean just that. Do you ever think about God?"

"Not really," Marlon said. He resumed shelving his books.

"Why not?" Karen asked. She was suddenly despondent and needed more than Marlon was giving.

"I don't know," Marlon said. "What's the point?"

"What do you mean?"

"I mean…why should I think about someone or something that may not even exist?"

"You don't believe in God?" Karen asked.

Marlon paused for a moment and looked at the book in his hand. *A Grief Observed* by C.S. Lewis.

"I don't know. I'm open to the possibility that there is a God, but logic tells me there probably isn't."

"So you're agnostic?"

"Sure."

"Do you want there to be a God?"

Marlon thought for a moment. "I'm not sure."

"Isn't that bleak?"

"Depends on how you look at it."

"What do you mean?"

"If I'm supposed to buy into the God that has been marketed by various religious institutions, then I'm forced to rationalize why He continues to allow so much hate, genocide, and intolerance to consume the world. If there isn't a God, then I guess I can feel better about why so many ugly things happen. So either God's a prick, or He doesn't exist." Marlon paused for a moment. Karen stared at him in disbelief. "I guess agnostic suits me because there really isn't any proof. Some people are so certain there is a God, but they're usually the ones who fly off the handle whenever you question Him. I think if something can cause someone to become so defensive, it speaks of doubt."

Marlon put Lewis's book on the shelf, nestled next to Jerome Lawrence and Robert E. Lee's play, *Inherit the Wind.*

Karen thought about Marlon's logic for a moment. She couldn't understand why, but his agnostic defense, as sound as it was, bothered her. Had Marlon known his answer would cause Karen so much discomfort, he would have offered a more diplomatic one. God, or the possibility of one, was so insignificant to him, he would have said anything (complimentary or otherwise) about God that would alleviate any anxiety his beliefs (or lack thereof) caused Karen. Marlon simply didn't think enough of God to care whether He really existed. As far as Marlon was concerned, God was just an insecure fictional character in a book with several plot holes. He didn't think God or religion was a high priority to Karen. Comments she made belittling religion earlier in their relationship led Marlon to believe she held his similar views.

One Sunday morning, as they sat on Marlon's front porch drinking coffee, they watched droves of people, dressed in their Sunday best, plod to church with their heads low and their gait labored. They looked like criminals marching to the gallows. Karen chuckled at their distressed demeanors and whispered, "Poor bastards" before taking a sip from her coffee. However, that comment, and others similar to it, were made *before* she had gotten pregnant out of wedlock. Now that she may face the wrath of God for her choices, she didn't think God deserved the same blasé attitude she earlier employed. Her sudden concern was lost on Marlon. At the moment, he only cared about organizing his books.

"Have you ever gone to church?" She asked.

Marlon thought for a moment. "My mom took me to Easter Mass once. I was just a kid. I don't really remember it. Another year, we went to a Christmas pageant. It was nice, but some spectators were upset that baby Jesus was black. The director shot back saying there weren't any Middle Eastern babies in the community. That just pissed the crowd off more. They wanted a North American Jesus, I guess." Marlon paused for a beat, recalling the memory. He chuckled and then added, "They served brunch after. Pretty good French toast."

"Do you ever pray?" Karen asked.

"No."

"Never?"

"Not in the sense that I get on my knees and ask for stuff."

166

"Why not?"

Marlon turned and looked at Karen. She stared hollow-eyed at a far wall. Marlon followed her gaze to the wall that kept her attention; it was empty, just a blank canvas not yet adorned with superfluous house décor. It finally occurred to Marlon that Karen's inquiries were rooted in something more serious than he first realized.

"What's going on?" he asked.

"I grew up catholic," Karen said. "You didn't know that about me, but it's true."

"Okay. Why are you telling me this?" Marlon asked. "Is being catholic important to you?"

"I don't know. I guess…"

"What is it, Karen?"

Karen's chin quivered. She quickly blinked, trying to stave off the invading tears.

"Do you think God is…upset with us?"

"Why would He be upset with us?"

"Because we…you know…"

"What? Because we're having a baby and we're not married?"

"Yeah."

"But we're getting married."

"But we're not married yet and we weren't when I got pregnant."

"I don't think God cares."

Karen was frightened, and Marlon's answer only amplified her fears. He wanted to laugh, to tell her she was putting too much stock in superstitions that were likely false, but he sensed she wasn't in the mood for blasphemy, no matter how sound. He gently put his hands on either side of her face and slowly turned her head back to him.

"Hey, look at me," he said. "God isn't disappointed with you."

Karen heard Marlon's words, felt the sincerity with which he said them, but she didn't fully believe him. He wasn't an authority. He wasn't a priest or a bishop or anything or anyone other than the guy who had gotten her pregnant. He didn't have the right to speak on God's behalf. Only the anointed could do that. There was no way to get Marlon to see the severity of their transgression. Defeated, she lowered her head.

"Yeah," Karen said, hollowly. "You're probably right."

"I know I am."

Marlon studied Karen a moment longer. She appeared to be past whatever was haunting her. She offered a weak smile and turned away. Marlon watched her for another minute and then returned to his books.

"Do you want a big wedding?" Karen asked.

"I don't care," Marlon answered, shelving another book.

"Where do you want to have the reception?"

"Wherever you'd like," Marlon said.

Karen sighed heavily. Marlon was too agreeable, too nice, too accommodating about everything. These were big life decisions. She didn't think it too much to expect her fiancé to be a little more invested in them. She bent over and pretended to rummage through a box. Marlon returned to his books, ignorant to the fact that Karen was softly crying.

"I don't want a big wedding," she said, standing up straight and wiping her eyes.

"Okay."

"In fact, I don't even care if we have a wedding."

Marlon turned to Karen. "Really?" he asked. He thought it was in a woman's feminine nature to want a wedding.

"It's not important to me," Karen explained. "I don't need to be put on display."

"Is it because you're pregnant?" Marlon asked. Karen lowered her head, validating his suspicion.

"We can wait until after the baby is born," Marlon said.

"No," Karen said quickly. "I don't want to wait until after the baby. I want to get married before. I just don't want it to be a big extravagant ordeal."

"Okay. Whatever you'd like."

"I just don't see the need to stress over something as ridiculous as a wedding," Karen explained. Marlon wasn't sure he believed her but felt it best not to press the issue.

"Okay," Marlon said. "We'll do something small."

"How small?"

"How small do you want?"

"What if we just went to the courthouse?"

"The courthouse? Really?" Marlon was surprised. "That's…yeah, that's small."

"Does that bother you?" Karen asked.

He never envisioned his wedding would be so…anticlimactic, but the more he processed it, the more he warmed to the idea. A courthouse wedding would be quiet, simple and to the point. It wouldn't need to be shrouded in decadence and forced interaction.

"Sure," he said. "A courthouse wedding. Why not?"

"Really?" Karen's eyes warmed. "You're okay with it?"

"Yeah, if it's what you want."

"Okay. When should we do it?"

"When would you—"

"Tomorrow. Let's do it tomorrow."

"Tomorrow?"

"Yeah, does that work?"

"Ah…yeah…that's sudden," Marlon said, quickly adapting to the scenario. "I'll have to call in a sub, but yeah, I could go tomorrow."

Karen offered a weak smile, nodded, and turned away. Marlon was perplexed. He thought he was giving her what she wanted and submitting all the right answers, yet she looked distant and disconsolate. Was she baiting him? Presenting different scenarios and hypotheticals to see how he would react to notions she didn't really want? He couldn't figure out what, if anything, he was doing wrong.

"Is something wrong?"

"No," Karen answered. "Everything is…exactly as it should be."

Marlon took a step toward her. "You sure this is what you want? A courthouse wedding?"

Karen turned and faced Marlon again. She glanced momentarily into his eyes and then stared past him as if trying to recall some lost memory. She shook her head, returned to the moment, and smiled.

"Yes," she answered, her voice hollow. "This is what I want. I want this more than anything."

"Okay," Marlon said. "I'll get a sub."

CHAPTER 17

Nichole's bed was still at Leroy's. It was a California king, pillow-top mattress outfitted with memory foam. She loved her bed. She missed her bed. It was the *only* thing about their relationship she missed.

Tired of trying to fit comfortably on Leroy's twin mattress, she purchased it a year earlier with her tax return. She wanted her bed back but had no way of knowing when Leroy would be gone so she could sneak into his apartment and steal what was rightfully hers. Besides, even if she could break in at an appropriate time, she couldn't move it alone. She was near her due date. Even routine tasks like tying her shoes now proved daunting and frustrating. Lexi offered to help with the mattress, and even said she could convince a couple guys from work to assist the transport, but Nichole feared the ramifications if Leroy were to come home and find mysterious men moving her bed from of his apartment. Needless to say, she would have to wait until after the baby was born to get her bed back. Until then, she slept with Lexi. Lexi's mattress was a queen, with no memory foam.

At four in the morning, Nichole's water broke. The damp sheets woke Lexi. She rolled over and shook her friend awake and accused her of wetting the bed. Twenty minutes later and they were on their way to the hospital.

Nichole cried and pushed as instructed. Lexi stood next to her throughout, holding her hand and wiping the sweat from her forehead with a cool washcloth. It was a textbook delivery. The doctor cut the umbilical cord and asked Nichole if she wanted to see the child. Nichole kept her eyes closed and said she was placing it for adoption. The doctor stared at her dumbfounded until Lexi yelled to him "No! She doesn't want to see the baby!" The doctor nodded to the nurse and then quickly exited the room, fearful that any further inquiries would warrant the same hostility. The nurse wrapped the child in hospital linens and cradled the baby against her breast. She turned to leave but stopped when Nichole asked if the baby was a boy or a girl.

"It's a beautiful baby girl," the nurse answered.

Nichole began to sob. There was an ambivalence to her tears; she was relieved to drop the burden that held her to Leroy, yet saddened that the child would soon belong to someone else. Somehow, she believed that if the baby were a boy, it would be easier to reconcile her choice to place it for adoption. As if the gender determined whether it was more closely associated with her or Leroy. He was vocal in his preference for a boy. Nichole always recited she just wanted the child to be healthy, but truthfully, she would have preferred a girl.

Lexi went to the nurse and spied the child suspiciously. There was something unusual about her, something incongruous. The nurse, sensing Nichole's uneasiness, asked if she would like to see the child. Nichole shook her head, averting her eyes from her child. The nurse nodded and exited the room. Lexi waited for the nurse to leave, told Nichole she needed to use the bathroom, and then slipped through the door to track down the nurse. She caught her just as she was entering the nursery.

"Excuse me, ma'am?" The nurse stopped and turned to Lexi.

"Yes?"

"Could I see her?"

"Sure."

The nurse rotated the baby and held her out to Lexi. Lexi took the child, cradled her, and curiously evaluated Nichole's newborn. Even at the beginning of her life, Lexi could see some of Nichole's features present in the child. However, even considering her biases, she couldn't account for any of Leroy's.

"Can I ask you something?" Lexi asked, keeping her eyes on the child.

"Sure."

"Why is she so white?"

"What do you mean?"

"The father is black," Lexi explained. "This baby doesn't look biracial."

The nurse looked at the baby for a moment and then back at Lexi. "Black or biracial babies are often born with lighter skin. It's not unusual."

"How long until her skin will get darker?"

The nurse seemed perplexed. "I can't really say."

Lexi looked at the nurse. "You can't or you won't?"

The nurse stole another glance at the child. "Maybe you should talk to the doctor."

"Look at her," Lexi said. She held the child toward the nurse. "Do you think she's a mixed race baby?"

"I'm not really allowed to discuss…"

"Right," Lexi said, pulling the child close to her, "I'll talk with the doctor."

Incidentally, the doctor suddenly rounded the corner. He spotted Lexi, halted for a moment, and thought to duck into another room, but there were none between himself and Lexi. He continued toward Lexi, and as he approached, he could sense something was wrong. "Is everything okay?" he asked.

"Do you think this baby is biracial?" Lexi turned so the doctor could get a better view of the child.

The doctored looked at the child briefly and then back at Lexi, not sure how to answer the question.

"The father," Lexi explained, "is black."

"I see," the doctor said. Lexi pulled the blanket away from the child's face. The doctor looked at the child closely. Nothing about her appearance indicated that she was biracial.

"I explained that black and biracial children are light skinned when they're born," the nurse said.

"Yes, that's true," the doctor said.

"Yeah, I get that, but look, I know the father, this baby doesn't look like him," Lexi said. "How long until she...you know...changes color?"

"It could take anywhere from a few hours to a few weeks," the doctor said.

"Is there any possibility that this baby isn't half black?" Lexi asked.

The doctor looked at the nurse. She shrugged, deferring to the doctor's authority. "At this stage, it's too early for me to answer that question," the doctor said.

"How long till you can answer?" Lexi asked.

The doctor anxiously shifted his weight from one foot to the other. "I think that...that, ah..." the doctor trailed off. He knew what he wanted to say, but feared Lexi's wrath if he said it. He straightened and looked at Lexi. "Look, I don't know your friend's sexual history. If you want to know for certain, bring the father in and we can test him. Everything else would just be conjecture."

"Nichole isn't speaking to the father."

The doctor paused. "Then I don't know what to tell you."

"If that baby isn't Leroy's, she'll want to keep her."

"Who's Leroy?"

"The father," Lexi said and then added, "Probable father."

"This is a conversation you need to have with Nichole. If you want to know who the father is, we'd need to get a DNA sample. It would be unprofessional of me to speculate as to the race of the father."

"Yeah, okay," Lexi said. "I understand."

The doctor offered a sympathetic smile and walked away. Lexi stole one more glance at the baby before handing her back to the nurse. The nurse started away and then paused and turned back to Lexi. "I don't think this baby is biracial," she said. "If your friend is only placing her for adoption because of the father, you should tell her to get a test. She may regret it otherwise."

"Thank you," Lexi said.

"I never said any of this," the nurse said.

"Of course not."

The nurse turned and walked away.

Lexi returned to the nursery an hour later to observe the baby one more time before speaking with Nichole. Lexi looked at the child for a long time. She still retained her white skin. Nichole's features seemed to have become more prominent in the last hour, while Leroy's were still obviously absent. She knew this could just be a mind trick since she was looking for reasons to believe the baby belonged to anyone other than Leroy. But the more Lexi looked at the child, the more she became convinced it wasn't Leroy's.

Nichole was sleeping when Lexi returned from the nursery. Lexi called for the nurse and asked that she return with the baby in fifteen minutes. Then she woke Nichole.

"I need to talk to you about your baby," Lexi said.

Nichole sat up. The soreness made it difficult to move.

"What about her?" Nichole asked.

"She doesn't look like Leroy."

"What are you talking about?" Nichole said.

"The baby is white, Nic."

Nichole heard the words, but she couldn't fully process them. Lexi repeated herself.

"What do you mean she's white?" Nichole asked.

"I mean she's white. There's no trace of Leroy in her."

"Biracial babies are born—"

"Yeah, I know," Lexi interrupted, "but I don't think she's biracial."

"He poked holes in the condoms, Lex."

"Have you been with anyone other than Leroy?"

"No. I was always faithful."

"I'm your best friend, Nic. You know there's no judgment here."

"Lexi, I'm telling you the...," but Nichole couldn't finish her thought. "Oh, god," she whispered. "Oh, god."

"Nic…"

"Where is she?" she asked desperately.

"Who?"

"The baby? I want to see her. I want to see if she's Leroy's."

As if on cue, the nurse walked through the door holding Nichole's baby. Nichole sat up, looked at the child from across the room, and knew that it wasn't Leroy's.

"Oh, shit," Nichole said. The nurse stopped, unsure how to proceed. Lexi turned and faced her friend. Nichole sputtered and gasped, choking on her words that wouldn't materialize. She held her arms out to the nurse frantically, indicating she wanted her baby. The nurse looked at Lexi for some guidance; she nodded. The nurse smiled fearfully and approached Nichole. She handed the baby over cautiously. Nichole cradled the child and looked down at her, studying and evaluating her features. "Oh my god," Nichole said.

"Give us a minute," Lexi said to the nurse. She nodded and slipped out the door. Lexi sat on the edge of Nichole's bed.

"It's not Leroy's, is it?" Lexi asked.

Nichole shook her head.

"Who's the father?"

"Look how gorgeous she is," Nichole said. She turned the child so Lexi could get a better view. "Isn't she perfect?"

"Nichole, who's the father?"

"I don't know," Nichole said, repositioning the child against her breast.

"You don't know? You've been cheating on Leroy this entire time?"

"I never cheated."

"Then how is it that you have a baby, Nic?"

"It never occurred to me it could be his."

"What are you talking about?

"Remember the bachelor party?"

Lexi stared stupidly at her friend for a moment, and then the memory of the bachelor party came roaring back to her. "Oh, shit," she said. "That guy? I thought you said you didn't sleep with him."

"I didn't think I did. I wasn't naked and neither was he. I couldn't remember anything from that night."

"So you did sleep with him?"

"I guess so."

"Shit, Nichole…"

"It's okay," Nichole said. "I'm not mad about it. I'm honestly relieved now. This baby isn't Leroy's, and I'm not placing her for adoption now.

"What?"

"I'm going to raise her alone."

"What about the father?"

"What do you mean?"

"I mean…that guy you slept with is the father."

"Yeah. So?"

"So don't you think he deserves to know?"

"No."

Lexi looked at Nichole in disbelief, but her stare went undetected. Nichole was so absorbed in her new child that nothing could break her focus. Nothing else mattered to her. She suddenly exuded life and happiness. Lexi had never seen Nichole so…alive. It almost frightened her. Nichole exhilarated in her sudden change

185

of circumstances. She was a woman reborn, a woman who suddenly had a reason to live. Nichole gave birth to her child, and in return, gave herself life, too.

A conflict arose in Lexi. She didn't want to rob her friend of her newfound happiness, but she felt an obligation to advocate the right course of action. Her friend just gave birth; the father deserved to know.

"You have to tell him, Nichole," she said.

"Why?"

"Because," Lexi began incredulously, "that is someone's baby, too."

"She's mine."

"She's someone else's too."

Nichole ignored Lexi's comment.

"Do you remember anything about the guy you slept with?" Lexi pried. "Did you get his name?"

"Marlon Brown."

"What?"

"His name is Marlon Brown," Nichole said. "He was named after Marlon Brando. I remember him telling me that." Nichole paused and then added, almost nostalgically, "I thought he was kidding."

"Did you talk about anything else? Anything personal? What he does? Where he lives?"

"I think his driver's license was from Oregon, but I can't remember for sure."

"Okay. That helps. I can ask my boss to pull the receipt records from that night. There will be a name from the credit card. If it wasn't his, it was one of his friends. We'll find him."

Lexi now had Nichole's full attention. "Find him?" she asked. "I don't want you to find him."

"He's the father."

"I don't want him to know."

"He deserves to know."

"Why?"

"Because…" Lexi started, but she couldn't offer more than her one-word weak rebuttal. She couldn't understand why Nichole didn't understand.

"This is my baby, Lexi," Nichole said. "I don't care who the father is. I wanted to give her to someone else when I thought it was Leroy's, and now that it isn't…well, this is my second chance."

"Nichole…"

"I'm not going to show up on some guy's doorstep and tell him he's the father. No. I've been saved from a lifetime of having to deal with Leroy. I don't need to make the same mistake again."

"Nichole, this Marlon guy deserves—"

"All I know about Marlon Brown is he sleeps with strippers. Does that sound like the kind of guy I need in my life? His involvement could just make things harder. I didn't get rid of Leroy just to find someone else exactly like him. I'm tired of making mistakes, Lexi. I'm done tricking myself into thinking I need a man to be complete. This, my baby, is my redemption. I can do this. I can raise her on my own."

Lexi had no rebuttal. She didn't know if Nichole was right, but her logic was sound. It was probably best that the father didn't know. Knowledge often cuts deepest when it's not sought after. Marlon Brown had his own life to live. He didn't need some stranger with a kid wrecking it. Some secrets needed to remain secret. Lexi nodded at Nichole and then leaned down and tickled the baby's stomach.

"So what are you going to name her?" Lexi asked.

"Abigail."

CHAPTER 18

The head didn't look like a head. The doctor saw it first and winced. The nurse saw it shortly after and shuddered, gasped, and quickly looked away. Her reaction went undetected. The doctor pulled her to his side and whispered for her to go find Dr. Philips. The nurse stole another glance at the child before quickly exiting the delivery room.

Marlon stood next to Karen, his hand in hers. She pushed and breathed as instructed. He dabbed the sweat from her forehead and delicately removed any wet strands of hair stuck to her face.

"Okay, Karen, you're doing great," the doctor said.

"Where did the nurse go?" Karen asked.

"She'll be back in a minute," the doctor answered. "I need another big push."

Karen gritted her teeth and pushed.

"One more."

She pushed again.

Dr. Philips came into the room just as the first doctor was pulling the baby from Karen's vaginal canal. Dr. Philips spotted the newborn and knew immediately. She took the child, doing her best to shield him from his Karen and Marlon.

"How is he?" Marlon asked.

"He's...," the doctor began but she wasn't sure how best to answer the question.

"Can I see him?" Karen asked. "Can I see my baby?"

Dr. Philips studied the baby for a moment and then told the nurse to take the child to the ICU. She attempted to hand the child to the nurse, but the nurse was too numb to react.

"Nurse!" Dr. Philips cried. The nurse blanched and awkwardly approached. She reluctantly reached for the child. Dr. Philips handed the baby to the nurse. The nurse exited the room carrying the child like a soiled garbage sack.

Karen noticed the exchange and caught a glimpse of her son. Marlon did, too.

"Oh my god," Karen said. Marlon stared at the door, frozen.

"Marlon...," Karen cried, "Did you see..."

Marlon looked at Karen. "Did you see his head?" she asked. Marlon nodded. The two doctors conversed in the corner of the room.

"What's wrong with our baby?" Marlon asked.

"His head…," Karen said.

"I saw…something…unusual," Marlon said to no one in particular.

The doctors continued to talk quietly, ignoring them.

It…," Karen said, almost choking on the words. "It's hideous."

Marlon started toward the doctors. "What's going on?" he demanded.

The doctors looked at Marlon, and then at each other, trying to decide who should offer an explanation.

"What's wrong with it?" Karen screamed, frustrated that their inquiries went unanswered. "Stop ignoring us!"

"Will one of you please tell us what is going on?" Marlon said, trying his best to appear calm.

Dr. Philips looked at Karen. "You need to rest."

"I don't want to rest. I want to know what's wrong with my baby," Karen cried.

"We don't know for sure yet," Dr. Philips explained. "I'm going to go run some quick tests. It shouldn't take long. Try to get some rest."

"Tests for what?" Marlon asked.

"To rule out certain birth defects."

"What kind of birth defects?"

"It didn't have a…skull," Karen whimpered. "It was just…just flesh…just raw…," she couldn't continue.

Marlon stepped to the doctors. "What's wrong with our son?" he asked, sternly. He wanted answers.

"It's too early to tell right now," Dr. Philips said, inching toward the door. "We need to run some tests. We'll be back shortly. Please try and get some rest."

The two doctors quickly slid out the door before Marlon or Karen could ask any more questions.

*****

An hour later, Dr. Philips returned. She entered the room quietly. Karen slept, while Marlon stood at the window watching some kids play basketball at a park across the street. Dr. Philips stood at the door for a moment. A full minute passed before she gently cleared her throat, and Marlon snapped his head in the doctor's direction. Karen didn't stir.

Marlon's eyes were bloodshot and defeated, his features haggard and unassuming. In the hour the doctor was away, it looked as if Marlon had aged ten years. The doctor looked down at the clipboard she carried as a means to avoid looking directly at Marlon.

"Should we wake your wife?" the doctor whispered.

"No," Marlon said. "Let her rest."

The doctor nodded. The silence grew, as did Marlon's frustration. He wanted answers, and Dr. Philips didn't appear to have them.

"Did you run the tests?" Marlon asked.

"Yes."

"So...what did you find out?" Marlon asked.

Dr. Philips looked up from her clipboard, forcing herself to complete the duties of her job. "Your son has a rare condition," she explained. "It's called anencephaly,"

"Anenc…," Marlon struggled with the pronunciation.

"Anencephaly," the doctor repeated. "It's an extremely rare birth defect. So rare, in fact, this is the first time I'd ever seen it at this hospital."

"What is it?"

"As the neural tube forms and closes, it helps develop the brain, skull, and spinal cord. If the neural tube doesn't close all the way, the baby is born without parts of the brain. That's what's wrong with your son."

"Wait," Marlon said, trying to make sense of what the doctor was telling him. "My son doesn't have a brain?"

"He doesn't have a cerebrum and his skull never fully developed."

"Meaning what?"

The doctor paused. She hated when everyday people didn't understand her advanced intelligence. She explained further, speaking slowly and in non-technical language. "He's missing the top of his head. His brain is exposed."

Marlon swallowed hard. "What...what can we do?" he asked.

"We...unfortunately, with cases of anencephaly, nothing can be done."

"So what are you saying? He's going to grow up without a skull?"

"No, I'm saying he won't grow up," the doctor said. She closed his eyes, and silently reprimanded herself for not choosing her words more carefully. Marlon didn't fully understand what he had been told. How could a child be born without a skull? How did this go undetected for the duration of Karen's pregnancy? Doctors could determine a child's sex, but in terms of having a child with a head, that escaped them? Marlon shook his head.

Dr. Philips shifted her weight from one foot to the other. She wanted to leave so Marlon and Karen could grieve alone. She felt out of her element standing awkwardly in front of Marlon. She was a medical doctor, not a behavioral therapist. *Be brief and concise and exit quickly.* Her own wisdom rattled around in her head. Easier said than done for sure. She stole another glance at Marlon. He looked distant and confused.

"Mr. Brown," the doctor continued, "your son…he won't ever leave this hospital. He's in the ICU now, but he won't live much longer. Best case scenario, he may make through the night."

"Through the night?" Marlon gasped. "That's it?"

"With this disease, yeah. There really is nothing we can do. I'm sorry."

The shock kept Marlon silent.

"Do you understand what I've told you?" the doctor asked.

Marlon nodded slowly.

"I will have the nurse bring him down in a few minutes," the doctor said. "You can spend whatever time he has left with him." The doctor put a sympathetic hand on Marlon's shoulder. She opened her mouth to say something else, but decided it was best to slip out the door undetected.

"I don't want to see it," a hollow voice said. Marlon turned. Karen was awake and staring at the far wall.

"What?"

"I don't want to see it," she repeated.

Marlon went to her. "He's our son, Karen," he said. He spoke clearly, but Karen gave no indication she heard him.

"It's not your fault, sweetie," Marlon said. "You don't think it's your fault, do you? There's nothing we could have done."

Karen didn't stir. She was catatonic and distant. Marlon reached down and took her hand. She gave no reaction to his touch. Her skin felt cold and lifeless.

"Karen," Marlon said. "Baby, please talk to me."

Karen slowly rotated her head and looked deep into Marlon's eyes. "It was a mistake," she whispered.

"What was?"

"Our baby. Us."

"What? What are you talking about?"

"People try to placate it. Call it a surprise or some other bullshit euphemism. No. It was a mistake. That…that thing we created."

"Karen—"

"It's our punishment."

Suddenly, the door creaked opened. Marlon turned. The nurse stood in the doorway holding their baby. Karen whimpered and turned her head away from the nurse. Marlon straightened and crossed to the nurse and took his child. Free of the child, the nurse turned and hurried out the door. Marlon cradled his son close to his breast. He could sense the fragility of his child's life. It may not be the life he envisioned, but it was life nonetheless, and there was no denying Marlon had a hand in creating it. He smiled at his child, and then took a step toward Karen.

"I don't want to see it, Marlon," she said.

Marlon froze. He stared at Karen for a long time, silently pleading for her to reconsider, but the longer he stood watching her, the more he understood that she did not intend to hold her child. The baby softly cooed, as if beckoning his mother to reconsider. Karen broke into angry sobs.

"Please," she cried. "Please leave."

Marlon stole one more glance at his wife, trying, and failing, to empathize with her anger. The child cooed once again. Karen gasped and shut her eyes. Marlon turned and walked out of the room.

He found a chair in the hall and sat down. He laid his son gently on his lap and looked down at his deformed face. The child's eyes maintained a distant glance, giving him a look of ignorance that was both innocent and endearing. The thin, inverted line of his mouth offered a perplexed smirk. He wasn't "normal" in the traditional sense, yet he had a hidden beauty that was not lost on Marlon. He stared at his child for a long time, seeing his and Karen's own traits in the distorted countenance of their baby. He loved the boy immensely. He loved him despite his appearance. His imperfection made him perfect. His abnormality made him whole. He was human, and Marlon was proud to be his father.

The child's distant eyes rotated suspiciously and ignorantly in their sockets and then settled momentarily on Marlon. A look of recognition seemed to fill the child's eyes. His thin lips struggled upwards into a broken smile. Marlon smiled back. He lifted his child, kissed him gently on the forehead, and wept.

PART TWO – SEVENTEEN YEARS LATER

CHAPTER 19

A student occupied each of the thirty desks that filled the classroom. Mr. Ned traversed the aisles, glancing over his students' shoulders, checking their exams and making sure no one cheated. As he made his way to the front row, he spotted a student's thong protruding from her pant waistband. Mr. Ned paused and slowed his step so he could better take in the sight. The panty wasn't much thicker than a shoelace. It spanned the student's back while another string, perpendicular to the first, dove down the student's butt crack becoming lost in the fabric of her pants.

The thong belonged to Abigail Sloan, Mr. Ned's promiscuous D- student. She was seventeen going on twenty-five. She wore shoulder-length, blonde-streaked hair that complemented her fair complexion void of the usual teenage acne or blemishes. She maintained a model's body and dressed in a fashion that showed as much of it off as the school's already lenient dress code would allow. She had established herself early as "the one" within the student body. "The one" was the label given to the girl at school who ranked first on every male's bucket list (or "fuck it" list as it soon became known). She had already surpassed most senior girls who had the advantage of being a year older. However, her status was quickly devolving. It was becoming common knowledge that it didn't take much courting to get Abigail Sloan into bed. Often, a bed wasn't even needed. A closet or any dimly lit area would suffice. She always wore clothes conducive to the act. Her short skirts usually just needed lifted an inch or two, and a minute later, the consummation was complete.

At night, Mr. Ned often thought of Abigail while he lay next to his slumbering wife. If he thought of her long enough, he entertained the idea of reaching for his wife and making some kind of advance, using Abigail as motivation to make love to the woman he no longer loved. He never did, though. He knew his wife would be more annoyed than aroused if he disturbed her sleep. On these nights, he often just climbed out of bed and retreated to the bathroom alone with his mental catalog of inappropriate fantasies.

Mr. Ned's rubbernecking became conspicuous to Abigail's best friend Carrie. Carrie was like Abigail—amoral and openly objectified by fellow classmates. Like Abigail, Carrie had an insatiable lust to elicit perverted stares from people like Mr. Ned. The problem was Carrie was not Abigail. She didn't have Abigail's seductive demeanor or a body that complemented such a disposition. She was the fallback girl, never the first choice, yet always managed to find herself on her back by the end of a party after enough booze had been consumed to make her look just appealing enough. Abigail liked Carrie because she worshiped Abigail almost as much as she envied her. Abigail was weak, but Carrie was weaker. When they weren't feeding each other's insecurities, they fed each other's egos. They were perfect for each other.

Carrie sat in the desk behind Abigail and to the left. She looked at Mr. Ned and followed his stare down to her friend's exposed thong. She shook her head, disgusted by her teacher, but also bothered that it wasn't *her* he had stopped behind. Carrie always made sure that her panty bands were slightly visible from behind, too.

Carried coughed, theatrically cleared her throat, and said "Pervert!" loud enough for the class to hear. All eyes, including

Abigail's and Mr. Ned's, shot to her. Carrie hunched over her test, pretended to read a question, and failed to suppress a smile. The class returned to their tests, unaware of the game Carrie was playing. Abigail craned her head up to look at Mr. Ned. He stared down at her and then glanced again at Abigail's thong before awkwardly moving on and sitting down at his desk. Abigail understood. She looked at Carrie, shook her head, and rolled her eyes. She was flattered but pretended not to be.

The bell rang five minutes later. Carrie and Abigail walked together to Mr. Ned's desk and dropped their exams on it. Abigail winked at Mr. Ned and smiled; he blushed and lowered his head and absentmindedly rearranged some papers from his desk. The girls laughed and then spilled out into the hall together.

"Do you think you passed?" Carrie asked.

"I'm pretty sure I bombed it."

"Abby, if you don't pass your mom isn't going to let you come to Tahoe this summer. You have to come. It's the summer before our senior year."

"I know."

"What are you going to do?"

"I don't know," Abigail said. "My mom is being such a bitch lately."

"What about your other classes? Are you passing everything else?"

"I think so. I convinced Mr. Robinson to let me retake my math final. I told Karl Stephenson he could finger me if he made me an answer key."

"Gross," Carrie said, smiling. It *was* gross, yet she couldn't deny feeling jealous of the fact that she lacked Abigail's sexual power. "Did he?"

"I took the test two days ago and I'm pretty sure I aced it," Abigail bragged.

"You are such a slut."

Abigail laughed, taking the insult as a compliment because she knew Carrie meant it as one. They arrived at Abigail's locker. She dialed in the combination and pulled it open.

"I don't know what I'm going to do about Mr. Ned's class," Abigail said, dropping her books in her locker. Glued to the inside was a mirror. She checked her face before grabbing the books for her next class and slamming the door shut.

"Maybe you should let him finger you," Carrie offered.

"I really should," Abigail said. "Did you see the way he was staring at my thong? I felt like he was eye raping me."

"Well, that might be the price you have to pay if you want to spend the summer in Tahoe with me."

Abigail sighed heavily. "I just don't understand my mom. She's so pathetic. Three weeks ago a guy took her out in a corvette. He took her to a Beyoncé show. Front row tickets."

"Damn," Carrie said. "I hope she marries that guy."

"I know, right? Well, the next day I asked her how the date went and she said he wasn't her type."

"Wasn't her type?" Carrie asked. "Any guy who drives a corvette and can score front row Beyoncé tickets is my type."

"She said he's all flash and no substance."

"What does that mean?"

"I have no idea."

"Maybe you could go out with him?" Carrie teased.

"I totally would, and I would let him do a lot more to me than just finger me."

"God, Abby," Carrie said, laughing.

"What? I'm sick of all these high school guys who are two pumps and done. I can't even get off unless I'm doing it myself."

Carrie nodded in agreement, but she couldn't fully relate. "I have to get to biology," she said. "Love you."

"Love you, too," Abigail said. They turned in different directions and started for their next classes.

Less than a minute later Abigail entered Mr. Robinson's math class. Upon entering, Mr. Robinson called Abigail to his desk. She rolled her eyes and crossed the room to where Mr. Robinson sat holding Abigail's makeup test. He held her test out to her. She snatched it up and looked at the score. Ninety-three. She studied the number for a moment, making sure that she read it correctly. Even she didn't expect to score *that* well. Mr. Robinson detected the surprise in her expression.

"That's impressive, Abigail," Mr. Robinson sneered. "Even you look surprised."

Abigail lowered the test and looked at Mr. Robinson. She could read in his smug expression that he knew she cheated. She also noticed a note of frustration because he couldn't prove it.

"You went from thirty-six percent to ninety-three," Mr. Robinson continued. "How did you ever manage to pull that off?"

"I studied really hard," Abigail said. She tilted her head and smiled, making no effort to hide the disdain she felt for her teacher.

"Sure you did."

"You're not accusing me of cheating, are you?" Abigail asked. Earlier in the year, Mr. Robinson accused a student of cheating. He couldn't prove it, but he failed the student anyway. The student's parents intervened and the school launched an investigation. When Mr. Robinson couldn't present any evidence outside of his intuition, the parents demanded Mr. Robinson's resignation. He insisted the student take another test to prove he really understood the material. The parents knew their son had cheated. He was a latchkey kid raised on Hot Pockets and video games. He was medicated and on every remedial accommodation the school offered. The parents even found the answer key in his backpack. But they knew Mr. Robinson didn't have any right to accuse their son of being a cheater, whether it was true or not, without proof. It was decided that Mr. Robinson could keep his job if he passed the student and didn't require another retake. He begrudgingly passed the student. That student is now in line to work at his father's tire store when he graduates. He'll make twelve dollars an hour until his mom forces her husband to promote him. That's the only way he'll ever make enough to move out of their basement.

"I never called you a cheater," Mr. Robinson said. "I was just wondering if you could tell me how you improved so drastically in just a week. I would love to employ your test taking skills with my other struggling students."

"I told you," Abigail said, "I studied really hard."

"Of course you did," Mr. Robinson said. "Well, my compliments to your tutor. I only hope that you didn't have to sacrifice too much in way of payment."

Mr. Robinson tilted his head and offered Abigail the same condescending smile she had given him a moment earlier. Abigail scoffed and started for her desk.

As Abigail turned, she noticed Karl Stephenson staring wide-eyed at her from the front row. He had heard the exchange between her and Mr. Robinson and was terrified she would label him as the culprit to Abigail's improved score. Karl was first in his class and had a full ride academic scholarship to Stanford waiting for him after graduation. His dad was a heart surgeon who lived in a studio apartment because he paid child support to three different women, including Karl's mom. Karl came from good stock, but he feared he might have inherited his dad's carnal proclivities in addition to his erudite ones.

Abigail held up her test for Karl to see and then blew him a kiss. Karl smiled coyly and stole a glance at Mr. Robinson, who stared back at Karl with complete understanding. Karl diverted his eyes back to Abigail who ran her hand down to her crotch and circled it before bringing it back up and sniffing her finger. Karl blushed and lowered his head. Abigail laughed and took her seat.

CHAPTER 20

Nichole sat at her desk filling out her monthly expense report. Due to her seniority, she had a cubicle on the fringes of the office floor. She had a beeline to the bathroom, break room, and most importantly, exit. When the day ended, she was able to leave briskly without getting caught into her co-workers' mundane conversations. However, her location didn't professionally distinguish her from the others. She had the same job title and responsibilities as everyone else, but unlike her coworkers, she didn't have to navigate her way through the cubicle maze to get to and from her workspace.

Next to her keyboard, and pinned to the corkboard to her left, were pictures of Abigail. The pictures showed the transformation of Abigail from innocent baby to promiscuous teen. The earliest picture showed Abigail, at two years old, staring hypnotically at a panda from their trip to the zoo. The latest showed her, at seventeen, at a friend's birthday party scowling at the camera. In the first photo, she wore a panda t-shirt with panda ears atop her toddler head. In the latest, she wore a sequined halter-top that didn't quite reach her belly button. Since Abigail's metamorphosis occurred under Nichole's parental jurisdiction, she was slow to see what her daughter had become since entering high school. She still viewed her daughter as the innocent, panda-loving child that sought comfort during lightning storms and thought chocolate chip pancakes were the greatest thing in the world. If there is one drug all parents are addicted to, it's their own ignorance.

Directly behind Nichole's workstation was the boss's office. His name was Harper and Nichole liked him, as did most of the workers. He wasn't obtrusive, and he didn't micromanage his employees. He treated everyone fairly and people earned their bonuses based on performance rather than nepotism or some other political imbalance. The solid oak door that led to his office usually remained closed with the blinds drawn. He liked to have his privacy as much as he extended it to his employees. When he did come out from his office, it wasn't to manage with an iron fist, but to inquire as to the needs of the office, while being open to any suggestions to make work less stressful without compromising productivity.

From behind her, Nichole heard Harper's door creak open. He approached from behind, looked about the office to ensure no one was watching, and gave Nichole a subtle tap on the shoulder. Nichole turned and looked at her boss. He wore a sincere smile and an expensive-looking suit that wasn't really expensive. He ordered most of his suits online from discount retailers, not because he couldn't afford to splurge on his wardrobe, but because he opted not to.

"Hey, Nichole," he whispered. "Do you have a minute?"

Harper didn't usually ask if someone had a minute. He was open about most things. If he needed something, he wouldn't whisper; he was never fearful about being overheard. He also never seemed to find it necessary to discuss things behind closed doors. He embraced transparency when it came to his dealings with his employees. He felt it was a sign of respect and appreciation. He was the kind of boss he would want if he had a boss.

"Sure," Nichole answered. She dropped her pen and leaned back in her chair and waited for him to continue.

"Not here," Harper whispered. He scanned the office. "Come into my office."

Harper turned and entered his office quickly. Nichole followed, a few steps behind, wondering what was so important that it needed to be discussed privately.

"Close the door," Harper said. "Have a seat."

Nichole closed the door and sat in one of the two chairs in front of Harper's desk. Harper circled his desk and sat down. Nichole spotted a folder with her name printed on the tab. Harper leaned forward and tapped the folder absentmindedly with his finger. He appeared nervous which made Nichole nervous. He didn't speak for a beat. He was lost in his own thoughts. When he finally glanced up, he found Nichole's eyes locked on him. He stopped his finger and sat back in his chair. He smiled at Nichole and laughed nervously.

"How are things?" he asked. "Good?"

"Yeah. They're...they're as they've always been."

"You're coming up on twenty years now, right?"

Nichole didn't think his math was correct, but as she quickly calculated the years in her head, she realized it was.

"Yeah, I guess I am. It will be twenty years in August."

"Are you happy here?"

"Yeah." Nichole studied Harper. "Is something the matter?"

"What do you mean?"

"I mean you're acting out of character, and it's kind of freaking me out."

"How am I acting?"

"Secretive."

"Humph."

Nichole thought her observation warranted a more enlightening response, but Harper didn't seem concerned to give her one. "Am I getting…fired?" she asked.

Harper laughed. It hadn't occurred to him that any break in his protocol would fuel such a hasty conclusion. "Oh, no," he said. "You are absolutely not getting fired. I was just trying to get a feel for what you thought of this place."

"I've been here since I was twenty. Why are you asking now?"

"Don't I always want to know how things are?"

"Yeah, but not privately."

"Good point," he said. He appeared ready to say something else but then paused. Nichole could tell he was figuring out the best approach to tell her whatever it was he needed to say. She couldn't, however, decide if the information he was withholding was good of bad. She stared at him and waited him out. He sighed heavily and leaned forward.

"We've been hitting really high numbers recently," he began, adopting his business demeanor. "Your numbers are higher than the rest, and they have been for a while now."

"Well…isn't that a good thing?"

"It's a great thing for corporate, but it's a bad thing for me."

"What do you mean?"

"They want to promote you."

"What?"

"We're opening operations in three other states. Arizona, New Mexico, and Utah. The Los Angeles offices have already filled the manager positions in Arizona and New Mexico, and they've asked me to recommend someone for Utah."

"You want me?"

"Well, if truth be told, no, I don't. I don't want to lose you. My numbers only look good because your numbers are good. I'm not stupid, Nichole. You're better at this job than I am, and if you leave, the higher ups will see that. But you deserve this more than anyone else. Your numbers are always high, you're loyal, you're...well, let's face it, Nichole, you would do a hell of a job out there. You're the best person for the job."

Nichole let the praise sink in. The recognition felt good, especially coming from someone who wasn't known for passing out praise on a whim.

"Utah?" she sneered. Utah was next door to Nevada, but as far as Nichole was concerned, it only served as an annoying obstacle between her home state and Colorado.

Harper laughed. "Yeah, I know."

"Isn't that where everything is closed on Sunday and the people wear magic underwear?" Nichole asked.

"If the rumors are true."

"Jeez, I don't know," Nichole said. "Utah?"

"It's actually a gorgeous state. I took the family skiing there a few years ago. It is a far cry from Vegas, though. We have liquor stores and strip clubs on every street corner. They have churches and dollar stores."

"That's not necessarily a bad thing," Nichole said. Secretly, she had been trying to get out of Vegas for the past decade. She knew it wasn't the best place to raise a child. But before she could seriously implement any kind of relocating effort, she blinked and was forty with a teenage daughter.

"No, it's not," Harper replied. "You could walk down the street without seeing smut pamphlets littered everywhere."

"My best friend used to be on those pamphlets."

"Oh, I'm sorry…," Harper began but stopped when he realized he had nothing to be sorry for. Just because Nichole knew someone on a smut flier didn't stop it from being a smut flier.

"Oh, it's fine," Nichole said. "She moved to Europe ten years ago. The trashy flyers were just a means to an end."

"Everything is a means to an end somehow, right?"

"That's one way to look at it. What's the salary?" Nichole asked.

"About thirty-five thousand a year more than you're making now."

Nichole's mouth fell open. "Plus commission?"

"Yeah. Commission, health, dental, retirement, vacation. Everything. Cost of living is lower there too. You could retire in ten years. It really is a great opportunity, Nichole. You've earned it."

Nichole was speechless. They sat quietly for a moment while Nichole processed what kind of life six figures could afford her and Abigail. She wanted the job. She had never wanted anything more at that moment, but she knew she couldn't accept it until she spoke to Abigail. She had always told Abigail they were a team. She meant it. If she took the job without her consent, she'd upset her daughter and prove to be a liar.

"I have to run it by my daughter first," Nichole finally said. She could already surmise what Abigail's response would be. No teenager wants to be uprooted before the start of their senior year. It would take some clever maneuvering on Nichole's part to get Abigail on board. A diplomatic approach would be her best bet.

"Absolutely," Harper said. "The job is yours if you want it. Take until the end of the month to decide."

Nichole nodded and stood to go.

"Hey, Nichole," Harper said before Nichole reached the door. "If you decide to stay here, I can increase your pay. It wouldn't be as substantial as the manager position in Utah, and I couldn't match the corporate benefits, but I would see what I could do."

"Thanks," Nichole said. She put her hand on the doorknob and then turned back to her boss. "If you were me, would you take the job?"

Harper smiled. "Yeah, but I hope you don't."

"Thanks, Harper."

"No problem. Oh, and it goes without saying, but don't say anything around the office. If you take the job, we'll give you a proper send-off, but if you decline, I don't want anyone else feeling like they were the second choice."

"I understand," Nichole said.

"Let me know what Abigail says."

Nichole nodded and snuck out the door. She didn't get much work done the rest of the day. She spent the afternoon going over all the ways to convince her daughter that moving to Utah was a great idea.

*****

Nichole entered her house under the burden of her workbag and Chinese takeout sacks. Abigail sat on the sofa watching television with her freshly painted toenails propped up on the coffee table to dry. Nichole dropped work her bag on the floor and placed the food on the kitchen counter.

"Hi, sweetie," Nichole said, but Abigail either didn't hear her mom or didn't feel the need to respond. Nichole hoped it was the former but knew it was most likely the latter. She retrieved two

224

plates from the cupboard and began portioning out the Chinese food. It was chicken lo mien. Abigail's favorite.

"How was school?" Nichole asked again, raising her voice so her daughter wouldn't ignore her again.

"Fine," Abigail answered, exhausted by the effort.

"How did you do on your English test?"

"Don't know," Abigail mumbled.

"I can't hear you. Use your words," Nichole instructed.

"I won't know till Thursday," Abigail yelled.

"What about your math test? Did you get your retake back?"

"Yeah."

"And…"

"I got a ninety-three."

"Honey, that's fantastic," Nichole said.

Abigail gave a small smile but quickly returned her attention to the television. Nichole finished portioning the food and walked with the plates to the sofa. She handed a plate to Abigail and then sat with her own dish at the end of the sofa.

"Can you turn this off?" Nichole asked. "I need to talk to you about something."

Abigail stared placidly at the television, ignoring her mother's request.

"Abby, turn this off," Nichole commanded.

"I'm listening."

"I want your full attention."

"You have it."

"Abby, I won't ask again."

Abigail rolled her eyes and sat forward to retrieve the remote. She switched off the TV, sat back on the sofa, and sighed audibly.

"I need to talk to you about something," Nichole said.

"What?" Abigail asked, throwing a dejected glance at her mom and shoveling a spoonful of rice in her mouth.

"I got a new job offer today at work. A promotion."

"How much money is it?"

"That's not important."

"Can I get a new car?"

"Abby—"

"Carrie's dad just got her a new Jetta."

"No, you can't get a new car. The one you have is just fine."

"It's four years old, mom."

"It's fine, Abby."

"You're so unfair."

Nichole thought to offer a rebuttal, to explain to her daughter how hard she *didn't* have it. She thought about explaining how when she was her age, she didn't even have a car of her own, along with several other luxuries she afforded her daughter. But she didn't want to be that parent. The parent whose greatest trait is failing to elicit pity from their offspring by reminding them just how hard it was growing up in a world that didn't care who you were. Abigail had the rest of her life to realize she didn't matter. She was still young enough to believe every innocuous task she performed was worthy of praise. Besides, Nichole didn't want to get into an argument with Abigail tonight. She was about to ask her to uproot and move to Utah; she needed her daughter on her side right now.

"Listen, Abby," Nichole began, "I got a job offer today. It's a great opportunity for me. For us."

"Okay."

"The job is in Utah."

Nichole watched Abigail's expression go from indifference to confusion to unrequited impertinence.

"What!" she cried. "We're moving?"

"Well, that depends. I wanted to talk to you about it first."

"I don't want to move. All my friends are here. I'll be a senior next year."

"This job could really improve our lives, sweetie. It could help pay for your college."

"I don't care about college."

"You should."

"Why?"

"You're going to college, Abby."

"Why? School sucks."

"It's important for your future."

"Just because you didn't go doesn't mean that I have to."

"I didn't go because I made some bad choices," Nichole explained. "I'm saving you from making the same mistakes I did."

228

"So I was a mistake?"

"I didn't say that."

As is the custom of any parent, Nichole never openly admitted that Abigail was a mistake. She once called her pregnancy an accident but had since opted for the more diplomatic label of "surprise." Words have the power to alleviate poor decisions, but inside the confines of her own mind, Nichole could never dissuade herself of the truth that Abigail *was* a mistake. There was no way to disguise it. Nichole slept with a random guy at a bachelor party and got pregnant. There couldn't be a clearer definition of a mistake. However, Nichole atoned for her mistake by dedicating her life to Abigail. She owned her impulsive decision and reaped the motherhood rewards of it. She knew she had screwed up, but the greater sin would be openly declaring Abigail the byproduct of the imprudent choice.

"This is all about you," Abigail said. "Everything is always about you. What about me? What about what I want? What am I supposed to do in Utah?"

"You'll do the same thing you do here. You'll go to school and when you graduate, you'll go to college."

"That's *your* plan, mom. It's not mine. How many times do I have to tell you I don't want to go to college? Why won't you listen to me?"

"What are you going to do with the rest of your life?"

"I don't know. I'll find a job. I'll do something, but I'm not going to school. I hate school. It's pointless."

Nichole chalked Abigail's disdain for going to college up to the ignorance of youth. She didn't want to go to college *now*, but she would thank Nichole later if she forced her daughter to seek a degree. Nichole knew better than most that there's nothing more pathetic than a woman who can't attain her own independence because she chose to be uneducated. She knew countless girlfriends in loveless marriages who stayed with their husbands simply because they couldn't afford to leave. Few had an education past an associate's degree. Outside of coloring one's hair at home or taking a turn carpooling kids to soccer games, most didn't have any viable job skills. They constructed their lives beholden to someone they

230

stopped loving because they didn't have the foresight or the parental guidance to make something more of themselves. Nichole needed Abigail to be more than a stereotype. Weak people are stereotypes. They seek other stereotypes and cling to them for fear of being alone. Nichole knew this because Leroy was one and he nearly turned her into one, too. Abigail needed to see this, but if she couldn't, then it became Nichole's job to shelter her from it. It was her parental obligation.

"Abby...," Nichole said, but she didn't have the fight in her to finish her thought.

"I don't even know where Utah is," Abigail cried.

Nichole laughed, blindsided by her daughter's ignorance. "And that's all the more reason why you should go to college. You should know where Utah is." Nichole tried to mask her comment as a joke, but she wanted it to sting. Her daughter needed to be smarter than she was.

Abigail grabbed a pillow from the sofa and flung it across the room. She sat back and burst into tears that came hot and fast and tore down her cheeks, tracing jagged lines down her face where the tears cut through her overdone makeup. She looked for something else to throw, hoping to punctuate further how upset she was, but she was out of pillows. Out of surprise, Nichole laughed, nettled by her daughter's behavior. Abigail, refusing to be the butt of any joke, threw her plate to the floor. It bounced on the carpet and pellets of rice jumped off her plate and into the carpet fibers.

"I'm not going," she sobbed. "You can go without me."

Nichole stared at her daughter, baffled as to how she had become so entitled, yet masked her incredulity that Abigail had become the very thing Nichole was trying to raise her not to be. Nichole looked at the spilled plate and dreaded the impending chore that she knew would be hers of cleaning it up. Sure, she could tell her daughter to do it, but she wouldn't. She would let the rice stay where it was for however long it took until Nichole finally caved and cleaned it up. Whenever Nichole tried to wage a war of attrition in regards to anything Abigail didn't want to do, Nichole always lost. Outside of politicians, teenagers are unprecedented in their ability to hold a grudge.

Somehow, through Abigail's childish outbursts, Nichole maintained her maternal compassion. She was a mother, so she always felt a desire to curb her daughter's distress. When she learned that Abigail wasn't Leroy's offspring, she promised that from that day forward, every decision she made would be for the benefit of her daughter. She owed her that. Her choices brought Abigail into this world, so it was her responsibility to give her the best life imaginable. If moving to Utah didn't fit that mold, she would stay where she was.

Nichole looked at the spilled food on the floor and sighed regrettably. She placed a mitigating hand on her daughter's leg. "You're my daughter and I love you. I won't go anywhere without you."

"Then we're staying," Abigail said; she wasn't asking.

CHAPTER 21

Marlon hated dating. He hated it more when it was setup. A setup

felt just like that: a setup, like he was being tricked into doing

something too ignorant to understand. A fellow teacher, Sarah, had

insisted for more than a year he go out with her friend Tiffany.

Marlon declined, citing that he was already seeing someone. (Seeing

someone seemed to be the most effective way to stop interlopers

from trying to set him up.) Sarah sensed he was lying but didn't call

his bluff. She simply employed a stronger strategy.

Tiffany had the same story every middle-aged single woman

in Utah has: married young, had a handful of kids, and while she and

her husband grew up, they grew apart. Kids marrying kids and

having kids. It was the Utah norm. Marlon had been out with fifty

women who had the same story as Tiffany. They all felt robbed of

their twenties because they spent it pregnant and tired. Their thirties

consisted of soccer games and dance recitals. Forty brings the

divorce, and they spend their childfree weekends at clubs trying to

reclaim two lost decades. Tiffany was no exception.

She was prudent enough to grant a no-fault divorce under the condition that her ex-husband foot the bill for a breast augmentation. The thought of trying to relive her twenties while in her forties scared her. It scared her more to imagine a man's reaction once he pulled off her shirt and noticed the stretch marks lining her stomach. The lifeless skin hung about her pouch just above her C-section scar—the constant reminder that she was the mother of four. Fake breasts would help deter a man's attention from the scars that chronicled her maternal history. Men didn't have these problems. The penis didn't adorn residual birthing marks. If a body transformation took place with a male, it was due to his own chosen lifestyle, not the trauma of fatherhood.

Surprisingly, even with all her baggage and faults, Tiffany found it rather easy to convince men to take her home, especially younger ones. All it took was a provocative smile or a revealing shirt to persuade a guy to leave with her. It was a bit off-putting, however, that they always needed to come to *her* house because most still lived at home.

Since her divorce, she'd spent the last year and a half at dance clubs trying to hide the crow's feet invading her eyes under strobe lights that flashed in rhythm to bad Katy Perry songs. Before her husband, she had only slept with one other guy, a boyfriend in high school who took advantage of her after the homecoming dance. She'd only been divorced for sixteen months and had slept with fourteen guys since then. All of them under forty, and all but two under thirty. She knew it wasn't love, but it comforted her to know that she was wanted, even if it was only for one night. The affirmation she felt at midnight outweighed the rejection she felt the following morning when the liquor wore off and the sun, peeking through her blinds, revealed to her young partners that she wasn't really thirty-three. They knew she wasn't all along, but they never questioned her fabrication. A dance club's function isn't to foster honest relationships. It's to put enough drunk people in a small enough space for the right amount of time to allow people to spin the right lie in an effort to get laid. The journey didn't matter so long as it ended with a cloudy orgasm.

There was one guy, however, that she was foolish enough to fall for. She didn't even learn his name until the next morning when he gently brushed a strand of hair from her face and asked what she would like for breakfast. Tiffany sighed and rolled over and told him his escape would be less awkward if he fled before she fully woke up.

"Why would I flee?" he asked.

"Isn't that how this works?"

"Not with me."

Tiffany sat up and looked at him. She was too old to play games this early in the morning and said as much.

"I'm not really thirty-three," she said.

"I know you're not."

"How old do you think I am?"

He thought for a moment. "Forty."

"I'm forty-one."

"Great. What do you want for breakfast?"

"It doesn't bother you that I'm forty-one?"

"No. I would rather be with someone I love than someone who's young."

Love. The word hung in the air, lingering there until she snatched it, believing that he must mean it in order to say it. She sat up and kissed him on the mouth, and when he didn't pull away, she took it for a sign that maybe this guy could work. Two months later and he was gone. No explanation. No back peddling. No lies to try and soften the blow. Just gone. Phone calls went unanswered, text messages, first asking how his day was, and then later propositioning him for sex, were deleted without any reply. He had gotten what he wanted and he simply didn't want her any longer. Her life as a mother, replete with laundry, dirty dishes and impromptu bouts of childhood sickness, weren't conducive to the life he wanted. Somehow it hurt more losing a guy after a couple months than it had losing a husband of twenty years.

Tiffany wasn't to be denied, though. After a week on her sofa watching *Sex and the City,* and scrolling through Facebook and Instagram publically liking her "friends'" posts while silently despising them and their artificial happiness, she was ready to try dating again. But this time, she wanted a change of scenery. The clubs weren't working; she wanted something more traditional. A romantic dinner and a movie followed by a promise to call—a promise that the man actually kept—would suffice. She no longer felt she needed to end the night on her knees or back in order to feel validated. She wanted something different. She wanted Marlon. He had to be different from every other guy for the unfathomable reason that he didn't seem interested in her.

Tiffany first noticed Marlon two years ago at a faculty Christmas party. She was separated at the time, but her divorce wasn't final. Sarah had convinced her to come, citing that it would be good for her to get out of the house around the holidays. Why stay trapped in a house with twenty years of falsified memories when you could spend the evening with 100 schoolteachers complaining about teenage angst and adolescent apathy?

Tiffany spotted Marlon across the room shaking hands with a colleague. He mouthed something and pointed to the exit. The colleague nodded and Marlon made his escape. Tiffany watched him leave and nudged Sarah.

"Who's that?"

"He's a fellow teacher," Sarah explained. "Mr. Brown. Marlon Brown."

"I wonder where's he's going."

"He has a reputation for leaving these things early," Sarah explained. "He's not very…gregarious." Tiffany looked at Sarah suspiciously, unfamiliar with the word. "He's not very social," she explained.

"He's handsome," Tiffany said, keeping her eyes locked on the exit in case he decided to reappear.

"Yeah, I know," Sarah said. "Everyone knows. He's often the topic of the math department's lunchtime conversations."

"Is he single?"

"Depends on who you ask. Three teachers have asked him out before, but he's turned each of them down claiming he's seeing someone. We all know it's a lie though."

Tiffany smiled. "Could you give him my number?"

"I'll talk to him."

And she did. Sarah spent the school year trying to convince Marlon to date Tiffany. Marlon had noticed Tiffany at the party, but he wasn't interested. Her designer knockoff dress looked gaudy and too formal for the occasion. He noticed how her eyes scanned the room in the same fashion a butcher looks over a display case of steaks. She was a hunter using her body as her weapon.

"She's just your type," Sarah told him the following week at school. Marlon laughed.

"Every woman thinks a sexy woman is every man's type," Marlon said.

"Isn't that true?"

Marlon entertained the notion of explaining Sarah's faulty logic, but he didn't see the point. Conversations where one party attempts to convince the other of something they don't believe frustrated Marlon. It's like accidentally opening your door to a Jehovah Witness. And like a religious zealot, Sarah was persistent. She often popped in on his prep period with new updates about Tiffany. Sometimes she would even ask questions that she knew Marlon had no way of knowing. (Did you know that Tiffany does

241

two aerobic classes every night at the gym? Did you know Tiffany was voted most likely to succeed in high school?) She emailed him selfies Tiffany took in front of her bathroom mirror at home. Often they were of her trying on new swimwear or underwear. In the emails, Sarah would tell Marlon, "Don't tell her I sent you these. She just wanted my opinion. If she knew I forwarded them to you, she would be sooooooo mad at me." Marlon found the approach pathetic. He had students that were more discrete with their philandering. Even though he couldn't deny that Tiffany was quite attractive, he couldn't fathom dating someone who made a habit of photographing herself in the bathroom. It reeked of desperation.

Sarah finally prevailed, though. One weekend Marlon got a nasty ear infection. He figured it would subside by Monday. It didn't. He thought he could find a sub in time to cover his classes. He couldn't. He went to Sarah and asked if she could cover his last period while he went to the doctor.

"I will on one condition," she said.

Marlon didn't need to ask what the condition was. He simply nodded while Sarah scribbled Tiffany's number on a post-it note.

"Take her anywhere that doesn't serve seafood," she instructed. "She hates seafood."

Marlon took her to the best sushi restaurant in town, partly as an act of defiance, but mostly because he knew he couldn't possibly take anyone seriously that didn't like good sushi.

He reserved a private room. In the middle of the room was the table sitting about a foot from the ground. The space under the table was a hollowed-out so people could sit comfortably with their legs dangling in the void. The walls appeared to be made of bamboo, but upon closer examination, one could see that it was plastic molded to resemble bamboo. The room offered an artificial privacy and elegance. It was Marlon's favorite restaurant.

"So what do you do for work?" Tiffany asked, even though she knew Marlon was a teacher. Marlon dwelled on the odd dating gesture of asking people questions they already knew the answers to. What puzzled him more was the level of interest the person employed when hearing the answers they already knew. The charade of caring.

"I'm a teacher."

"What do you teach?"

"English."

"Oh, I hated English in school," Tiffany said. "It was so boring."

Marlon reacted by not reacting. What was there to say to the person that hated your profession?

The server appeared and asked what they would like to drink. Tiffany ordered wine and Marlon asked for water. He thought to order wine himself but didn't want to risk drinking too much. Tiffany struck him as the type that finished her drinks rather quickly and then insisted whomever she was with follow suit so she could justify ordering more.

"I'm an esthetician," Tiffany said after the server left. Marlon hadn't asked what she did; she volunteered the information unprovoked. "I make ugly people gorgeous," she added.

Marlon looked at Tiffany, wondering if her comment was a joke. It didn't appear to be.

"That sounds like something you would be good at," he said sardonically.

"What do you mean?"

"You seem to take a lot of pride in your appearance," Marlon said.

His eyes scanned Tiffany's body and stopped for a moment at her chest. She wore a button-up shirt with the top three buttons conspicuously undone. Her bra pushed her breasts together and up, making her already ample bosom appear to be even more ample. She looked at Marlon looking at her. She assumed he liked what he saw; most guys did. He neither liked nor disliked what he saw when he looked at her. He continued staring at her breasts simply because they were there, much in the way one stares at someone's mouth when they have something stuck in their teeth. He was as indifferent to her physical appearance as he was to the plastic bamboo walls. Both simply served as something for the eyes to gaze upon.

"I do take a lot of pride in my appearance," Tiffany said. She traced the fold of her shirt down to her breasts and gently ran her finger along the line of her bra. Marlon looked up, conscious that he had kept his eyes locked on her breasts for too long. He thought to offer an apology but decided against it. He didn't care that he had been caught staring. Women like Tiffany wanted men to stare. Their livelihood depended on it. They didn't drop three months' salary on alterations *not* to be ogled.

"Well then, your career suits you," Marlon said.

The waitress returned with the drinks and asked if they had settled on what to order. Tiffany made a face and said she wasn't a huge sushi fan. She suggested Marlon just order whatever he liked and she would pick through the raw fish to the rice. Marlon ordered three rolls and the waitress left.

"So I have a confession to make," Tiffany said.

"What's that?"

"I googled you."

"Why?"

"Just to see who you are."

"And?"

"Nothing."

"That sounds about right," Marlon said. "I'm nobody."

"You're not on Facebook either. Or Instagram."

"Of course I'm not."

"Why not?"

"Why would I be?"

"It's fun."

"It is?"

"Yeah."

"What's fun about it?"

"You get to share your life with your friends."

"Can't you do that privately?"

"Sure, but why not make it public?"

"Your question is also your answer," he said.

"Huh?"

"The whole world doesn't care."

"But your friends do."

"No, actually, they don't," Marlon said. "They pretend to, but they do not care that your kid carved a pumpkin or that you got a speeding ticket."

"You couldn't be more wrong."

"Okay," Marlon mumbled.

"Do you want to take a selfie?"

Marlon looked at Tiffany. Evidently, she wasn't kidding because she already had her phone in her hand.

"I'm not taking a selfie," Marlon said.

"Why not?"

Marlon paused and shook his head.

"Come on," Tiffany said. "It will be fun."

"No."

"Why?"

"Does your ego really need to be fed right this minute?"

"What do you mean?"

"Suppose you posted a selfie and none of your friends liked it."

"That would never happen."

"Suppose that it did," Marlon said. "What would you do?"

"I'd delete it. It would be embarrassing."

"Exactly. Your ego needs to be fed. You need affirmation to feel relevant."

"What's wrong with that?"

Tiffany's ignorance perplexed Marlon. "Nothing, I guess. I just don't want to be part of it."

"Come on," Tiffany said. "I already told all my followers I was going out with a hot guy tonight." Tiffany winked at Marlon. "Now I have to show you off."

"I'm not interested."

"Please."

"How many friends do you have?"

"Over a thousand."

"You have over a thousand friends?" Marlon asked.

"Yeah."

"Bullshit."

"Rude!" Tiffany said and laughed. "Here, I'll show you." From her phone, she pulled up her Facebook page. Once loaded, she handed her phone to Marlon. Marlon stared at her outstretched phone for a moment before taking it. She wasn't lying. She had close to twelve hundred friends. Marlon nodded and handed the phone back.

"Want to see my latest profile pic?" she asked, and before Marlon could answer, she thrust the phone back at him. A picture of Tiffany in a two-piece swimsuit filled the screen. Her newly augmented breasts pushed against the inadequate fabric of the suit. Her boobs spilled out the top and bottom of the bikini top, while two pink inadequate patches held the contraption together by a thin pink string. The patches covered her nipples and not much more.

"It has over four hundred likes," Tiffany bragged. "It has over a thousand on Instagram. I want to get to two thousand."

"Why?" Marlon asked.

"Because…" Tiffany started but didn't say more because she felt it was obvious why she would want two thousand people to like her picture.

"Well, that's…admirable," Marlon said.

"Do you want to see my Instagram page?" she asked.

"Not really," Marlon said and handed back her phone. Tiffany took it, hurt that Marlon didn't ask to see other pictures from her page, or try and pry into her social profile by scrolling through her news feed. She had purposely added more photos of herself before their date in the hope that she could show him the parts of her she felt best objectified her. She couldn't believe Marlon wasn't even interested in her update about him. She posted that she was going on a date with a "hottie" (a fire emoticon included). She punctuated the post with a selfie of her date outfit. She figured he would be flattered if he saw the post. She would have acted embarrassed and pretended to want her phone back, while secretly encouraging him to continue down her newsfeed. It stung that he didn't feign more interest. She'd uploaded last year's Halloween costume. She dressed as a slutty cop and received over 600 likes. Below that was a photo of her meeting a local celebrity. Nearly a thousand people liked that. Marlon needed to see these because Tiffany needed her life validated.

She reluctantly placed her phone on the table. She wanted it nearby in case he changed his mind about a selfie.

"You really need to get on social media," she said.

"Why?"

"You can stay connected to you friends."

"I am connected with my friends."

"All my friends know I'm on a date right now," she said. "Do your friends know what you're doing?"

"No. I want it that way."

"Are you, like, secretive or something?"

"Just private.

"Why?"

"I don't need people knowing what I had for dinner."

Tiffany had planned on taking a photo of their dinner when their sushi arrived. She wanted her friends to know that she had finally tried it. Marlon's sour mood was ruining that opportunity for her.

"Do you really think you have as many friends as you think you have?" Marlon asked.

"What do you mean?"

"I mean do you really think you have twelve hundred friends?"

"Yeah."

Marlon was baffled and his stare indicated as much. Tiffany was baffled too, but more so because she didn't understand why Marlon had such a hard time understanding her popularity.

Their waitress arrived and dropped off a bowl of edamame. Marlon was thankful for the distraction. He quickly grabbed a pod and sucked the soybeans from the shell. Tiffany eyed the beans curiously but didn't take one. She looked lovingly at her phone. The soybeans were begging her to photograph them.

"So you're divorced?" Tiffany asked.

"Yeah."

"What happened?"

"It just...didn't work out," Marlon said. He discarded the empty bean shell and grabbed another one.

"Marriages today rarely do. I'm mean, that's why we're here, right?" Tiffany laughed awkwardly and took a long drink from her wine. "My ex-husband is a real asshole. After nineteen years, he told me he had enough. I think he was fucking his secretary. I know what you're thinking. He's such a cliché, right? The pathetic part is she's not even that cute. I mean, yeah, okay, she's like, ten years younger than me, but you should see her body. Can you say cellulite?"

Tiffany laughed at her own critique. Marlon stayed silent, sucking on the edamame, while looking bored and distant.

"What's wrong?" Tiffany asked.

Marlon didn't answer because he didn't hear her question. "Huh?' he asked.

"What's wrong?" Tiffany asked again.

"Wrong? Nothing is wrong. I was just…listening."

"What did I say?" Tiffany tilted her head and narrowed her eyes, ready to pounce if he couldn't successfully answer.

"You said that, ah, that…," Marlon rubbed his temples "…that your ex-husband is an asshole."

Tiffany softened her eyes and lowered her shoulders, duped into believing Marlon had actually heard her. He hadn't. He just assumed it was a safe bet that Tiffany had called her ex an asshole. That seemed to be a reoccurring theme with most of his dates. It's a paradox women want to go out with men to complain about how much they hate men. Most men even nod at the critique, believing the act of agreeing is the surest way to the bedroom. Women interpret the agreement to mean *this* guy must be the exception. He's the exception because he recognizes the fault with every other man, so he must have figured out the way not to replicate them.

"You were listening," Tiffany said. "I thought I lost you for a second."

Marlon's attentiveness touched her. He felt a tinge of guilt for tricking her into believing he had been listening to her. He could sense that most guys she dated didn't hear what she said. They just nodded at the appropriate places. Marlon's feigned interest had just placed him into uncharted waters. All he had to do now was keep playing the part of the active listener and he was certain to get laid. Unfortunately, for Tiffany, it was a prospect that held zero appeal for him. He didn't want to experience 10 exciting minutes only to survive the torturous thousands that would surely follow. The next day text messages that would be run-on sentences filled with emoticons and misspelled words. Her hinting that she had nothing going on the following weekend. The blowback when he didn't take the hints, and then the effort to placate his ignorance by agreeing to another dinner. God, it was all so exhausting. Marlon didn't want to misrepresent himself, so he decided to come clean.

"Actually, I just guessed that was what you said," he explained. "I wasn't listening to you, Tiffany. I haven't really been listening to you since we've sat down."

Tiffany stared at Marlon in disbelief. He didn't think her shocked expression needed to be so…shocked. Inexplicably, it made him feel a little uncomfortable and even sad. He shifted in his seat.

"You're pretty enough, sure," Marlon went on, "but I think we're both just wasting the other's time here, don't you?"

Tiffany thought for a moment and then said, "That's a harsh thing to say."

Marlon nodded. "We're both middle-aged divorcees. Haven't we earned the right to be harsh?"

"You're not attracted to me?"

"What?" Marlon said. "That's what you think this is about?"

"Isn't it?"

"No."

"So you are attracted to me?"

Marlon groaned. "Sure…you're…cute."

"Cute?"

"Cute isn't good?"

"Puppies are cute."

"Look, I…I'm not sure what you are after here."

"Tell me I'm beautiful or sexy or anything other than cute."

Marlon knew what she wanted, but he couldn't bring himself to give her what she was after. After a moment he answered, "You look like every other woman that's trying to fill a void with her appearance."

"What does that mean?"

Marlon sighed, and then, without warning, yawned. Initially, he tried to fight the yawn, but somehow that seemed to make him even more tired and thus intensifying the gesture. He finally decided to surrender to his exhaustion and let it overtake him. He opened his mouth wide and expelled the pent-up breath like a lion waking from a deep slumber. He opened his eyes and saw Tiffany staring back at him, wide-eyed and expecting.

"What?" Marlon asked.

"Am I boring you?"

"Well…"

"What did you mean when you said what you said?"

"I can't remember what I even said."

"You said…," but Tiffany couldn't remember exactly what Marlon had said either, only that it seemed offensive. "I can't remember what you said. Something about my appearance."

"Oh, right. Yeah, you look…stereotypical."

Tiffany stared at Marlon in disbelief. "You are such an asshole," she said. She snatched her phone from off the table and dropped it in her purse.

"What did I do?" Marlon asked.

"Who talks to a woman like that?"

"But isn't there a part of you that likes that I'm being honest?" Marlon asked. "I mean, I'm not just pretending to be interested in you just to fulfill some carnal desire. Isn't that worth something?"

"You want praise for being rude?" Tiffany asked incredulously.

"No. For being real. For...for not caring that you're sexy."

"You don't care that I'm sexy?"

"That's not what I'm saying."

"What are you saying?"

"Being sexy is only a plus if there's more to you than that."

"You have a lot of nerve," Tiffany said, throwing her purse over her shoulder. She was about to storm out of the room when Marlon reached across the table and took her by the arm.

"Why do you hate your husband?" Marlon asked.

"What?"

"Why do you hate your husband?"

"He...he cheated. He lied to me."

"He wasn't honest?" Marlon said.

"No, he wasn't."

"You want honesty in a relationship?"

"Yes!"

"Then why are you walking out on me?"

"What?"

"I'm being honest with you. I'm not placating things just to get laid. Isn't it refreshing?"

"No. It's…you're…"

"You don't want honesty, do you?" Marlon asked.

"I do."

"You do until you don't. Until the truth stings, then you run from it."

"I'm not running from anything."

Marlon leveled his eyes on Tiffany. "Tiffany, give me an honest moment."

"What?"

"Give me an honest moment."

"What do you mean?"

"I mean…tell me all the things about you that you don't want me to know."

Tiffany stared at Marlon for a long time, trying to make sense of what he was after. This was a game she had never played before, and she hated that she didn't understand the rules. Tiffany liked simplicity because she was a simpleton. Dating only made sense when she knew what the guy was after. She understood *that* game; she knew *those* rules. Marlon was rewriting the rulebook. Tiffany just wanted affirmation from a man that she was worth something. Even if Marlon didn't think it, what would it hurt to just indulge the lie? That's what dating was supposed to be. Lying to make another feel validated: it was the most human thing about humans.

"Please," Marlon pleaded again, "give me an honest moment. Tell me something about you that you don't want me to know."

"Why would I do that?" Tiffany asked.

"To filter through all the bullshit," Marlon explained helplessly. "To transcend all the dating crap we put ourselves through and just be completely open and authentic. We could sit here and pretend to be interested in things we really don't care about, or we could be real with each other and tell each other the things we don't want the other to know. Let's put it all on the table now so there aren't any surprises later."

Marlon finished his speech and looked at Tiffany hopelessly. She looked confused and her confusion was compounded because she wasn't sure what it was she was actually confused about. Was Marlon mocking her or revealing himself? Was he trying to make a connection or was this a scathing evaluation? She couldn't tell. Everything that came out of his mouth sounded like a paradox.

"I've never been talked to like this on a date."

"Of course you haven't. All the guys you've been out with told you everything you wanted to hear because they wanted to sleep with you."

"Wow. You are such a jerk."

"Tell me I'm wrong," Marlon pleaded. "Slap me and tell me I'm wrong. Show me there's life in you."

Tiffany opened her mouth to tell Marlon he was wrong, but couldn't say the words. In the split second between his request and her rebuttal, she thought of the young man who had recently broken her heart and the countless other guys who had slept with her only to sneak out of her bedroom shortly after it was over. Marlon was right. Tiffany was just a means to an orgasmic end for the guys she dated. Still, he didn't need to be so blatant about it and his pompous disposition didn't help mitigate the sting from his words. She wanted to cry but somehow kept herself together. Had she allowed herself the release, Marlon would have swept her up in his arms, thankful for the opportunity to feel the sincere vulnerability of another human being. He would have taken her home, tucked her into bed, and kissed her affectionately on the forehead. The next morning, he would have called her and asked if he could see her again. He would have done anything to feel alive at that moment with another person, to know that he still had the capacity to feel something, anything. But Tiffany was resilient, subscribing to what she thought was wanted: unremitting stoicism. She choked back her tears, pushed them to the recesses of her heart with the refuse of her broken marriage and subsequent one night stands.

"You ask any woman what they want in a relationship and they always say honesty," Marlon went on. "Well, here I am being completely honest with you. How many times have you taken your phone out on a date and pulled up a picture of you in a swimsuit or some other revealing outfit and passed it across the table to some guy hoping to get a reaction?"

Tiffany stared at Marlon. She had nothing to say, but her curiosity of where his diatribe was going kept her glued to her seat.

"You knew what you were after," Marlon continued, "and I bet they all acted the same, prompting you to show them more pics that garnered more shallow responses about how hot you were. That's what you wanted from me earlier, and I didn't give it to you because I want to know *who* you are as a person, not what you are as a potential fuck."

Marlon's vulgarity hit Tiffany like a ton of bricks. Her chin quivered and Marlon reached for her, urging her to embrace the emotional release, but she pulled away.

"You're such a…," Tiffany started, but couldn't finish her thought. Marlon was right and the realization invoked something in her. What's more, she actually found herself getting turned on by the scathing nature in which he was belittling her. What did it reveal about her that even as Marlon ridiculed her vulnerability, at that moment she wanted more than ever to leap over the table and kiss him passionately?

"Just…just give me an honest moment," He pleaded. "Please."

"I don't know what you mean by that," Tiffany said, raising her voice to match her frustration.

"Look, I'll go first," Marlon said, trying to make clear what he was after. He leaned forward. "When I was eleven I cut the head off my sister's favorite Barbie and flushed it down the toilet."

"What? Why?"

"Because I was eleven and stupid."

"I don't understand…"

"It hurt my sister so badly. I wish I hadn't done it. I'm ashamed."

"Then why are you telling me?"

"That's the point."

"What's the point? I don't understand what you're after."

"I…I'm…," Marlon struggled, "…trying to reclaim what I lost…," Marlon whispered. Suddenly his eyes grew hot and tears started from them. He thought to wipe them away but lacked the effort it would take to do so. He looked at Tiffany. She couldn't understand his tears, where they came from and what they meant. He silently willed her to reach across the table and place an affectionate hand on his cheek. He would have done anything at that moment to feel the touch of another human.

"This is really weird," Tiffany said, uncomfortable with the situation.

Defeated, Marlon lowered his head. "I think you should go," he said.

"Are you...did I hurt you?" she asked.

"No," he said. "Just go."

Tiffany quickly stood and left the room. On her way out, she passed the waitress carrying their plate of sushi. Tiffany awkwardly side-stepped her, spied the raw fish and increased her step. The waitress watched her go, unsure if she should say something or mind her own business. She pushed opened the curtain and found Marlon sitting with his chin resting on his chest. The server placed the rolls on the table.

"Are you okay, sir?" she asked.

Marlon didn't look up. "Yes. You can bring the check."

CHAPTER 22

Abigail scored fifty-four on her English exam; she needed sixty to pass. Mr. Ned walked right up to her, pulled her paper from the top of the stack and dropped it on her desk. The giant 54, red and circled, stared back at her. The marking of Mr. Ned's red pen had bled down the paper like a wound leaving a streak of red residue. It seemed to signify so much more to Abigail than a failed score. Fifty-four was a sentence of boredom and anticlimactic happenings for the summer ahead. She glanced up at Mr. Ned. He shrugged his shoulders and moved on. Abigail couldn't tell if he was happy, sad, or indifferent in regards to her failing his class. He didn't know either. If given the choices, he would have answered that he was somehow all three.

Carrie whispered Abigail's name. Abigail turned and Carrie raised her eyebrows. Abigail held up her exam. Carried studied the number. "Shit," she said. "What are you going to do?" Abigail shrugged. She didn't know what she was going to do, only that she needed to figure out something. She turned back and faced the front of the room. Mr. Ned was staring wide-eyed at her. When their eyes met, he quickly looked down, picked up a pencil from his desk, and pretended to write something. Abigail kept her eyes fixed on the top of Mr. Ned's head. She had an idea.

*****

Mr. Ned's prep period was at the end of the day. If Abigail could catch him before he went home, maybe she could convince him to change her grade. She knew her mom would ask about her test when she got home. Abigail needed to act fast.

She went into the girls' bathroom after lunch and applied a fresh layer of makeup. She wore a button-down shirt and skirt. The skirt extended to the middle of her thighs. She appraised herself in the bathroom mirror and sneered at her complexion. She looked too modest for the job ahead. She undid another button and opened her shirt collar further, exposing the black lace of her bra. Her skirt was short, but not short enough. She folded the waistband over twice and looked at herself from behind. A hint of her buttocks emerged beneath the hem of the skirt. She faced the mirror again, reached up the skirt's fold, pulled her thong down her legs, and stepped out of it.

She shoved the underwear into her backpack and retrieved her perfume. She gave her neck two sprays and her breasts one. She pocketed the perfume and gave herself another overview. Satisfied, she started for Mr. Ned's class.

Mr. Ned's desk was in the far corner of the room, concealed from the window that looked into his class from the door. Abigail knocked softly on his door and then gently pushed it open without waiting to see if he would admit her himself. He sat placidly at his desk playing solitaire on his desktop. When he noticed Abigail, he quickly closed the game, out of some unfounded fear that she'd report him for not spending his time constructively. He sat up straight, looked at Abigail's attire and tried his hardest not to stare.

"Is it a bad time?" Abigail asked. She tried to appear innocent and coy and succeeded at neither.

"Shouldn't you be in class?" Mr. Ned asked.

"I thought I could talk to you about my grade," Abigail said. She closed the door behind her and started toward Mr. Ned. She walked slowly and with purpose, placing one high-heeled shoe in front of the other like a model on a runway.

"I don't allow retakes, Abigail," Mr. Ned said. After his first year teaching, Mr. Ned resolved he would no longer allow exam retakes. He didn't see the point. It only made more work for him. What did he get out of giving students two opportunities to fail?

Abigail finished her seductive walk and sat down in a chair across from him Mr. Ned. She opened her legs slightly and watched as Mr. Ned's eyes furtively investigated the hollow space between her legs. She smiled and then slowly crossed one leg on top of the other. Mr. Ned quickly looked away.

"Could I do anything for extra credit?" Abigail asked, biting on her lower lip.

"There's ah…I don't offer…," Mr. Ned began but trailed off. Abigail ran her fingers up her thigh to where her skirt ended and her legs began. He understood what Abigail was after.

"The thing is," Abigail began, "my friends are going to Lake Tahoe this summer and my mom won't let me go if I don't pass all my classes. You would really be helping me out if there was something I could do to raise my grade." Abigail slid her skirt higher up her legs and looked at Mr. Ned desperately.

"You shouldn't be in here with the door closed," Mr. Ned said, trying to resist the urge to look at her smooth, shiny legs. Her audacity was beyond reproach. "This is highly inappropriate."

"What is?"

"What you are doing?"

"What am I doing?"

"Just…just stop it, okay."

"Do you want me to leave?" Abigail asked. She sounded hurt and uncrossed her legs to elaborate the false threat of leaving. She made to stand, but just sat with her legs opened so Mr. Ned could reconsider her question. She slightly arched her back and spread her legs wider. Mr. Ned naturally looked at what she was displaying, but quickly turned away when he saw that she wasn't wearing underwear. He shuddered and tapped into every ounce of self-control to avert his eyes from Abigail. He tried to pick up a pencil from his desk, simply because he wanted something to do that took his stare away from Abigail, but fumbled at the task and it fell to the ground and rolled toward Abigail. She bent over slowly, letting her shirt fall open, and picked up the pencil, keeping her eyes on Mr. Ned the entire time. She stood and walked to Mr. Ned. She got to his desk and gently put the pencil on top of it. Mr. Ned could smell her perfume. He turned away from her.

"You're sure there's nothing I can do to raise my grade?" Abigail asked again.

"Abigail, this is…this is highly inappropriate," Mr. Ned managed to say.

"You already said that."

"Well, it is."

"No one will know."

"There's nothing to know."

Abigail took a step closer. Their knees touched. He turned and looked at his knee touching Abigail's naked one. His eyes slowly inched up her legs, to her stomach, her breasts, and finally settled on her eyes. She stared at Mr. Ned; all innocence had fled her. She wanted him. She stared deep into his eyes and slowly began to lift her skirt.

"How…how old are you?" Mr. Ned choked.

"Eighteen," Abigail lied. She leaned closer to him and whispered, "I promise I won't tell anyone."

"I could…I could lose my job," Mr. Ned mumbled. He shook his head and turned away from her.

Abigail advanced, forcing Mr. Ned's knees apart and stepping between them.

"Don't you believe me when I say I promise I won't tell?"

"Tell what?" Mr. Ned said. He seemed to have regained some of his composure. "I don't know what you're talking about. You need to leave."

Abigail put her hand on Mr. Ned's leg and turned him toward her. He resisted at first but gave up the fight rather quickly. He spun around in his chair and found himself at eye level with Abigail's breasts. She took Mr. Ned's hand.

"Feel how wet I am," she said.

She guided his hand up her skirt. He let her lead him, feeling defenseless and rationalizing that somehow, he was the victim to her whims. He swallowed hard and closed his eyes and let her guide him. He felt what she wanted him to feel. She closed her eyes and moaned. He shuddered and explored what she was so willing to

offer. When he opened his eyes a moment later, he saw the principal

staring back at him, her mouth opened and her eyes wide.

CHAPTER 23

From the corner of her eye, Abigail could see her mother's white knuckles clutching the steering wheel. Every minute or so Nichole would sigh heavily and open her mouth to speak, before deciding against it, and assuming a tighter grip on the wheel. Abigail sat in the passenger seat with her arms crossed, sulking. She looked at the blurred trees that passed in various flashes of color outside the window. Thus far she succeeded in not crying, but it was a struggle to keep the tears at bay. She wasn't sad because she got caught with a teacher's hand up her skirt; she was sad because now there was no way Nichole would let her go to Tahoe for the summer. Her mother would strip her of her liberty and relegate her to a summer spent under Nichole's watchful eye.

The light ahead turned yellow. Nichole pressed on the accelerator, then reconsidered her decision, and pushed hard on the brake. The seat belts caught, and they skidded to a stop just as the light switched to red. Stranded in the middle of the intersection, angry commuters quickly laid on their horns. Nichole looked in her rearview and backed through the intersection, avoiding all eye contact with the other drivers.

"What were you thinking?" Nichole finally asked.

"I don't know."

"You don't know?" Nichole repeated. "Jesus, Abigail. What kind of answer is that?"

"He came on to me," Abigail mumbled.

"What?"

"He came on to me," she said more clearly.

"He came on to you?" Nichole repeated incredulously.

"Yes," Abigail said. She looked at her mom desperately. Nichole scoffed and shook her head. Abigail tried crying, unsuccessfully, in a pathetic attempt to garner some sympathy. "I was scared," she said. "I didn't know what to do."

"What were you even doing in his class? You should have been in Spanish."

"He told me he needed to talk to me about my test. The next thing I know he has me down and he's trying to...to take advantage of me."

"God, Abby," Nichole cried.

"What?"

"That's not the way he told it."

"So?" Abigail asked. "You're going to believe him? Some fifty-year- old perv who tried to rape me?"

"I didn't say I believed him," Nichole said. The light turned green and she sped through the intersection. "All I said is your version is a lot different than his."

"Yeah. Because he's a liar."

"The principal saw it, Abby. He didn't have you pinned down."

"The principal's a bitch, mom!" Abigail yelled. "How can you believe those people over your own daughter?"

"God, you are something else, you know that."

"What does that mean?"

"It means…," Nichole started but didn't have the energy to explain what was so obvious to everyone but Abigail. "Well, you're done there. Two weeks left in the school year and you get kicked out."

"What!" Abigail sprang forward, forcing the seat belt to contract. "That isn't fair."

"What do you want me to do about it?"

"Fight for me. Tell them—"

"Tell them what, Abby? The principal saw you."

Abigail slumped back into her seat. This time she didn't need to force the tears; they came freely. She glanced at her mom to see if her theatrics gained her any motherly sympathy. She couldn't tell.

"Do I still get to go to Tahoe?" Abigail asked with a little hope and a lot of sorrow.

Nichole spied her daughter from the corner of her eye. "You're kidding, right?"

"What?"

"No, Abby, you don't get to go to Tahoe."

Abigail whimpered but remained silent for the rest of the drive home. Ten minutes later, Nichole pulled into the driveway and turned off her car. Abigail stayed slumped in her seat, crying. Nichole turned to her daughter and watched her cry. She did feel some sympathy for her, but not enough to reconsider her decision.

Nichole reached for Abigail, but Abigail hit her hand away and

slouched further in her seat.

"Don't touch me," Abigail said.

"Abby…"

"You are such a bitch," Abigail said.

It was the first time Abigail had ever called her mom a bitch,

yet somehow it sounded so natural coming from her, Nichole was

surprised this was the first time she ever offered the insult. Nichole

wasn't sure why, but the comment didn't sting as much as she felt it

should. She actually laughed at the absurd remark.

"Yeah, I'm the bitch because I won't let my daughter, who

shoved her teacher's hand up her skirt, go on a summer trip."

Abigail sat up and wiped her face. She looked at her mom.

"Well, what do you expect, Nichole? I'm a whore because my

mom's a whore."

When Abigail called Nichole a bitch, it didn't sting, but when

she called her a whore, compounded with her actual name, it had the

opposite effect. The word didn't hurt; the delivery did. Abigail meant what she said. Nichole clenched her fists and took a deep breath to collect herself. She counted to ten and then opened her eyes.

"Don't say things you'll regret later," Nichole instructed.

"You are a whore, mom," Abigail said evenly. "That's why I don't even know who my father is."

"Abby...watch it."

"Or what, mom? What are you going to do?"

"I'm your mother," Nichole said, patiently.

"I wish you weren't."

"That's real original, Abby. Be the self-loathing teenager who hates her mom. Next are you going to tell me you hate me?"

"I do hate you."

"Of course you do."

"I hate who you are."

"And who am I, Abby?"

"A slut that fucked some stranger at a party and now here I am. A fucking slut born from a fucking slu—"

The slap wasn't a conscious action. It just happened, like absentmindedly scratching an itch. It wasn't clear whether it surprised Nichole or Abigail more. Nichole immediately retrieved her hand and used it to cover her opened mouth. She stared dejectedly at her daughter, trying to make sense of what she had just done. Abigail froze and stared blankly back at her mother. Nichole's handprint stood visibly red on her daughter's cheek where it tried, unsuccessfully, to dissolve into her pale skin. Once the shock of the action dissipated, Nichole reached for her daughter.

"Oh, god, Abby. I'm so sorry."

Abigail pushed her mom away, unclicked her seatbelt and scrambled out of the car. She ran inside her house, darted down the hall to her room, fell on her bed, and sobbed.

*****

Abigail cried for most of the night. Nichole wanted to go in and speak with her but felt it best to wait until she calmed down. Besides, Abigail had her door locked and Nichole knew no request, no matter how sincere, would result in her opening it. Around midnight, when Abigail quietly emerged from her room to use the bathroom, Nichole snuck into her room and sat down at Abigail's corner desk. A minute later, Abigail came back into her room and locked the door behind her. When she turned back around, she noticed Nichole sitting in the corner. She thought to tell her to get out but decided her silence was cutting her mom more deeply than any words she could think of. Abigail ignored her mom and walked to her bed and laid down with her back facing Nichole. Nichole rose from her chair and sat on the edge of her daughter's bed. She placed a remorseful hand on her daughter's leg, fearful that it may cause Abigail to pull away or become violent. Abigail didn't respond to her mother's touch.

"I'm so sorry for what happened in the car, sweetie," Nichole said. Abigail stayed resolutely quiet and still.

"I'm taking that job in Utah," Nichole said. She felt her daughter stiffen. Abigail rolled onto her back and looked up at her mom. Fresh tears were forming in the corners of her eyes.

"What?" Abigail said.

"I'm taking the job," Nichole repeated.

Abigail wanted to protest, but couldn't formulate a word. Her chin quivered and she closed her eyes, causing the buildup of tears to run down her cheeks.

"You can be pissed and call me names and hate me forever, but I'm taking the job," Nichole said. "It's a great opportunity for us and I'm not letting it slip away. I'm tired of Vegas. I'm tired of this town."

"It's not fair," Abigail said, weakly.

"Abby, for the past seventeen years everything I've done has been for you. I know I've made mistakes. I'm doing the best I can, though. I've turned down two proposals from two really great guys because I promised myself when I had you, I would always put you first. When my best friend moved to Europe and asked us to come, I stayed for you. I've given you my life, and I've given you a great life, but now I'm doing something for me. You're defiant, Abby. You're promiscuous and you have no respect for me or yourself. You're angry all the time, and I don't know why. What do you have to be angry about? Where did all this hate come from? I don't know what I've done to make you hate me so much. I don't know how you've become this…pissed off entitled teenager that feels everyone owes you something. I'm sure I'm to blame on some level. I know in many areas I've failed you as a mother, and for that I am sorry. I mean that. I am sorry."

Nichole waited for Abigail to say something, but she remained silent, refusing to extend her mother the gift of speech. Nichole removed her hand from her daughter's leg and placed it in her own lap. She was defeated. She didn't know how to communicate with her daughter anymore. She reluctantly got to her feet and then leaned down and kissed Abigail on the forehead. Abigail neither received nor rejected the kiss; she just remained stoic and indifferent. Nichole started for the door and then turned back to her daughter.

"Utah will be a fresh start."

Abigail took in a deep breath. "I don't want a fresh start," she cried. "You can't make me go."

"Actually, I can, Abby," Nichole said. "You're not eighteen for seven more months, so legally, you have to do what I ask. If you want to come back here in seven months without a car, without a place to stay, without a job and without a dollar to your name, you can. You can come back here and be free of me forever. But until then, you're coming to Utah with me." Nichole paused to see if Abigail had anything further to say. She didn't. "Oh, and one more thing. You will need to take a summer English class to make up the credit you lost. I emailed the principal a few hours ago. They have an eight-week summer course you can take to earn your credit. It starts at the first of next month."

Abigail shot up. "You're making me spend my entire summer taking an English in Utah?"

"Yeah, I am. Deal with it."

"That's not fair," Abigail cried.

"Abby, I have one job to do as a parent and that's to make sure you have better opportunities than I did. I'm not making you take an English class. You are. You're the one who made the decisions that have led to this moment. Accept the life you've created for yourself. I'm going to ride your ass every day until you graduate. After that, if you want to throw your life away, go ahead, but until that time, you're stuck with me."

Abigail sank back onto her bed. "I hate you so much."

"I know you do," Nichole said and closed the door behind her.

CHAPTER 24

Marlon sat with his feet propped up on his desk and his book in his

lap. There were seven students in the classroom. Four were reading,

two were sleeping and one, Samantha, was texting. Marlon caught

Samantha's texting from the corner of his eye. He thought to tell her

to put her phone away and stay on task, but he lacked the energy to

do so. It was only the first day of summer school, and he already felt

burned out. He wondered why he volunteered to teach it again this

year. Only the dregs took it, the students whose ambition never

quite surpassed their parents' insistence that they make something of

themselves. They offered nothing, contributed nothing besides

consumerism and unrequited teenage angst. They were pissed

without knowing why and naïve about how pissed they were. Life

was hard because it required effort. Most gave up early, learning

instead how merely to exist by sleepwalking through life on a

preordained course set up by a parent or a boyfriend or girlfriend that

would soon become a spouse and then soon after become an ex-

spouse. In many respects, Marlon's own life was slowly beginning

288

to mirror his students. His contempt for them was almost on par with their contempt for everything he stood for. He had all the answers they weren't looking for, just as they probably had, presumably, all the solutions to his problems. Even though they appeared to be on different sides of the spectrum, teachers and students often have more in common than they would like to admit.

Just as Marlon was returning to his book, Abigail walked in. She wore short white shorts and a shorter top. From behind, Marlon could see the outline of a red thong pressed against the transparent fabric of her shorts. Her shirt snugged her adolescent breasts, highlighting two erect nipples that stuck out from the material like a hitchhiker's thumb. Marlon lowered his gaze and noticed her bellybutton piercing contrasting sharply against her tan stomach. Typical summer school student, Marlon thought. Two of the boys that were reading looked up and appraised Abigail with stereotypical pubescent approval. One of them nudged his sleeping friend and pointed at Abigail. The newly awakened student rubbed his eyes, looked at Abigail, and then rubbed them again. Behind him, Samantha took stock of the new girl, too. Samantha was the B-version of Abigail. They wouldn't be friends, couldn't be friends because they were too much alike. Their most prominent trait was hating anyone who resembled them. Samantha had, moments earlier, elicited her own lustful stares from the boys in the class as she entered wearing her own belly shirt. Now she was just an afterthought.

Abigail knew the class was watching her. She relished the attention because she knew the guys in the class wanted her and the girls wanted to be her. She let them stare and assess her before giving the room a contemptuous sneer to let them know she was out of their league.

Marlon sighed, dropped his book on his desk and lowered his feet. Abigail approached him; her summer registration receipt fluttering in her hand. She held it out to him, but he didn't take it.

"What's your name?" Marlon asked.

"Abigail."

Marlon looked at his role and found her name.

"From Las Vegas, huh?" Marlon asked.

"Yep," Abigail answered, bored.

On the floor next to Marlon's desk was a box. He reached inside and retrieved a copy of *1984*. On the edge of his desk sat a stack of work packets. He pulled the top packet from the stack and handed the book and stapled papers to Abigail.

"Ever read *1984?*" he asked.

"Nope."

"One of the greatest books ever written. You have six weeks to finish it along with that makeup packet. You need to be here every day from nine to eleven. If you're more than ten minutes late, you'll be marked absent and you won't get your credit. Every Friday we'll have a quiz on a section from the book and every Wednesday we'll have a vocabulary test on terms from the book. You'll find the vocab list in your packet. Any questions?"

"Sounds boring," Abigail said, weighing the book in her hands.

"That wasn't a question," Marlon said. "That was an observation. Do you have any questions?"

Abigail sneered and shook her head.

"The book isn't boring, but the curriculum is," Marlon explained. "If you're passionate enough, write your congressman and let him know." Marlon paused. He sensed Abigail didn't understand anything he was saying. "I'm Mr. Brown," Marlon said.

Abigail nodded and then turned to walk away.

"Tell me three things you're knowledgeable about," Marlon said. Abigail stopped and turned around.

"What?"

"I like to know something about my students. Tell me three things you're knowledgeable about."

"I...I don't know."

"Yes, you do."

"What?"

"Don't ever say 'I don't know' when you do know. That's lazy. Reserve your 'I don't knows' for things you don't actually know. For example, name three Supreme Court Justices.

Abigail thought for a moment. "I don't know any."

"Very good. You don't know. Now, tell me three things you're knowledgeable about."

Abigail rolled her eyes before settling them back on Marlon, hoping that her annoyance could work as reason enough not to offer an answer. He looked at her and waited an answer. She sighed and said, "Fashion, wake boarding, and dancing."

"You're only knowledgeable about two of those things," Marlon said quickly.

"Which two?"

Marlon turned toward his desk. "If you don't already know, I don't want to be the one to tell you. Exploiting your body isn't fashionable. It's ostentatious. This may be summer school, but we still have a dress code. Follow it. Ever since you walked in here, Scott and Chuck haven't stopped staring at you."

Abigail looked over the class and found Scott and Chuck staring back at her with their mouths opened. They quickly lowered their heads and pretended to read.

"Don't flatter yourself, though," Marlon continued, picking up his book. "The real accomplishment would be to get Braxton to wake up. Not even coming in here without a bra could do that."

Abigail looked back over the students and extrapolated that the student softly snoring must be Braxton.

"The first thirty minutes of class is for reading," Marlon said. "*1984*. Get started."

Abigail was perplexed. Teachers didn't usually address students in such a scathing manner. Was this the Utah custom? Was everything so backwards here that teachers had permission to criticize a students' wardrobe if it didn't adhere to the Utah adage of "modest is hottest"?

Abigail looked at the cover of her book. It looked so plain. Just four numbers strung together to make the year that served as the title. Underneath in smaller type, the author's name. She examined it from the side. It looked thick. She opened to the last page. 320 pages. She had never read an entire book before and had no idea how one even got through a series of words and paragraphs that could go on for three hundred and twenty pages. She knew enough people in Vegas that she never had to do her own work. But here, in this foreign land, she was all alone. Even if she could use her talents to get one of the other students in the class to do her work, she doubted any of them were up for the task. Summer school wasn't an accelerated program. It was a last resort, the final straw, the short bus reserved for the apathetic. Abigail felt hopeless.

She glanced back at Marlon. He had returned to his own copy of the Orwell classic. She could see sections of his book earmarked and highlighted with indecipherable notes scribbled in the margins. Abigail looked back at the other students. The boys still stared at her, mentally letting the few clothes that covered her body disintegrate under their gaze. Samantha stared, too. She kept her head tilted to the side and she chewed her gum condescendingly. Abigail scoffed at her and made her way to her seat. It took every ounce of her strength not to cry.

CHAPTER 25

Marlon sat on a table at the front of the classroom. His students stared up at him with placid, dead eyes. They wanted to put their heads down and go to sleep, but knew the second they did, Marlon would yell for them to wake up. Or even worse, he wouldn't say anything and let them take their nap, only to fail them for not paying attention. At the moment he was trying, unsuccessfully, to facilitate a discussion from *1984*.

"What does Winston mean when he says that if a change is going to occur, it needs to happen with the Proles?"

Marlon's question, like most, received blank stares. Most students will just wait out the teacher. Wait for him to answer his own question and continue with the irrelevant lesson. Marlon wasn't like most teachers. He didn't mind the silences brought upon by student disinterest. He waited them out.

Nervous ticks—students tapping pencils or clicking pens—started to flood the classroom. Marlon scanned the nine student faces staring back at him. They were zombies, but with less motivation. Samantha expelled an animated yawn, adding emphasis to let Marlon know that he, and his class, were beneath her. Marlon spied Samantha with pent-up hostility. He zeroed in.

"Sam, what do you think?" Marlon called her Sam because she insisted on the first day he call her Samantha.

"I don't know," Samantha answered, not even attempting to come up with an answer to appease her teacher.

"How's that working out for you?" Marlon asked.

"What?"

"Not knowing things?"

"Huh?"

"Tell me something you do know."

"I know this book is boring."

The other students laughed and Samantha smiled. She didn't intend to gain the approval of her peers with her comment, but now that she had it, she savored it. Once the laughter died, the students looked at Marlon and wondered how he would handle the criticism. He looked back at Samantha with a bemused smirk.

"Fair enough," Marlon said, setting his book down next to him. "Who else thinks this book is boring?"

Reluctantly, after gauging that Marlon wouldn't be too upset with their honesty, the students slowly put their hands in the air. Marlon nodded, stood and went to the whiteboard. He drew a large triangle on the board, followed by two horizontal lines, slicing the triangle into three uneven sections. The first section, at the top by the point, was very small. The second section was a little bigger, and the third section at the bottom was the largest. He turned back to his students.

"This triangle represents the society in *1984,* but it also represents our society today," he said. "The top section is Big Brother, or the one percent. We've heard that term a lot lately, haven't we? The one percent. Well, they're at the top of the pyramid. The next section is the inner Party, or the rich. The "haves" if you will. And the bottom section represents the Proles, or us. Now, as you can see, because of numbers, the power lies with the Proles, but Big Brother's inner party, or the one percent, keeps them so dumb and happy and ignorant they don't realize the power they have. Just like we don't realize the power we have."

Marlon looked at Samantha. She still looked bored and lost.

"Sam, does this make sense?" Marlon asked.

"Not really," she said and popped her gum. She hoped her apathy would elicit the same reaction her earlier response had. It did not.

"How does the one percent keep us dumb and happy?" someone asked. Marlon turned in the direction of the voice. It was Abigail. She seemed genuinely interested. Marlon pounced on her interest.

"They give us a false consciousness," Marlon answered.

"What's that?" Abigail asked. The other students shifted in their seats and looked at Abigail, curious as to why she seemed sincerely fascinated in something as boring as a book. Some of the boys sat up, hoping to gain Abigail's favor by feigning interest.

"The false consciousness consists all the things we have in our life that keep us from thinking," Marlon explained. "It's all the bullshit we clutter our lives with to help convince ourselves that we are relevant and our lives are worth living."

Some of the students snickered upon hearing Marlon curse, but they quickly fell silent when they sensed he wasn't trying to be funny.

"If we weren't so pacified because of the one percent," Marlon continued, "then we could change the structure of the pyramid. We are the ones keeping the rich wealthy and the one percent in power, just like the Proles keep Big Brother in power. We're ignorant to our own strength."

"I still don't understand," Abigail said. "What things does the one percent give us that keep us from changing the structure of the pyramid?"

"Think of how the average person spends their time," Marlon explained. "Think of what you would be doing if you weren't in this class right now. You would be on Facebook or Instagram showing off your new tattoo. You would send your "friends" text messages with emoticons letting them know every detail of your day. Chuck would take a shit and then tweet about its size."

Marlon flashed Chuck a smile. The class burst into laughter, this time making no attempt to suppress the joy they felt from hearing their teacher swear. Even Samantha couldn't keep from laughing. After the joke's merriment subsided, Marlon continued.

"We go and see cheesy movies and listen to bad music and watch violent television shows," Marlon said. "This is how we get through the day. They keep us dumb and happy. They are produced and marketed to us by the one percent to ensure that we continue to be hypnotized enough into believing a new iPhone will finally make us complete. The one percent keeps us sedated so we don't ever question our shitty existence. We just accept that things are the way they are because that's just how it is. Orwell is trying to show us that we have the power to change our lives, but we're too indifferent to do anything about it. It would need to be a group effort, but too many of us are asleep."

"I'm not asleep," Samantha interjected. "I'm going to climb the pyramid. I'm going to be part of the one percent. I'm going to be rich."

"Of course you believe that," Marlon sneered. "You listen to enough Jay-Z to believe that money will make you happy, and you think you have the necessary skills to get to the top. But you're not innovative enough to climb the pyramid. Your greatest trait, like everyone in here—myself included—is your ability to be whatever society asks you to be."

"You don't know that," Samantha said after a beat. She felt that Marlon had just insulted her but she wasn't sure how. "I can get to the top."

"How?" Marlon asked.

"I'll work hard."

"What does that mean?"

"It means…you know, that…hard work will pay off."

"There's about ten million illegal immigrants in this country that would disagree with you. Hard work is a small part of getting to the top, but privilege will get you farther than your work ethic. And you are not privileged."

"How do you know?"

"Because you're in a public school. You have been your entire life. Your parents—"

"My parents are divorced," Samantha interjected. "I live with my mom."

"Okay. Your mom can't afford to give you an education with smaller classes and personal tutors. Instead, she, like most people in the grueling race to the middle, enrolled you in the public school system because it's cheap daycare. All that is expected of you is, at best, to become a tax paying citizen."

A few of the boys snickered. They didn't fully understand what Marlon was saying, but the way in which he said it, led them to believe laughter was the appropriate response. Samantha was offended. She had always believed school was supposed to be a safe space. If Marlon was going to teach her something that didn't reinforce her narrow beliefs, she deserved a trigger warning. What right did he have to expose her to the reality of the world? Even if he *was* right, it upset Samantha to hear it, and by god, her feelings mattered!

"Okay," Samantha said, "since you have all the answers, how does one get to the top of the pyramid?"

"You have to create something that the masses—the Proles—cannot live without. Some things, like cures for diseases, more efficient household products, and softer mattresses have a positive effect on society. While others, simply exist to trick us into believing we're more relevant than we actually are. Facebook, Instagram, selfie sticks, Pokémon, Youtube. Invent a product that allows the masses to publically share their regurgitated ideals and their manufactured happiness, while simultaneously sedating them, and that can help you get to the top, too."

Samantha scoffed. "I can do that."

"Oh, yeah? What are you going to create?" Marlon asked. "What super awesome idea is floating around in your head right now? What do you have to offer the world?"

"I don't know yet. But I'll come up with something."

"Are you an outlier?"

"What?"

"An outlier?"

"What's that?"

"The fact that you don't know tells me you aren't one."

"Huh?"

"What makes you unique?" Marlon asked. "What puts you above everyone else? This is the third summer I've had you in class. How do you expect to climb the pyramid when you can't even pass a high school English class?"

"This class isn't important. I don't need to know about some stupid book that was written, like, a hundred years ago to be rich."

Marlon looked at Samantha a long time, debating whether to continue with his point or just drop it before he said something that could possibly get him in trouble.

"You're right, Sam," Marlon said. "You don't need to understand what's in a book to be rich. Most people in the one percent are illiterate anyway." Marlon looked over his class, willing them to find the irony in his comment; none did.

"You'll see, Mr. Brown," Samantha said. "You'll see in five years when I'm rich and you're still just a high school English teacher."

Samantha's comment cut Marlon deeply but not for the reason that she intended. Her belittlement was aimed at his paltry salary, but that wasn't what stung. Her insight that he'd still be stuck teaching high school is where the insult struck him. Teaching used to be an honorable profession. Twenty years ago when Marlon told people he was studying to become a teacher, they would nod and tell him teaching was a noble and respectable profession. Today, the answer was met with pity and wonderment as to why he didn't choose something more rewarding—financially and intellectually. Marlon had worked long enough to experience the paradigm shift. He couldn't dispute the mockery that his profession had obtained when he considered how easy it was to graduate high school. It required minimal effort, and often, if the student had an overbearing parent, it didn't require any. Now, nearly twenty years into his career, Marlon found himself part of an institution that rewarded apathy and indifference, while intelligence and innovation became lost in the folds of mediocrity. Marlon's job wasn't to educate; it was to filter kids through the system so the higher-ups could boast about high graduation rates. Samantha's observation stung simply because it forced Marlon to recognize his own insignificance. He wasn't anything more than a glorified babysitter with an advanced degree.

Samantha's comment still hung in the air as Marlon returned from his reverie. The class stared at him, anticipating how he would respond. He again weighed the risk of saying what he wanted versus saying what his profession would allow. He bit his tongue and gave way to professionalism and said, "Only part of your comment will be true, Sam."

"Which part?" Samantha asked. Marlon looked at her smug face for a long time. Why was it that the average never saw themselves as such? Marlon thought. Something suddenly came alive inside of him. Samantha was baiting him and he was dangerously close to taking the bait.

"I'll still be a high school teacher, but you sure as hell won't be rich," he said evenly.

Samantha scoffed. "Yeah, I will. See, I don't even need to create something to get rich. I can just marry a rich guy. You don't have that chance. No woman wants to marry a high school English teacher."

Marlon chuckled. His restraints were quickly falling away. "The only guys that would marry you are the guys that are just like you. And trust me, they won't be rich."

"I could get any guy I want," Samantha argued.

Marlon laughed because he knew Samantha actually believed her absurd comment. Ignorance is always funnier when it's mixed with irony. "Okay, Samantha, enlighten me. When do you expect to get married?"

"I don't know. Twenty."

Samantha couldn't even recognize how much of a cliché she really was. She was two years away from the Utah norm that encouraged kids to get married so they could live under the illusion that they were adults.

"The divorce rate in this country is more than half," Marlon explained. "That number skyrockets if you get married before you're twenty-five. Now you're naïve enough to think that those statistics wouldn't apply to you, so let me make sure we are absolutely clear on one point: You are not exceptional. If anything, you are as generic as they come."

Samantha stared at Marlon for a long time. She appeared either upset or confused. She was a little of both; she felt Marlon had insulted her, but like earlier, she couldn't tell for sure how. Nonetheless, she stared at Marlon blankly for a full minute trying to decipher what his words meant. She couldn't make them make sense.

"What do you mean?" she finally asked.

"You are not exceptional," he said slowly, emphasizing each word. "Your marriage will fail. Just like every other undertaking you attempt."

"You don't know that."

"*That* is one of the few things I do know," Marlon said.

"Okay," Samantha said, refusing to let the conversation die. "Tell me what my life will be like then? You're so smart. Why don't you tell me what's in my future?"

Marlon stood silently for a long moment, evaluating his situation. He went through all the possible future scenarios he envisioned for Samantha but knew he couldn't vocalize his insight. He wished at that moment that they were outside the classroom. He would have given anything to be someplace where he wasn't restrained by his position. In the end, he simply gritted his teeth and said, "My position doesn't allow me to truthfully give my opinion on the matter."

Samantha smirked, feeling like she had just gained the upper hand in the argument. She was on a roll and wasn't going to stop now. The arrogance of youth was on her side. She spied her classmates sitting restlessly, wondering where the conversation would go next. She understood the dynamics of the situation. She was bound by nothing, whereas Mr. Brown was constrained by a history of litigious parents and easily offended teens. Samantha could say what she wanted without fear of reprisal. She had free reign to be as big a bitch as she wanted. It was the opportunity of a lifetime. She sat up straight and said, "That's because you're a fucking loser school teacher that drives a Hyundai."

The class held a collective breath. Samantha leaned back in her chair with an elevated sense of superiority. She smiled and then cut into the silence by theatrically chomping her gum. Abigail and the others sat on edge, waiting to see how Mr. Brown would react. Marlon stared at Samantha for a minute, trying to talk himself out of saying what he wanted so badly to say. He turned and started for his desk, but then abruptly stopped and turned back to Samantha.

Fuck it, he thought. *She started it.*

With deliberate, metered steps, he slowly approached Samantha. He arrived at her desk, placed his hands on either side of it, and leaned down until he was inches from her face. He could smell her perfume. It smelled like apricots, weed, and desperation.

"Sam, in ten years your best years will be behind you. Guys will no longer feel inclined to buy you drinks, and girls will pity you instead of envy you. You'll have saggy tits and a bank account that isn't ample enough to have them adjusted. Your weekends will be spent at clubs where you'll escape your shit existence at the bottom of watered down cosmopolitans. Guys will sleep with you because guys will sleep with anyone. You'll mistake the sex as love, but they'll accurately label it as what it is: a sloppy lay from a saggy dunce. You'll have three to five dipshit kids from three to five different dipshit dads who wanted to give you a money shot but couldn't pull out fast enough. You'll name your kids something unique like 'Unique' or 'Storm Cloud' or 'Starship' in the hope that their creative names will mask how fucking stupid they are. They'll be raised on corn dogs, Pop Tarts, and videogames. You'll be too busy on your knees behind dumpsters in poorly lit alleys to be a good parent. But fortunately for you, and unfortunately for the rest of us, you're dumb enough to think you can mask your parental shortcomings by tattooing your children's names in some generic calligraphy down your back. That, to you, is how you show love. You'll hit and curse your kids, but they'll never doubt you love them because you spent $200 getting their names permanently smeared onto your sweaty skin. Your kids will grow up to be just like you: retarded and horny. Which means you'll be a grandmother before you're forty. After that, you'll spend your latter years in a rascal navigating the aisles of Walmart looking for deals on Nutella and Mountain Dew until you ultimately die from a gun accident involving your grandson Gunner."

Marlon paused. No one spoke. No one even breathed. He kept his eyes leveled on Samantha and after a beat, leaned in closer and finished with: "You don't hate *1984* because it's a boring book. You hate it because you're too fucking stupid to recognize your role in it."

Marlon stood up straight but kept his eyes on Samantha daring her to say something else. She didn't. She stared back at him with wide eyes that spoke of disbelief and frightened entitlement. Marlon turned and started toward his desk, and then paused and added: "And I drive a Honda, not a Hyundai."

He let his words settle into the suffocating air and then continued to his desk. He took his time, basking in the elation that was his. This was a teaching highlight for him. Even the knowledge that Samantha would probably go to the principal wasn't enough to diminish the high he felt. He felt lighter, more at ease. Marlon had twenty years' worth of pent-up frustration, and it felt good to purge himself of it. If he got fired for it, if the principal wanted to speak to him about it, so be it. He already had his defense: "I'm a teacher. You hired me to teach. I taught."

Abigail watched Marlon walk back to his desk, fascinated by his audacity and drawn to his honesty. He sat in his chair, picked up his book from his desk, and began reading. Abigail's eyes darted to the cover of her own book, which she suddenly eyed with a newfound curiosity.

CHAPTER 26

Marlon didn't know it, but his scathing critique of Samantha inspired Abigail. Maybe it was because she had never heard a teacher be so honest toward a student before. Maybe it was because, like most people, she simply enjoyed it when people quarreled. There was something pleasing about observing an argument between two people. You can sit back and enjoy knowing that other people have problems too, and often theirs seemed to supersede your own. Or maybe Abigail realized that, if she was completely honest with herself, she recognized that everything Marlon said to Samantha could have just as easily been said to her.

Abigail wasn't bright, but she certainly wasn't stupid either. She understood that if it weren't for her body, she wouldn't be able to control men as easily as she did. A little skin, the right perfume, and a knowing smile could just about get her anything from the other sex. After all, if it weren't for her nosey principal, she would be in Tahoe right now with her friends, and all it would have cost her was a little finger assault from a sexually-repressed school teacher.

Everyone would have come out ahead. Instead, she was in Utah taking a summer school class from a begrudgingly honest teacher.

Truth be told, Marlon Brown fascinated Abigail. And it wasn't just because he was handsome when most teachers weren't. It was that his disposition was more at ease and confident than every school authority Abigail had ever known. She sensed there was more to his story. He had to be more than just a high school English teacher. How did he arrive at the place where he conveyed his indifference toward his students without fear of reprisal? Abigail wanted to strip him of his artifice and uncover who he was and what he was hiding. And she knew if she were to be successful, she would have to do so on his terms. She would have to enter into his realm and pretend she wasn't an intruder, that she belonged on the same plane. She couldn't employ her usual tactics to get close to Marlon. He would see right through them. She would need a new approach. She would have to read.

At home, Nichole was still trying to settle into their new house. In the aftermath of Abigail's indiscretion, Nichole wasted no time supplanting themselves from Vegas. She put her condo on the

316

market and by the end of the week, she had two offers. Each substantially less than what she was asking. She took the higher of the two and they next day flew to Utah to meet with a real estate agent her boss had recommended. They drove to a quaint, mountainous neighborhood and Nichole made an offer on the first house she looked at. She called Abigail with the news. Abigail cried, told her mom how unfair she was, and hung up without saying goodbye. Two weeks later they were pulling a U-Haul across the state line and into their new life. Nichole watched the Nevada horizon recede from her rearview. She tried to compartmentalize how she felt leaving her home, but ultimately she felt nothing. Nevada would become a footnote in her life; she would make Utah her story. She reached over and placed her hand on Abigail's leg and gave it an affectionate squeeze. Abigail turned away and began playing on her phone.

Nichole still hadn't made appointments to have the cable or Internet hooked up. She told Abigail that as soon as all the moving boxes were unpacked, she would call for service. She assumed the lack of technological stimulation would encourage Abigail to help her mother unpack, and just by way of proximity, it would bury the hatchet between them. But instead of bonding by unpacking, Abigail spent every minute in her room alone while her mother sorted through all the boxes by herself. So with no television or Internet to keep her occupied, Abigail read for the first time in her life. And what's more, she liked it, both because the novel was gripping, but even more so because it would work as the link she needed to approach Mr. Brown.

And so from the living room, Nichole worked on the boxes. Every so often her eyes shifted to Abigail's door in the hope that her daughter would emerge and ask if she could help. Abigail stayed concealed, though, only coming out to use the bathroom or scour the refrigerator for food. Nichole thought to let the food run out and use that a means of communication, but her motherly nature couldn't reconcile such a passive aggressive tactic. A mother's job is to feed and provide for her children. Nichole would continue to feed Abigail, she just wouldn't let the television or Internet raise her daughter any longer, unless of course, she was willing to forgive

Nichole. Only through forgiveness could Abigail obtain the euphoria of entertainment.

Nichole pulled the flaps apart from an unmarked box. Inside, buried beneath newspapers and bubble wrap, was various Christmas décor. Nichole retrieved an object from the box and began peeling away the dated newspaper sheets, eventually uncovering a Christmas ornament Abigail had made in elementary school. It was a Christmas tree made of solid plaster about the size of a cell phone. It was haphazardly painted green, the bulbs that littered it were painted red and yellow. The workmanship was shoddy and irresponsible, the ideal markings of a child. The thing was hideous, but it retained an ostentatious innocence because Nichole's child was the artist. It was a symbol of what Abigail used to be: carefree and filled with wonderment. Nichole turned the ornament over and found Abigail's name and grade level stenciled on the back. *Abigail. 2nd grade.* Abigail's teacher placed each student's ornament in a gift box and then gave the students to rest of the afternoon to wrap it. The sloppy wrapping job made the gift all the more adorable. Abigail presented her mother with it Christmas morning. It was the perfect gift.

Nichole studied the ornament for a moment and smiled, recalling the excitement Abigail displayed once Nichole unwrapped the box Christmas morning. Nichole gave the ornament to Abigail and asked her to hang it on the tree, which she did, front and center. The ornament represented a simpler time. A time when Nichole still had the capacity to fix things with unicorn Band-Aids and chocolate sundaes.

Nichole re-wrapped the ornament in the old newspapers and put it back in the box. Nostalgia washed over her. She turned and looked at Abigail's closed door and sighed. The stubbornness of adolescence. Nichole navigated the living room clutter and walked to Abigail's door and gently knocked.

"Abby? Sweetie, are you busy?"

Inside, Abigail lay on her bed reading her book. She heard her mom but didn't think enough of her inquiry to answer. Nichole knocked again, tried the door, and was surprised to find it unlocked. She pushed it open and peeked inside.

"Are you busy?" Nichole asked again.

"Yeah," Abigail mumbled and continued reading.

"What are you reading?"

"It's a book for school."

"How is school?"

"I don't know."

"What are you learning?"

"I don't know."

"You don't know?"

"Stuff."

"What kind of stuff?"

"Just…stuff."

"English stuff?"

"Yeah."

"What book is that?"

"It's called *1984.*"

"Is it any good?"

"It's all right."

"What's it about?"

"I don't know."

"You don't know or you don't want to tell me?"

Abigail stayed silent.

"How's your class going?" Nichole asked.

"It's fine."

"How's your teacher?"

Abigail paused, thought about Mr. Brown, and answered, "He's all right, I guess."

"What's his name?" Nichole continued with her interrogation.

"Mr...," Abigail trailed off, lost in a passage from the novel.

"Mr. what?"

"God, mom," Abigail said. "You would know all this shit if you came to registration with me."

Nichole laughed. "Does that make you feel old, Abby? To say 'shit'? Where did you pick that up? Talking back to your parent? Some MTV reality show chronicling the lives of entitled teenagers?"

Abigail shook her head.

"I couldn't go to your registration. I had to—"

"Work," Abigail interjected. "That's all you ever do."

"I'm just trying to get settled in, sweetie. This new job will take some getting used to, okay?"

Abigail stayed silent. "Okay?" Nichole asked again, raising her voice.

"Okay. God, I heard you. What do you want from me?"

"I want you to talk to me."

"I am talking to you."

"It's like pulling teeth getting you to say anything."

"What do you want me to say?"

"Tell me about school."

"Summer school is fantastic," Abigail said derisively. "My teacher is awesome. The other students in the class are wonderful. I love Utah."

"Have you made any new friends yet?"

"Nope."

"Have you tried?"

"Everyone here is lame."

"Kids are kids, Abby. They're just like the ones in Vegas. You all think you're unique, but you're all the same. Right now, in

323

every other state, there is a mother trying to connect with her child and she is being dismissive and thinking how hard her life is. You can stay mad and feel victimized, all while living in a house with heat, electricity, running water and a fridge full of food. And if you get tired of dealing with all those hardships, you can hop in your car and drive somewhere to get away from me for a few hours. But as long as you're here, I'm going to keep inconveniencing you by asking questions because I want to know what is going on in your life. And try as you might, I know somewhere inside that pissed-off head if yours, you still love me."

Silence. Abigail heard her mom, and felt the slightest pang of sadness from the reality check, but she was still an ungrateful teenager who had been programmed not to admit her faults even when they've been so clearly manifested. She pretended to read her book, but the words suddenly lost all focus.

"Are you hungry?" Nichole asked. "We could go grab something to eat. I noticed a Mexican place down the street."

"I'm not hungry."

"Want to help unpack some boxes? I could use an extra hand."

"I can't. I have too much homework."

Nichole sighed, at a loss with her daughter. "Okay. I'll take the hint."

Nichole turned away and began closing the door behind her. Abigail sat up, ready to tell her mom she was sorry and would love to go grab a bite to eat. But as her door sealed shut, Nichole's cell phone rang. Abigail sprang from her bed and stepped into the living room. Nichole had her phone pressed to her ear, telling the person on the other end pertinent information about second quarter numbers and other business jargon that meant nothing to Abigail. She watched her mom for a moment and then returned to her bedroom to read.

CHAPTER 27

Marlon gave exams on Fridays. He corrected them over the weekend and returned them the following Monday. For the first time in her life, Abigail knew she aced a test (without cheating). She had already finished *1984* by the time Marlon passed out the weekly exam. She filled in the answers quickly, relishing in the excitement of actually knowing the material. She finished first, stood, and took her test to Marlon. She handed it toward him with a knowing smile. Marlon sat reading a book. He absently grabbed the test and placed it on his desk without even extending the effort to see which student had handed it to him. Dejected, Abigail returned to her desk and sat down. She kept her eyes fixed on Marlon. He spent the period reading without ever looking up.

The weekend was torture. The anxiety and excitement overwhelmed Abigail. She needed the confirmation of what she already knew. She wanted to see the look of approval on Mr. Brown's face on Monday when he handed back her test. The impending exhilaration was almost enough incentive for her to try in all her classes. It was remarkable how far a little ambition could take a person.

To her chagrin, Marlon waited until the end of class to return the exams. By either coincidence or unabashed torment, he passed her test back last. He made his way to her, stopped, and stood over her desk. He slowly extended the test in her direction. She snatched the paper and flipped it over. Ninety-eight percent. Abigail looked at the score and then to Marlon. He stared back at her for a moment and then nodded in approval. She was speechless. She looked back at the score. Ninety-eight. She was so excited she wanted to scream.

"Nice job," Marlon whispered and even offered a wink. Abigail blushed at the compliment and swallowed hard. Marlon turned and went to the front of the room, checking his watch as he did so. It was still early, but he excused his class for the day anyway. The students quickly gathered their belongings and shuffled out of the class before Marlon could reconsider. Abigail stayed seated for a moment, looking at her test, and basking in her accomplishment. She wished things between her and her mom weren't as they were. It would be nice to go home, show her mom the test, and hear the praise that would follow. The recent dynamics of her and Nichole's relationship made her sad. Her sadness quickly dissipated, however, when she recalled why she was still angry with her mother.

Abigail carefully put her test into her backpack and stood. She glanced at Mr. Brown; he had his back to her erasing the whiteboard. She watched him guide the eraser over his written notes and wondered if he ever grew tired of writing the same information year after year on a giant white board for students not to understand. It almost made her sad to think of the effort that went into something that students never appreciated. She had an overwhelming urge to speak with him. His physical presence and intellectual gravitas frightened and fascinated her. Mr. Brown re-wrote the book on what it meant to be a teacher.

"What do you think of Utah?" Marlon asked, still erasing his notes. Abigail couldn't tell if his question was asked out of some unwritten teacher obligation, or if he genuinely wanted an answer to his question.

"It's okay," she answered. "Kind of boring."

"I'm sure most places are compared to Vegas."

"Have you ever been?"

"Yeah. A few times." Marlon turned and faced Abigail. "So did you actually read the book or just the Spark Notes?"

Marlon's question surprised Abigail. Being accused of cheating hurt, especially when, for one of the few times in her schooling, she actually did the work. She was about to defend her score when Marlon knowingly smiled at her.

"I finished it last night," Abigail said. "I stayed up till two in the morning reading it."

"You don't need to be done with it for a few more weeks, you know?"

"I know. I just didn't want to stop reading."

"So what did you think?"

"Honestly?"

"Yeah."

"I hated it. I hated that Big Brother won."

"Winston was weak," Marlon said. "Big Brother had to win."

"Why?"

"Because Big Brother always wins. If he didn't, it would just be…Hunger Games."

"I like Hunger Games."

"So do I, but that's not the point. Orwell let Big Brother win because if he didn't, it wouldn't have been accurate. In life, Big Brother wins."

"Yeah, I guess," Abigail said, "but it was just so bleak. I thought for sure Winston and Julia would find a way to defeat Big Brother. It made me sad when they confessed. It seemed so…," Abigail searched for the right word, and then settled on one already offered by Marlon, "…weak."

Marlon nodded. "Exactly."

Abigail studied Marlon for a moment, lost in her own thoughts. "Can I ask you something, Mr. Brown?"

"Sure."

"Do you think I'm weak?"

"In what way?"

"In the way you think Winston and Julia are weak."

"I don't know how to answer that. Winston and Julia were in a situation where the only option was failure. They were up against something bigger than themselves."

"Okay," Abigail said. "Well, then do you think I'm weak in the same way you think Samantha is weak."

Marlon thought about the question for a moment. "Why do you need affirmation that you're better than Samantha?"

"I don't."

"Your question indicates you do."

"I guess because...I see a lot of myself in her."

"And that troubles you?"

"Well, yeah."

"Why?"

"The way you described Samantha...I just see that so often. I don't want that."

Marlon nodded and then simply answered, "No."

"No? What do you mean 'no'?"

"I don't think you're as weak as Samantha."

"Why?"

"Samantha wouldn't have stayed up till two in the morning reading a book. You stayed up because you connected with it on some level. Weak people only make connections with other weak people. They latch on to each other because they keep them in their smallness."

Abigail wanted Mr. Brown to elaborate, to explain what he meant by smallness, but felt that if she asked him to explain further, he would view her ignorance as a sign that maybe she was like Samantha.

"Are *you* weak?" Abigail asked.

"On a lot of levels, yeah," Marlon answered.

"What levels?"

"I'm not going to answer that," Marlon said, smiling.

"Can I change my answer?" Abigail asked.

"What answer?"

"When you asked me to name three things I'm good at. I said fashion, wake boarding and dancing, and you said I was only good at two of those. I want to change my answer."

"Okay."

"I'm also good at seeing behind peoples' masks."

"What do you mean?"

"Like Julia in the book. I can read people."

"Julia was wrong about a lot."

"She was right about Winston," Abigail countered.

"Yeah, she was," Marlon admitted.

"I knew O'Brien was bad the moment Winston looked at him. I see who people are below the surface. I can look behind their masks."

Marlon chuckled because he knew what Abigail was after. She was baiting him, hoping he'd ask what she saw when she looked at him. It was now up to him whether he took the bait. It was what she wanted, but Marlon rarely felt inclined to give students what they wanted. If he caved to their wants, his classes would consist of movies, naps, and trips to the nearest convenient store. That's what the "cool" teachers allowed. Marlon wasn't a cool teacher. However, this was different. Abigail was trying to make a human connection, no matter how transparent she was in the effort. Marlon had to respect that.

"Okay," he said, smiling. "I'll bite. What's behind my mask?"

"You sure you want to hear it?"

"Sure."

Abigail took a step toward Marlon. "You're lonely," she said.

Marlon appraised the feedback, smiled and nodded. "Go on," he said.

"You can only connect with people in books. That's why you teach summer school. If you weren't here, you would be forced to spend the summer alone. You enjoy coming here and putting people like Samantha and me in our place. It makes you feel better about your lonely life."

Marlon's smile vanished. He stared back at Abigail blankly. She couldn't read his expression, and suddenly she wasn't sure what had inspired her to be so honest. The words just came to her, and she didn't realize what she had said until they had already spilled from her mouth. She shuffled her feet nervously and waited for Marlon to give her a reaction, but he just stood listlessly, staring back at her. Abigail grew uncomfortable.

"Sorry...I...I didn't mean to...I should go," Abigail stammered. She turned and awkwardly started away. She stopped at the door and looked at Mr. Brown briefly, hoping he would break his silence, but it was clear he had no intention of doing so. Abigail stepped into the hall and then ran for the nearest exit. Marlon went to his desk and sat down. In front of him sat his copy of *1984*. He picked it up and turned it over in his hands, ruminating on what Abigail's words.

CHAPTER 28

The next four weeks of summer school were anticlimactic. Marlon gave typical, district-approved assignments that contained little higher-level thinking. The students—for the most part—completed them, half-heartedly perusing their books for worksheet answers and keeping their markings clear and inside the lines of the state-sanctioned bubble sheet tests. Everyone stayed on track to graduate while earning their English make-up credit, and Marlon got his stipend for the extra summer work. It was lifeless and monotonous. He gave information, and the students retained it long enough to regurgitate it onto a test so the school could document that learning occurred. Minimal effort for maximum reward. It was textbook public education.

Abigail passed the class with an A, her first ever. She never scored lower than ninety on any of the tests. For the summer essay she wrote about the benefits of pop culture and received eighty-seven percent. It was an average paper, and any other student would have earned an average grade, but Abigail needed at least eighty-seven percent for an A, so that's what Marlon gave her.

Abigail paid close attention to Marlon those last four weeks. He was distant, preoccupied, and lifeless. He no longer tried to facilitate class discussions. He no longer asked open-ended questions in an attempt to get the students thinking. He resigned all attempts to engage the students in upper-level discourse. He simply gave an assignment, asked if there were any questions (usually there wasn't), and then returned to his desk where he read for the remainder of the class. He was everything the school board wanted him to be: boring, robotic, and teach perfectly according to state standards. He didn't ruffle any feathers, and he didn't spark any level of thinking. He just circled the drain and collected his paycheck. Everyone came out ahead, except the students. Of course, they wouldn't have wanted it any other way. Let them memorize answers and they're fine. Ask them to think, and it's pulling teeth.

The most Marlon talked during the remaining four weeks was on the last day. He returned the student essays with their final grade printed on the front. He handed Abigail's essay back last, gave her a furtive glance, and walked to the front of the classroom.

"Congratulations on staying on track to graduate," Marlon said. "You now have a week until you have to be back here for your senior year. Stick it out. You're almost finished with high school." Marlon paused. He felt he needed a stronger closing line, so he added: "Don't trip at the finish line." He had heard so many other teachers recite the same adage a million times. Each time it made his skin crawl. Was he becoming such a textbook teacher that even state-approved platitudes were seeping into his lexicon? He silently cursed himself for offering something so banal. "Enjoy the rest of your summer. You're free to go." The students sprang from their seats and rushed for the exit, thinking that if they left fast enough, they could still reclaim a sliver of the summer Mr. Brown's class robbed from them.

Abigail remained seated and waited for the other students to exit the room. She stared at Marlon for a long time, silently willing him to look in her direction. He wouldn't. He was busy mulling over and organizing a stack of papers cluttering his desk. Abigail felt some unknown inclination that she needed to apologize for her comments a month earlier. She detected she had hurt him, and she couldn't explain why, but it bothered her that she may be the reason for some of his suffering. Prior to their conversation a month ago, he seemed so sure of himself. He exuded confidence, not in a condescending way, just a demeanor that he didn't need assurance from anyone other than himself. It didn't make sense that she could wound him like she did.

Once the class was empty, she gathered her things and approached Marlon. She arrived at his desk, stood, and cleared her throat. He didn't look up.

"So I got my school schedule yesterday," Abigail said. "It looks like I have you for senior English."

"Yeah," Marlon said, still pretending to shuffle through a stack of papers. "They give me all my summer students. It's a district policy. I'm supposed to keep tabs on you to make sure you stay on track to graduate."

"I've never really liked English, but I did like your class."

"Good. I'm glad to hear it." Marlon glanced at Abigail for a moment and then quickly looked away.

Abigail could sense she wasn't wanted. She turned and started for the door, but then quickly turned back and returned to Marlon's desk. She wanted closure, and she wasn't going to leave until she got it.

"Can I ask you something?" she asked.

Marlon looked up at her, perturbed to see her standing at his desk again. He shuffled a few more papers, and when he knew he could no longer keep up the charade, he leaned back in his chair and answered, "Sure."

"Did I...offend or upset you with what I said a few weeks ago?"

Marlon looked at Abigail for a long time and then answered, "No."

"Your teaching style changed ever since our talk," Abigail said. "Did I have anything to do with that?"

Again Marlon offered his patented blank stare. "Nope."

"You're a great communicator, you know that?" Abigail said. "Your wife is a real lucky woman." Abigail turned and headed for the door.

"I don't have a wife," he called after her.

Abigail stopped. "What?"

"I don't have a wife."

Abigail stood at the door and looked at Marlon. She couldn't tell if his response was an attempt to illustrate how she had inaccurately judged him again, or if he was confiding in her something that most students didn't know. His expression offered nothing by way of an explanation. He remained, as always, stoic and indifferent. He kept his eyes leveled on Abigail for a moment before abruptly turning away.

Abigail returned to his desk. "Is that true?" she asked. "You really don't have a wife?"

"Yes, that's true."

"I thought everyone in Utah was married. Isn't it a law or something?"

"For some, sure," Marlon quipped. "I wasn't offended by what you said to me. I don't get offended. That's for religious zealots and Millennials. I was just…surprised."

"Surprised by what?"

"That you were able to peg me so accurately. Most students aren't introspective enough to see anything outside of themselves."

"I don't even know why I said what I said. I was out of line. I'm sorry."

"Don't be," Marlon said. "It's just hard sometimes to have a mirror held up to you."

"What do you mean?"

"You showed me the error of my ways."

"I didn't mean to."

Marlon offered a weak smile. "I wasn't always lonely, but you're right, I do have an easier time making connections with fictional people."

"Why?"

"They always say the right things. They have the principles and attributes I want in myself and other people, so it's comforting to get lost in them. I've only met one other person like that and…well, she left."

"Was that your wife?"

Marlon nodded.

"Did she die?" Abigail asked.

"No."

"Where did she go?"

"It doesn't matter. She isn't coming back."

"How long ago did she leave?"

"Thirteen years."

"You've been alone since then?"

Marlon nodded again. He wasn't sure why he was opening himself to Abigail. It wasn't like him to disclose personal elements to his students. He liked to maintain an air of mystery. He figured the less his co-workers and students knew about him, the better. Inexplicably though, he felt comforted taking to Abigail. He trusted her, but he couldn't explain why.

"Do you have kids?" Abigail asked.

It was a simple question, and Marlon tried to answer, but every time he opened his mouth to utter the word 'no,' he couldn't bring himself to do it. *No* didn't suffice. What would? *Kinda? Sorta? Use to?* If he couldn't will himself to give a simple, one-word answer, how could he ever possibly explain that he did have a son, but he died from a rare birth defect? He was a one in one-hundred-thousand child. An anomaly sent to people to test their faith. Faith in what? He didn't know.

People knew of Marlon's child. The gossip made the rounds years ago, but no one ever broached the subject directly to him. Not until Abigail. She didn't know the horrific details, so she didn't know it was a question best left unasked. Marlon couldn't settle how best to answer it. A routine, recited response wasn't preordained and calibrated for moments like this. A simple explanation eluded him, and the effort required to retell the stories surroundings his failed attempts at fatherhood were too exhausting. So instead of saying anything, he simply shook his head.

Abigail sensed there was more to Marlon's answer, but she could also sense that his withholding was for good reason. She was in uncharted territory with Marlon. She wanted to reciprocate the gesture, to reveal to him something that proved she was fractured and hurting too. She inched closer to him. Their knees were almost touching. Marlon's thoughts consumed him so indelibly that he didn't notice how close his student suddenly was to him.

"I've never met my father," Abigail said. "I don't even know who he is. Sometimes I make up conversations we'd have if I ever met him. He always seems to say the right thing, too. At least in my head, he does." Abigail paused for a moment and then added: "If I ever met him, I don't know if I would be mad at him or happy to see him or…what…"

"What happened? Why don't you know who he is?" Marlon asked.

"It was a one-night stand. My mom got pregnant and she never saw him again."

"Does he have a name? You could try and find him."

"My mom says she never found out his name. They met at a party, flirted a little, drank a lot and…now here I am."

"Sounds like a hell of a guy."

"My mom finally told me about him when I was ten. She couldn't keep dodging my father questions. When she first told me it was a one-night stand, I was mad at him—my dad. I hated him. I thought that he had abandoned me, but as I got older, I realized it was silly to hate him. He doesn't know about me. And besides, he only did what any guy would do."

"What do you mean?" Marlon asked.

"I mean...I get it," Abigail said. "A beautiful woman comes on to him. It's Vegas. He's probably there on vacation and knows he'll never see her again. What guy wouldn't take advantage of that situation? He doesn't know that he got my mom pregnant. She was just a vacation lay. Just a good time, you know. Who can blame him?"

"You can, Abigail," Marlon said.

"Yeah, maybe, I guess. Maybe I just tell myself he's not a prick so I feel better about myself. I don't know anything about him. Maybe he's a really great guy who just had a moment of weakness. Or maybe he's an asshole and I'm better off not knowing him."

"Those are both very real possibilities."

Abigail looked away, lost in her mind and the battles waged there for so many years. When she spoke again, her voice gave way to her emotions. "I just wish I could know if I'm the way that I am because of who he is."

"Do you like who you are?" Marlon asked.

"I...don't...know," Abigail said. "I just...if my dad is some horny prick going around having one-night stands, what does that make me? I mean, I'm part of him, you know?"

"It makes you whatever you want to be. You're not defined by a man you've never known."

"I know one thing about him. He takes advantage of women when he can. Sounds like maybe the apple didn't fall far from the tree, huh."

"I'm not sure what you mean by that," Marlon said.

Abigail laughed. "Sure you do. You judged me correctly the first day I walked in here."

"I didn't judge you."

"You told me I looked like a slut."

"No," Marlon said, "I said you needed to abide by the dress code."

"That's a nice way of saying I look like a slut."

"What label would you give your wardrobe?"

"I know what I'm doing when I get dressed."

"I don't doubt that."

"People only like me because I'm pretty," Abigail said, lowering her voice. "If I was ugly or ordinary, I wouldn't have anything. I wouldn't be anyone."

"You think you're someone now?" Marlon asked. "Just because you're attractive?"

"People like you if you're hot. They'll do things for you they wouldn't normally do. They like you more if you put out."

Marlon scoffed. "They only like you for that moment. Once it's over, you're just a story to tell. A punch line."

Abigail's eyes watered. "I know. But that is the only thing I've ever been good at." Abigail dropped her chin to her chest and softly cried. She took a clumsy step forward and instinctively, Marlon stood and caught her. Abigail wrapped her arms around him and cried heavy sobs into his chest. It had all happened so quickly that it wasn't until he was holding her that Marlon realized he was *holding* her. It was all innocent enough. He was simply comforting a student in need, but did *she* understand that? His annual ethics review suddenly took on much more significance. *Teachers should never have any physical interaction with a student. Ever.* He was breaking the cardinal rule. He felt Abigail's fingers dig into his back, gripping him tighter in case he thought of letting her go. She liked feeling her body pressed against his. His touch felt good. A warm welcome when everyone else only offered cold goodbyes. Abigail was lonely, a stranger in a strange land with any sense of semblance lost in a Vegas fog.

The real surprise was Marlon *liked* holding Abigail. It didn't feel sexual; it felt...paternal. He knew on the surface that holding her was inappropriate, but below the surface, it meant something beyond the superficial. He was doing the right thing, the human thing. Offering comfort to the afflicted. He gave a shoulder when others turned their backs. Marlon knew it best never to venture into these waters, but he didn't resist Abigail because her tears indicated she needed this more than Marlon's requirement to stop it.

And then, with no forewarning, her lips were on his. Marlon pulled back and pushed Abigail away. She tripped and fell to the ground. Her beady, red eyes stared up at Marlon dejectedly.

"What are you doing?" Marlon asked.

"I...I...," Abigail stammered. Wounded and afraid, she tried to get to her feet but couldn't find her footing. "I thought that you wanted to," she whispered.

"Wanted to what?" Marlon asked. He looked hard at Abigail.

Abigail whimpered and cowered under his stare. Marlon sighed and whispered, "Oh, god." He turned away from her, counted to ten, and when he turned back, she was gone. Marlon went to his door and looked into the hall. Abigail ran down the hall, crying harder than she had moments earlier when she was in his arms.

"Shit," Marlon said.

CHAPTER 29

The next day Marlon did the prudent thing and told the principal

everything. Explain it all and let the pieces fall where they may, he

told himself. He had a good reputation, and the more he thought

about it, the more he convinced himself no one was to blame for

what happened. He comforted a student, she misinterpreted his

agenda, made a pass at him, and he stopped things before they could

progress any further. He presumed as long as he went to the

principal first and offered full disclosure, they could bury the

incident without taking any further action. It looked better than if he

kept it secret and it leaked to the wrong people. The details would

spiral out of control if left to the public to pass judgment. *Did you*

hear Mr. Brown kissed that new student? I heard they made out. I

heard they had sex. I heard... Marlon didn't think Abigail would

tell anyone, but he couldn't take that risk. She was a seventeen-year-

old girl; if there was one person a secret wasn't safe with, it was a

seventeen-year-old girl.

So a week before the new school year, Marlon recounted the episode to the principal. He explained himself and then defended his actions. Once finished, the principal sat silently for a moment before nodding and telling him what he wanted to hear: "You did the right thing by bringing the matter immediately to me."

"I don't know who this girl will tell. I didn't want you to get a distorted version of the truth," Marlon said.

"This actually isn't the first encounter this particular student has had with a teacher," the principal said.

"What?"

"She got in some trouble with a teacher at her old high school."

"You're kidding."

"I wish I was. The principal walked in on her with a teacher's hand up her skirt."

"What happened?"

"The teacher lost his job and Abigail's mom uprooted her here."

"Wow," Marlon whispered. "So what do we do now?"

"We need to tell Abigail's mom."

"I was afraid you were going to say that."

"Imagine how it would look if what happened got back to her and she found out I knew about it," the principal explained. "You covered your ass by coming to me first, now I need to cover mine by going to her before she gets some altered version of the truth."

"I'm sorry, Dr. Evans," Marlon said.

"It's all right. We just need to stop this before it becomes more than what it was. My biggest concern is the district's new summer school policy."

"What do you mean?"

"The district wants all summer school students to keep their summer school instructors through the school year."

"Yeah."

The principal leveled her eyes on Marlon. "Should I be concerned if Abigail remains in your class?"

"Of course not," Marlon answered, bothered that he even had to defend himself.

"It's not you I'm worried about, Marlon," the principal said. "She's an impressionable, smitten seventeen-year-old girl. You know how the mind of a teenager works. I need to know that I have nothing to worry about if she remains in your class."

"Dr. Evans, trust me. I won't have any problems with Abigail remaining in my class. I can guarantee that on my end."

"Well," Dr. Evans sat back in her chair, "I would very much like to sweep this under the rug as soon as possible. I don't want to get the district involved. Let's get the mom in here and see if she expects us to make any modifications to her daughter's schedule. Hopefully, she'll want to resolve this as quickly as we do."

Nichole met with the principal and Marlon the following day. When she asked Dr. Evans why they needed to meet, she answered that it would be best to discuss it in person. "Did something happen with Abigail?" Nichole asked over the phone. "We can discuss everything tomorrow," the principal answered. "What did she do?" Nichole wanted to know. "We'll discuss it tomorrow," the principal answered. Nichole hung up the phone and went to Abigail's room.

"I just got a call from Dr. Evans," Nichole said.

"Who's Dr. Evans?"

"Your principal."

"Oh."

"She needs to meet with me tomorrow. Do you have any idea why?"

Abigail looked at her mom and then picked up her phone and started texting. Nichole snatched the phone from her daughter.

"Did something happen?" Nichole asked.

"No," Abigail whispered.

"Why would she need to meet with me?"

"I don't know. Can I have my phone back?"

"You can have it back after my meeting," Nichole said, slamming the door behind her.

*****

Nichole arrived to the meeting before Marlon. The principal admitted her, offered her a chair on the opposite side of her desk and then engaged her superficial small talk until Marlon arrived. Nichole nervously indulged Dr. Evans, and suddenly found herself explaining Las Vegas weather patterns when someone knocked on the door.

"Just a moment," the principal yelled toward the door. She looked back at Nichole. "You were saying?"

"Ah…what was I saying?" Nichole asked.

"Something about hundred degree days in July."

Nichole waved off the principal. "It's not important."

Dr. Evans offered a sympathetic smile and crossed to her office door. She opened it and Marlon stood outside.

"Hello, Mr. Brown," the principal said. "Please, come in."

Marlon entered and closed the door behind him. Dr. Evans was already back in her chair by the time Marlon turned and faced Nichole. "I'm Mr. Brown," Marlon said, extending his hand. "I was Abigail's summer school teacher."

Marlon didn't recognize her. She was as foreign to him as any random stranger on the street. Just another parent whose presence only mattered because she happened to be the mother of a student. However, to Nichole, there was something oddly familiar about Mr. Brown. When their eyes locked, there was a brief moment of recognition, but he looked away too quickly for her to catalog it. She needed more time unraveling her mental resources to determine where she had seen him before.

"Nice to meet you," Nichole said, shaking his hand. Marlon released her hand and took the empty chair next to Nichole.

"I thought it would be best if Mr. Brown were here," the principal explained.

"What is this about?" Nichole asked.

The principal and Marlon exchanged a glance, trying to decide who should begin. The principal, exercising her authority, nodded to Marlon.

He turned to Nichole. "There was a...incident with your daughter a couple days ago in my class," Marlon said. Nichole shifted in her chair and faced Marlon.

"An incident?"

"Yes," he said, clearing his throat. "On the last day of class, she stayed after everyone else had left. We were discussing the course and then she...she...advanced and then...kissed me."

Nichole heard the words, and she felt the gravity of what Marlon had said, but they were somehow lost on her. She knew she had seen this strange man before. She needed to remember where. Everything suddenly became lost in the haze of trying to remember when she had previously met Marlon.

"Nothing happened," Marlon continued. "It didn't escalate any further. I know how impressionable teenagers can be so I brought the matter immediately to Dr. Evans. I figured it would be best to put everything on the table so there wouldn't be any surprises later."

Nichole continued staring at Marlon. Through her fog, she noted that he was no longer speaking. If he wasn't talking, he must be waiting for her response. She turned away for a moment and processed his words.

"My daughter came on to you," Nichole said, but neither Marlon nor the principal could decipher if this was a question or a statement.

"In a manner of speaking, yes," Marlon said.

"How did it happen?"

"I just told you."

"Tell me again," Nichole said, forcing herself to pay better attention to the retelling.

"Like I said, class had just ended and Abigail told me how much she enjoyed the class, and then after talking for a couple minutes…she just…kissed me. I immediately pulled away and she ran out of the room."

"Just like that?" Nichole asked. "Just innocent talking and then she kissed you?"

Marlon swallowed and cleared his throat. He looked at the principal for support and received none.

"She…," Marlon began, choosing his words carefully, "…prior to the incident she was telling me, confiding in me, things about her personal life, about her…past."

"What kind of things?" Nichole asked.

Marlon shifted in his seat. "Maybe you should talk to Abigail about it," Marlon said.

"Maybe you should just tell me," Nichole countered. There was an edge to her voice. "You can't call me in here, tell me you kissed my daughter and then expect me not to get the details."

"She told me she's never met her father," Marlon said. "She said doesn't know who he is."

Nichole sighed and closed her eyes. "She told you that?"

"Yes."

"Anything else?"

"No. She seemed pretty distraught about it and then started crying. I tried to console her and I think she misinterpreted my intentions. That's when she...kissed me."

No one spoke for a moment. Nichole processed the story while Marlon and the principal waited for the aftermath.

"Mr. Brown has been here for nearly twenty years," Dr. Evans said. "He's one of my finest teachers. I think it speaks to his character that he brought the matter to me immediately. He's a good man, and I have no doubt that the events played out the way he described. A student came on to him, and he stopped it before anything else could happen." She paused briefly and looked at

Marlon. He nodded to the principal, grateful for her support.

"Now," she continued, "I would like to put this matter to rest. I think it should be noted that I have spoken with Abigail's old principal and he informed me that she was involved in a similar scandal a few months ago."

"Scandal?" Nichole repeated the word incredulously. "It wasn't a scandal."

"Oh, would you care to share what happened?" the principal asked with an air of condescension.

Nichole narrowed her eyes at the principal. "Is that really necessary?"

"It could be if—"

"My daughter is a good student."

"Her transcripts don't share your sentiment," the principal said.

"What does that mean?"

"She did have the highest percent in my class," Marlon said, coming to Nichole's defense for reasons unknown. The principal shot him a look. Marlon turned away, momentarily forgetting that the principal was on his side.

"Look, I want this issue resolved quickly and amicably," the principal said, feeling the meeting slipping away from her. "The school year starts next week. Can we just agree that something happened that shouldn't have and it won't happen again? Let's just move on from this little…indiscretion. I don't think Abigail needs to be suspended, and I don't think any further action needs to be taken against Mr. Brown. His reputation alone tells me this doesn't need to be made into something bigger than it already is."

Nichole looked at the principal and then to Marlon. She felt ambushed but couldn't explain why. She wanted the same thing they did, so why did she feel threatened? After a moment, she nodded and said, "I can move on from this."

"I would like that," Marlon said eagerly.

"Good," the principal said.

"I do have one other concern, though," Nichole said. "I noticed on Abigail's schedule that she has Mr. Brown this year for English."

"Yes...," the principal said, clenching her jaw.

"Well, what if...what if something happens again."

"It won't," Marlon said.

"I'm not implying that you would ever try and do...what I mean is...," Nichole trailed off, unable to approach what she wanted to say. "Okay, yes, in the interest of full disclosure Abigail did come on to a teacher at her old school. My concern now is what if she comes on to you again?"

Marlon leveled his eyes on Nichole. "I'm a professional," he said. "I will act as one."

"If you were such a professional, how did this happen in the first place?" Nichole said.

"I—" Marlon began, but the principal cut him off.

"We did look into placing Abigail into another English class," the principal explained, trying to diffuse the issue. "Unfortunately, as a result of district policy, summer students are paired with their summer instructors. This helps the instructor keep the student on track to graduate. I would very much enjoy *not* going to the district and explaining why Abigail should be placed in another English class. I think you can understand why that wouldn't be a good idea."

Nichole nodded. "I understand."

"Trust me," Marlon said. "You will not have to worry about anything else happening between your daughter and me."

"Look, I'm sure you're good at your job," Nichole said. "Hell, you actually got Abby reading for the first time in her life. I didn't mean to imply…I just…sometimes I think she does these things just to spite me. She's angry with me for uprooting her the summer before her senior year. Now we can't even have a conversation without her telling me how much she hates me."

Marlon and the principal both nodded but didn't feel they needed to add anything to Nichole's revelation. Nichole and Abigail's personal matters were out of their jurisdiction. Parents often felt inclined to disclose family matters to teachers and administrators. Marlon learned that most people just want someone to listen and offer an emphatic ear. Nearly twenty years of teaching taught him the best approach was to stay silent and nod appropriately.

"Sorry," Nichole said, sensing the uneasiness in the room. "I wasn't trying to make my problems your problems. Thank you for letting me know what happened. I'll talk to Abigail. She won't be a problem again."

"Great," the principal said, getting to her feet and ushering Marlon and Nichole out of her office. "It should be a good school year."

Nichole followed Marlon out of the principal's office and into the hall. She kept stealing glances at him trying to place him, but by some cruel trick, the more she dwelt on it, the more foreign he seemed to her. He was like some suppressed memory trying to fight its way back into her consciousness while she unknowingly built barriers to keep him at bay.

"Look, I'm sorry about all of this," Nichole said. They arrived at the school's main entrance. "Abigail doesn't respect authority. She doesn't respect much of anything, actually."

"I'm just relieved we can put this behind us," Marlon said. "This is a teacher's worst nightmare."

"It pains me to admit that I'm not surprised this happened. Not because of you. Because of her. She's so…defiant.

"Most teenagers are."

"Do you have kids?"

Marlon paused. "No," he said, and then quickly changed the subject. "Abigail really is a bright girl. She's probably the best summer school student I've ever had. She sees things in books and people that most don't. She's quite…perceptive."

"Thank you for saying that. I was shocked when I saw she got an A in your class. I would have been happy with just a passing grade. She has struggled lately with school. That was one of the reasons I moved her out here. A fresh start, you know?"

"Sure."

Nichole still appraised Marlon and still came up empty. "Do we know each other?" she finally asked.

"I don't think so."

"You look vaguely familiar to me."

Before Marlon could respond, a fellow teacher, Mr. Gibson, approached from behind. Nichole's back was to him, but Marlon spied him advancing. He stopped a few feet behind Nichole and looked her up and down. He nodded approvingly and winked at Marlon. He lifted his hands and pretended to cup Nichole's ass. He smiled at his own behavior. Marlon looked away. He hated Mr. Gibson.

Every high school has a token pervert teacher. Zion High's was Mr. Gibson. He was thirty-seven going on sixteen. He became a teacher because he wanted to return to the time in his life when he felt most relevant.

It wasn't a secret that, in many student circles, Marlon and Mr. Gibson were viewed as the "hot" teachers at the school. Mr. Gibson relished the adoration he elicited from the student body. Marlon felt being attractive in the eyes of teenagers held about as much honor as being elected mayor of a town teeming with pedophiles. Once, when a student told him of the numerous girls that had a crush on him, Marlon shrugged and said, "Sounds like I'm the cream of the crap." When Mr. Gibson received similar praise, he wanted to know specifically which students thought he was attractive. Later, the named students received friend requests from

Mr. Gibson on Facebook. All the students accepted, allowing them access to a variety of shirtless selfies and other photos that presented Mr. Gibson in the all-too-generic Facebook light. No one could believe a teacher could live as he did. Summiting Kilimanjaro, running the Great Wall of China marathon, and surfing in Australia. Mr. Gibson broke every teacher mold—except he didn't. The exotic vacation photos, conveniently taken at a distance, weren't of him, but of his older brother. A brother too busy living for himself that he didn't bother manufacturing every event on social media, and thus didn't know that his brother was plagiarizing his life.

Because Mr. Gibson felt he was on par with Marlon, he tried hard to befriend him. The dance club and drunken party invitations he offered Marlon had certainly diminished over the years, but it wasn't uncommon for Mr. Gibson to still knock on Marlon's door at the end of a workday and ask if he had any plans. Marlon always did, and they never involved Mr. Gibson. At first, Marlon would invent a lie (family's in town, nephew's birthday, grandma's funeral), but now he simply said no without any attempt to placate his rejection. He couldn't be friends with a guy like Mr.

Gibson. How could he like someone who sneaks up on unsuspecting parents and evaluates their ass while Marlon tries to have a conversation?

Mr. Gibson lowered his hands once he realized Marlon did not intend to acknowledge his gesture. He looked Nichole over once more and then walked past Marlon and Nichole.

"How was your summer, Marlon?" he asked as he passed.

"Fine," Marlon answered, brusquely. Mr. Gibson slowed his walk and waited for Marlon to ask him how his summer was, but Marlon remained silent. He didn't want to hear about whatever exotic location he pretended to have visited. Mr. Gibson crept by and entered the office, somewhat put out by Marlon's indifference. Marlon watched Mr. Gibson enter the office and then shook his head once he was out of sight. He looked back at Nichole, who was staring back at him with large, bewildered eyes.

"Your name is Marlon?" she asked incredulously.

"Yeah," Marlon answered. "Not like the fish, though."

"Like the actor."

"Yeah."

"Marlon Brown," Nichole said, mouthing the words, remembering the name she tried for eighteen years to forget. Understanding dawned on her. She was looking at the father of her child. Her daughter's teacher. The one Abigail kissed. God.

"Yeah, it sounds awfully close to Marlon Brando, doesn't it?" Marlon said. "That's not by mistake. My mom was a huge Brando fan."

"Oh my god," Nichole said, flushed.

"Are you okay?"

"It's you," Nichole whispered so softly that Marlon didn't hear her.

"Excuse me?"

Nichole backed away slowly, fearful that if she made any sudden movements Marlon would somehow understand her sudden trepidation. Marlon watched her suspiciously. He asked if something was wrong and took a step toward Nichole. She turned and ran out of the building.

The parking lot blistered. Lost in her own thoughts, Nichole weaved in and out of the cars trying to find her own. She stumbled upon it by chance. She riffled through her purse in a mad hunt for her keys, but couldn't focus enough on the task to successfully retrieve them. The more she tried to compose herself, the more she failed. Her breathing increased, as did her frustration. Her heart raced. She tried to calm herself. She took deep breaths and closed her eyes, but she couldn't escape her panic. She threw her purse to the ground; its contents scattered on the dark asphalt. She screamed and quickly put her hand over her mouth to muffle her cries. She kicked her car, swore at the ensuing pain and swore more at the world and everything in it. She ran a frustrated hand through her hair and surveyed her scattered belongings. She stooped down and began gathering her valuables. Her hands shook as she absentmindedly grabbed her things. She was on the verge of a larger breakdown, and she could feel it coming like a wave whose only purpose is to capsize anything in its path. Finally, surrendering to the circumstances, she fell to the ground and burst into sorrowful, angry sobs. She didn't fight the catharsis. She expelled eighteen years' worth of anger and confusion and resentment. She yelled and screamed and cursed and wondered why the world was punishing her.

*****

The living room was dark. Pitch black, save for the street light that shone weakly through the front window. Nichole stared hypnotically at the front door waiting for her daughter. She intermittently took sips from the glass of red wine balancing in her hand. The bottle on the table next to the sofa was empty.

Abigail was at the school's annual bonfire to celebrate the upcoming school year. She wasn't thrilled to go but knew any chance to get out of her house was worth taking. She anticipated Nichole telling her no when she asked permission and was surprised when she said it was okay. "Really?" Abigail asked.

"Yeah," Nichole said. "It'll be good for you to meet new friends. Besides, after how well you did in summer school, I think you've earned it."

Of course, Nichole granted her daughter permission *before* she knew Abigail made a pass at her teacher. Had she known earlier that her daughter had come on to her father, she certainly would have made her stay home.

Nichole took another drink. The wine wasn't working. Somehow, the alcohol was amplifying the image of Abigail kissing Mr. Brown. Instead of becoming lost in an inebriated haze, the incident became *more* lucid, as if Nichole had witnessed the encounter firsthand. Nichole mentally surveyed the contents of her cupboards and medicine cabinets, searching for something stronger than wine. She had nothing but aspirin and cough drops.

Abigail came home just after midnight. She smelled like campfire, perfume, and marijuana. She turned on the light and found her mother sitting on the sofa.

"Holy shit, mom," Abigail said, startled. "You scared me."

Nichole kept her eyes fixed on the far wall, staring at nothing in particular. She was aware of her daughter's presence, but the wine had robbed her of the energy required to have the conversation she had been waiting up all night to have.

"Were you waiting up for me?" Abigail asked. Nichole had never waited up for Abigail before.

Nichole turned and looked at her daughter. She wore a miniskirt and a white halter-top with no bra. Nichole could see the dark circles of her daughter's nipples through the shirt. She looked like a whore who confuses being a whore with fashion. Nichole studied her daughter with awed curiosity and tried to determine when exactly it was that she had succumbed to complete depravity.

"I need to know that nothing else is going to happen between you and Mr. Brown," Nichole said evenly.

"What are you talking about?"

"I know you kissed him, Abigail."

"No, I didn't."

Nichole sighed. "Enough with the lies. I met with the principal and Mr. Brown today."

"He came on to me."

"So you did kiss him?"

"No...I...he..."

"I don't care how it happened. I just need to know that nothing will happen again."

"Tell *him* that. He's the pervert."

"Goddamn it, Abby!" Nichole cried. "Enough!"

"What?"

"If he came on to you, why did he stop it? Why would he go to the principal and tell on himself?"

"That's...I don't know," Abigail said. "Maybe to save his ass."

"Come on, Abby," Nichole said shaking her head.

"Why do you hate me so much?" Abigail asked. She was close to tears.

"I don't hate you. I want to protect you. I want to help you."

"By thinking I'm some slut who comes on to her teachers?"

"This is the second time, Abby."

"It wasn't my fault!"

Nichole laughed. "Then who's to blame?"

"They are, Mom!"

"Who, Abby? Who are you even talking about?"

Abigail tried to explain but discovered even she wasn't sure who she was talking about. Instead, she scoffed and turned away.

"Look at how you're dressed, Abby. What message are you sending to people? What are you hoping to accomplish by going out like that? I can see your nipples for crying out loud. You look like you just spent the night working the street corner."

"Fuck you, mom," Abigail cried. She folded her arms across her chest in a feeble attempt to cover herself. She started to her room, but Nichole sprang from the couch and cut her off.

"I need to hear you say it," Nichole demanded. "I need to hear you say you won't make another pass at Mr. Brown."

Abigail tried pushing past her mom, but Nichole grabbed her by the shoulders and shook her violently.

"Say it, Abby."

"You're drunk."

"Say it!" Nichole screamed. "Say you're not going to try and fuck your teacher!"

Nichole shook Abigail again. Abigail didn't try to defend herself or resist the brandishing. She fell limp in her mother's hands until Nichole stopped shaking her. When the shaking ceased, Abigail lifted her head and looked at her mom.

"What if I do, mom?" Abigail said meekly. "What if I do come on to him? What are you going to do about it?"

Nichole was defenseless. Abigail knew her mother had no power over her. She could do what she wanted. Spite was her motivator, and she was in great supply. She hated her mother. She hated Utah. She even hated herself although she didn't know it. Hatred, in its purest form, can only hurt. Abigail wanted to hurt everyone that tried saving her from herself. Nichole couldn't stop Abigail. She was a moving force with too much momentum.

"Honey, please..." Nichole pleaded.

"Don't you see, mom. I'm just like you. People only care about me because I'll sleep with them. That's the whole reason I was even born into this shitty life."

"Shitty life?" Nichole repeated incredulously. She staggered backward and slumped onto the sofa. "I have given you everything."

"Yeah, and you took it away by moving me out here."

"Abigail, you're my life. Everything I do is for you."

"Then why can't we go back home?"

At a loss, Nichole shook her head. She stood, wavering for a moment until her faculties restored enough equilibrium for her to stand straight. "If you want to leave, I won't stop you. You can do whatever you want. You do anyway. You want to go home? Then go. Maybe you will be better there. At least he's not there."

"Who?" Abigail asked.

"What?"

"You said 'at least he's not there.' Who are you talking about?"

Nichole shook her head. "Forget it."

Nichole turned around, staggered to her room and closed the door behind her. She walked to her bed and fell face first onto the mattress and promptly fell asleep. Her sleep was so sound that she didn't even stir when Abigail entered thirty minutes later. She entered with the notion of apologizing, but when she saw her mother sleeping, she decided against it. Instead, she gently removed her mother's slippers, pulled back the comforter and placed it over her mom.

CHAPTER 30

Marlon normally spent his lunch period in his own room. It was forty-five minutes of the day he could be alone without students bothering him about deadlines and makeup work. The principal, however, had hijacked the first two weeks of school. She required all teachers to spend their lunch period in the teachers' lounge the first ten days of the school year. She called it "Break Bread by Breaking the Ice" week. It was an effort to help teachers become familiar with their colleagues (new and old) while also promoting cross-curriculum planning. Marlon tolerated it, simply because it was easier than not. He'd worked for five different principals during his teaching career. They all had clever titles and plans for not-so-clever ideas. The trick, Marlon learned, was to endure it rather than defy it.

Marlon's room was just down the hall from the teachers' lounge so he was usually one of the first to arrive. He'd sign in—yes, the principal took roll—and then retreat to a corner table with a novel. The luxury of teaching English was that reading was part of his curriculum, so if someone inquired as to what he was doing, he could simply answer that he was planning future lessons. This left him free from discussing his uneventful summer, but more importantly, it freed him from having to feign interest in his colleagues' generic stories of their summer trips to Disneyland or the Grand Canyon. Needless to say, Marlon was now forty-one. He'd been "breaking bread to break the ice" for five years now, and not once had he ever used the time for its intended purpose.

Just as Marlon's custom was to arrive early so he could get a corner table, Mr. Gibson was usually ostentatiously late. This allowed him to enter under everyone's watch. If he made eye contact with a man, he'd give a subtle nod. For women, he always winked. He'd make his way to the sign-in sheet while addressing the room and giving a reason for his tardiness. He never missed an opportunity to be the center of attention.

The first day of the new school year emulated the first day of the past five. Marlon sat in the corner alone huddled over a book. Ten minutes later, Mr. Gibson strolled in and said he would have been on time, but he had to upload his most recent marathon time to his Garmin connect profile. Sadly, no one had any follow-up questions to Mr. Gibson's pretext. After he signed in, he scanned the room for a place to sit. He spotted Marlon reading in the far corner. Mr. Gibson started toward Marlon. His step was casual and it indicated, falsely, that he was a man of importance. He pulled a chair from Marlon's table and then leaned down and whispered into Marlon's ear, "Abigail Sloan."

Marlon stiffened at the name and looked up. "What?"

"Abigail Sloan," Mr. Gibson repeated, shooting Marlon a knowing smile. Marlon felt hot with embarrassment. *Does he know?* Marlon wondered. He glanced at Mr. Gibson with raised eyebrows.

"I don't know what you're talking about," Marlon said eagerly, realizing that his answer may have sounded suspicious.

"She's a transfer student from Vegas," Mr. Gibson explained in hushed whispers. "She's in my first period class. Smokin' hot body. She's wearing this little number today," Mr. Gibson whistled softly and looked to make sure no one was eavesdropping, "short skirt with a sequined top. Tits out to…well, you get the picture. I'm telling you, man, this girl could be in Hustler. I looked up her schedule. You have her tomorrow during sixth period. Abigail Sloan. Let me know what you think."

"Are you really talking to me about a student?" Marlon asked incredulously. "A teenage student?"

"Wait till you see her."

"I don't need to see her. She's an adolescent."

"Not this one, man. This one…she could easily pass for twenty. She knows it too."

"She knows what?"

"How hot she is. You can tell just by the way she walks. She knows she'll never have to work a day in her life."

"You disgust me."

"Bullshit," Mr. Gibson said, smiling. He thought Marlon's demeanor was just part of some customary ethics game that all teachers played but none really observed the rules. "Don't sit there and try and tell me you never look at some of the students who come through here."

"I don't," Marlon answered, looking Mr. Gibson straight in the eyes.

Mr. Gibson stared back at Marlon and wondered if he was actually telling the truth. He laughed awkwardly. "Well then, my friend, you are missing out."

"I'm not your friend. Why are you even sitting here?"

"I'm...breaking the ice, right?" he sneered.

"You're pathetic. You're a...fucking pervert."

"I...," Mr. Gibson began, but upon further examination realized that he may have crossed a line with Marlon. "I...was only kidding, man."

"About what?"

"About...you know, this new student."

"No, you weren't."

"Look, man, sorry I bothered you." Mr. Gibson pushed his chair out and scanned the room for a new spot.

"Aren't you married?" Marlon asked.

"Yeah."

"So why are you looking at your students if you're married?" Marlon asked, not attempting to lower his voice. Mr. Gibson blushed and surveyed the room to see if anyone paid them any attention. Everyone seemed to be lost in their own conversations. He lowered back into his chair.

"There's nothing wrong with looking," he whispered.

"There is when who you're looking at someone that is underage."

"She's a senior, man. She'll be legal in a couple months."

Marlon gauged the seriousness of Mr. Gibson's comment. Mr. Gibson shrugged his shoulders and smirked. Marlon shook his head. He leaned in close to Mr. Gibson. "Get the fuck away from me."

Marlon opened his book and tried to resume reading, but he couldn't focus on the words that lined the page. Mr. Gibson stayed seated, too confused to move. He waited for Marlon to break character, to suddenly smile and tell him he was just messing around, but the longer Mr. Gibson waited, the more he understood that Marlon really did want him to leave.

"Fine," Mr. Gibson said. "I get it." He stood and crossed the room to another table.

CHAPTER 31

The first day of the new school year was over. Marlon sat at his

desk going over his class rolls, trying to memorize student names

from their class picture. He didn't hear Nichole come in. The day

had just ended and the oppressed excitement of two thousand high

school students filled the halls and flushed out any noise Nichole

made when she entered Marlon's classroom. She stood in front of

Marlon's desk for over a minute waiting for him to notice her. After

the minute passed unsuccessfully, she felt foolish standing there

shuffling her feet and thought to sneak out of the room and then re-

enter, this time knocking to interrupt his focus. However, thinking

of the embarrassment that would be hers if Marlon happened to look

up as she was sneaking out and then wonder why she left just to re-

enter prevented her from leaving. Nichole didn't know what to do

other than stand there stupidly and think of solutions that only

caused her more bewilderment. Fortunately for her, as she was over

analyzing another course of action, Marlon lifted his head looked at

her.

"Ms. Sloan," he said, surprised. "Can I help you with something?" Marlon stood and extended his hand, but then wondered if the gesture appeared too formal and quickly retreated it.

Nichole stared at him for a long time. She saw her daughter in his features. The prominent nose, the deep-set eyes, the full lips, the high forehead and the straight white teeth. So straight people often assumed he must have had braces as a kid. Nichole wasn't sure if the wave of familiarity that overcame her when she saw Marlon a few days earlier was from the bachelor party so many years ago, or because she was looking at the male equivalent of her daughter.

"Can I help you with something?" Marlon asked again, unsure if she had heard him the first time.

Nichole stopped her evaluation of Marlon and regained her focus. "I was just wondering how Abby was today."

"I have her on B-days. I won't see her until tomorrow."

Nichole nodded like she understood, but Marlon wasn't sure that she did. He wondered if Las Vegas had the traditional A and B-day schedule or if they used an alternative one.

"Is there something I can help you with?" Marlon asked for the third time.

"Would you like to go get a cup of coffee with me?"

Nichole's question threw Marlon. "Ah, coffee? Right now?"

"Sure."

Marlon thought for a moment. "You mean like…a date?"

"No, not a date," Nichole said quickly. Her fast response deflated Marlon. His disappointment was foreign to him. He rarely wanted to go out with anyone.

"I just need to talk to you," Nichole said.

"Okay. Yeah, I could go for a coffee," Marlon said. "I know a great place."

Fifteen minutes later and they were at the same coffee shop where Marlon had first met Karen. Despite the painful fallout of Marlon and Karen's marriage, he still liked the coffee shop. It let him remember her before the dead children. When she loved him and wanted nothing more than to be loved by him. He still believed in the day that she would walk back into the shop, see him at their familiar table, and ask for their life back. It was a pleasant fantasy, even if Marlon knew it wouldn't ever happen.

They sat next to the table that Marlon used to sit with Karen. He would glance at the vacant table intermittently, replaying in his mind conversations they had shared.

Across from him, Nichole added one sugar packet to her coffee. Her hands shook. She stirred the white crystals until they dissolved into the dark liquid. She gripped the cup with both hands and brought it to her lips. She burned her tongue and softly cursed and returned the cup to the table.

"So what did you want to talk to me about?" Marlon asked.

Nichole mentally searched for the best approach to say what she needed to tell Marlon but came up empty. She began unconsciously tapping her finger on the table. Marlon assumed this meeting had something to do with his encounter with Abigail. He wondered if Nichole wanted to investigate the matter further, without the supervision of the principal. Buy why? Did she feel Marlon was withholding certain information? Did Abigail give Nichole a different version of the story and now she was fact checking? Marlon waited for the questions that were soon to come. He waited for three full minutes before Nichole finally looked up from her coffee and spoke.

"Did you go to a bachelor party in Vegas about eighteen years ago?" Nichole asked. The question was so unexpected that it took Marlon several seconds to register what she had even asked.

"How would you know that?" Marlon asked.

"You did, didn't you?"

"I..."

"Remember how I asked if we had met before?"

"Yeah."

"We have. Your mom named you after Marlon Brando. Her favorite movie is *On the Waterfront*."

Nichole let her words reach Marlon and watched as understanding dawned on him. "You're the stripper," he said.

"I wasn't a stripper."

"You're the stripper that wasn't a stripper," Marlon said.

"Yeah."

Marlon tried to speak but couldn't.

"I realized it the other day when that teacher called you Marlon," Nichole explained. "You looked familiar to me, but I couldn't place you until I heard your name."

In his mind, Marlon traveled back eighteen years to the party. He recalled the hotel suite. The bar. The two women entering wearing trench coats. He returned to the coffee shop and looked across the table at Nichole. He recognized her. He felt a tinge of embarrassment. "Wow. What a small world, huh? How long ago was that? It must have been at least—"

"Eighteen years," Nichole said. There was an air of regret to her tone. Her mood suddenly changed. Marlon understood this meeting wasn't about reminiscing. There was something larger at stake. She began tapping her finger again and Marlon waited for the next revelation. A minute later her finger stopped and she lifted her eyes and looked at Marlon.

"She's yours, Mr. Brown...er...Marlon."

Marlon was confused. "She's mine? Who?"

"Abigail," Nichole said. "She's your daughter."

Marlon looked at Nichole for a long time. "What are you talking about?"

"I got pregnant that night."

"What?"

"We had sex and I got pregnant," Nichole explained.

Marlon paused. Her words weren't registering. "What?"

"I got pregnant at the party," Nichole repeated.

"What…what is this?" Marlon asked.

"What do you mean?"

"Have you been looking for me all this time?"

"No. God, no. I didn't think I'd ever see you again. I had forgotten all about you until a few days ago."

"So…this is all just a coincidence? You moving to Utah and enrolling Abigail at my school? In my summer school class?"

"Yeah, actually," Nichole said. "A coincidence. One great big coincidence. I thought you lived in Oregon."

"I moved."

"I didn't know that."

"How do you know she's mine?"

"What?"

"How do you know she's mine? I mean, no offense, but don't strippers kind of have a reputation for sleeping around?"

"I don't know. I don't know a lot of strippers."

"Do you need money? Are you here because you need me to help take care of you?"

"No, it's not like that at all," Nichole said. "We don't need you to take care of us. In fact, we don't need anything from you. I don't want anything from you."

"Then why—"

"And I was telling the truth when I said I wasn't really a stripper. I was only there because my friend needed someone to go with her. That was my first and only time."

"Seriously?"

"Yes. I wasn't sleeping around."

"You had a boyfriend. I remember you telling me you had one. How do you know he's not the father?"

"I thought he was."

"You had him tested?"

"No, I never had him tested."

"Then how—"

"Because he's black," Nichole said brusquely. "You were the only other person during that time I slept with."

Marlon sat back in his chair. He glanced at the table to his left, the table that represented Karen. He felt like this was a trick and somehow she was responsible. He recognized the faulty logic to that rationale, but it still made sense because she served as the source of so much other angst in his life. He turned back to Nichole.

"So did you put her in my class to…what exactly? Introduce us?" Marlon asked.

"No. Like I said, I had no idea you lived here or worked at the school. This was all by coincidence. I swear."

Marlon could tell she was telling the truth. His mind suddenly refocused on Abigail and the interaction he had with her. "Oh, god," he said, with a sudden realization. "She came on to me. She kissed me."

"I know. That's why I decided to tell you."

"What do you mean?"

Nichole spoke slowly, choosing her words carefully. "I don't know that she won't...come on to you again."

"What?"

"I think she might make a pass at you just to get back at me."

"Why would she do that?"

"She's defiant."

"Defiant? Does she know who I am?"

"No."

"And you're afraid she might come on to me just to upset you?"

"Yeah."

Marlon leaned forward. "I don't understand."

"Look, until last week I had completely forgotten about you. You've never crossed my mind since the day I had Abigail. Honestly, I was happy that you were the dad because I knew, or at least I thought, you would never have to know. If I had it my way, I would have lived with you as my secret for the rest of my life. You were always supposed to be a mystery to her. But here we are, and I need something from you. I need your word that nothing will ever happen between you and Abigail and you will never reveal who you are."

"God, she talked to me about her dad."

"I know."

"The entire time she was talking about me."

"I know."

"She has no idea who I am?"

"No. And it needs to stay that way."

"Then why even tell me any of this?"

"So that you'll reject her if she ever comes on to you again."

Marlon scoffed. "Do you really think I would take advantage of a student?"

"You took advantage of me," Nichole countered.

"That's not fair. That was mutual and you know it."

"I don't even remember that night."

"Neither do I."

"Do you remember having sex with me?" Nichole asked.

"No. Do you?"

"No."

"I didn't force you."

"I know you didn't, but nonetheless, here we are."

"This is…just…incredible."

"Look, I'm not trying to make you explain your actions from eighteen years ago, Nichole said. "I know I'm just as much at fault. I've talked with Abigail. I'm trying to teach her right from wrong, but the truth is I feel like I've lost my daughter. I don't know who she is anymore. She does things just to defy me. She doesn't think. She…" Nichole trailed off. She wanted to cry but fought the urge. "Look, I'm sure you're a great guy. But all I know about you is that you sleep with strippers. That's all I have to go on. I don't know you. I don't know anything about you, but I know my daughter. I felt the best way to protect her was to tell you who she is."

"I would never take advantage of a student," Marlon said.

"I'm just protecting my daughter."

Marlon could sense Nichole's desperation. She was just a parent exhausting all avenues to save her child. Marlon understood her plight.

"So what do we do now?" he asked.

"You help my daughter get through her senior year so she can graduate, and then we'll be out of your life forever."

"Just like that, huh?"

"Yeah. Just like that. You don't have to accept a larger role in this."

"What if I want one?"

"You can't have one. I've kept you a secret for seventeen years and it needs to remain that way."

"I don't get a say in this?"

"No." Nichole looked at her watch. "I have to go," she said, getting to her feet. "I know this is a lot to take. I'm sorry you had to find out this way. I just..." Nichole didn't know what else to say, so she didn't say anything. She waited a moment to see if Marlon had any more questions. He looked straight ahead, lost in his own thoughts. Nichole nodded and then started away.

Marlon turned and called after her: "Why didn't you ever try and find me after you knew your boyfriend wasn't the father? I had a right to know."

Nichole stopped and faced Marlon. "Would you have tried to find you?" she asked.

He couldn't argue with her answer. No, he wouldn't have tried to find him. He was everything a woman wouldn't want in a man or a father. He went to Vegas and had sex with a strange woman. Why would she try and find him? She didn't know him. The only memory she had of him was pushing drinks toward her so she could drown her sorrows before stumbling into bed together.

Nichole could see that her answer stung Marlon. It was unintentional, but it still cut him. He turned away from her and stared at the table in the corner. She took a step toward him and almost put a consoling hand on his shoulder and then stopped. Her job was done. Nothing else needed to be said. It wasn't her duty to mitigate how he felt about what she told him. Her job was to protect her daughter. She'd done that. She turned back around and walked out of the coffee shop.

CHAPTER 32

Marlon spent most nights alone, with only his thoughts and the memory of Karen to keep him company. Now, however, new thoughts invaded his mind. Thoughts of choices made and actions taken. Thoughts of what might have been and could have been, compounded with the choices that never should have been. There was that old adage about how even though you may be through with the past, the past isn't through with you. The axiom suddenly took on much more significance. Marlon made a choice eighteen years ago to take advantage of an inebriated woman, and now he found himself in his own twisted Oedipus soap opera. On many accounts, books dictated Marlon's life; now he found his life worthy of one. He thought on the irony and tried to let it alone but didn't hold the capacity to bury something that had taken eighteen years to resurface. His mind raced, trying to find the proper place for the situation that was now his. He thought of Karen and how he wasn't able to produce a living child with her. She had thought them cursed for the babies they didn't bring into the world. What would she think now if she knew Marlon had achieved the task with another woman only months before their failed offspring? What would he think if he knew the truth about Karen? That she now had two healthy children of her own in another life with another man. Marlon suspected she may have been able to move on more easily than he. That maybe she did find someone else and they had a nice house, a couple children, and youth sporting events to fill their weekends. The beautiful chaos that accompanied family life. He never did any serious investigation into the life Karen may be living now. Never typed her name into Google or made a Facebook account to try and find her. He was afraid of what the search may reveal. The only element in his life that kept him alive was the absurd belief that Karen would one day come back. Just walk back into the coffee shop and say she was ready for round two. He was like Gatsby, pathetic and waiting for a life that had already passed him by.

The first year after Karen left was the hardest. Each subsequent one got a little more manageable until he had placed enough time between his past life and his current one to function without her memory breaking him down. It took him three years after Karen left to go on another date. He met a woman for lunch. It lasted less than thirty minutes. She asked if he would call, he said he would, and he never did. With every woman, he tried—and failed— to replicate what he had with Karen. One woman, after having made it to a fifth date, he even asked to stay the night. She agreed, and she and Marlon had awkward, passionless sex. She slipped out in the middle of the night and never heard from him again. By the time he reached forty, he realized he preferred being alone. He wasn't lonely when he was alone. He was pensive and passed the time reading or writing, discovering new characters from another's imagination and then forming his own from the inspiration of great writers before him. He relished his solitude, took comfort in it. But now that he had the knowledge that he was a father, he suddenly felt isolated and lonely. When Karen left, he was certain his life was through surprising him. He had lived blissfully in the time leading up to the faulty delivery. The aftermath nearly killed him. It had taken him nearly fifteen years to recover from Karen's exodus. He believed himself finished with despair. It was a harsh awakening to realize he was wrong.

He wished Nichole hadn't told him he was the father. What was he supposed to do with that information? A person can't be told they're responsible for someone, and then in the same breath be asked to relinquish all responsibility. It wasn't fair. It would have been better for him to remain ignorant. Why tell him and not Abigail? If Nichole's concern was her daughter's promiscuous nature, why not tell *her* of his identity and allow him to remain in the dark? Surely a daughter wouldn't make a pass at her own father. Marlon cursed himself for not presenting this logic to Nichole. Not that it would have mattered in retrospect. He could have only presented his argument *after* she had already revealed his identity. Still, she should have known better.

From the stillness of his kitchen, Marlon's microwave beeped, compelling him to suspend his thoughts of Nichole and Abigail He stood and retrieved his TV dinner and sat at his table. He used the plastic cutlery that came with the meal to try and cut through the genetically modified steak and potatoes. The fork snapped at the base of the meat, sending a plastic splinter across the table. Marlon stared at the steak, envious of its strength. He picked up the meat with his hand and ripped off a piece with his teeth. He chewed it long enough to know that it wasn't worth the effort to swallow. He spat the wad back into the plastic tray and went to bed hungry.

He woke a couple hours later. He tried to fall back asleep, but too much cluttered his mind. He switched on his bedside lamp and grabbed his laptop from his bedside table. He logged into his school grade book and retrieved his class rolls. A series of student pictures, arranged alphabetically, filled his screen like a page from a yearbook. He scrolled through the photos until he found Abigail's. He clicked on her face and the other pictures surrounding hers quickly minimized while hers expanded to the four corners of the computer screen. Marlon stared at the photo for a long time, studying Abigail's different features and trying to find his own in hers. He couldn't see himself in her, but he did see another version of himself. The version that didn't survive. His and Karen's child—

"the baby that wasn't a baby." That's what Karen called their son. She let slip that was how she thought of "it."

The admission came during their final counseling session. Marlon looked at Karen incredulously and then stood and walked out the door, ignoring the counselor's guidance to stay and talk about Karen's revelation. Marlon drove to a deserted church parking lot and sat alone in his car for three hours. Karen never called, and Marlon spent the night at a hotel. The next day when he returned from work, ready to apologize and make amends for his abrupt exit, all her stuff was gone. She picked the closet clean and ransacked the bathroom in haste. Marlon tried calling, but she wouldn't answer. He left messages, but they were never returned. He sent texts and emails, but she deleted them without even reading them. His persistence finally led Karen to get a new number and email address, leaving the coffee shop as the only connection Marlon still had to her. He went there every day in the hope that she would choose to come back into his life. She never did, at least not yet. He still kept hope, so he still went, and somehow, even though he knew she would never return, it still stung every time he walked through the door and didn't see her waiting in the corner for him.

The longer Marlon stared at Abigail's picture, the more he saw his dead son in her countenance. He named him Howard, after the architect in the Ayn Rand novel. He felt it fitting since *The Fountainhead* was the first book Karen was reading when Marlon first saw her. He named him without telling Karen. The birth certificate arrived in the mail just as Marlon arrived home from work. He found Karen crying on the kitchen floor with the certificate balled up in her hand.

"How could you?" she screamed. "How could you name something that wasn't even human?" She threw the ball of paper at him; she would have thrown more if there were anything in the vicinity.

After she managed to get to her feet, she packed a suitcase and left. Three days later she returned. He didn't ask where she went or what she did. He just listened as she told him she loved him and she needed things to work. Marlon wanted that, too. She revealed how hard it was to be around Marlon. He reminded her of what they had lost. Marlon offered no rebuttal. He felt numb. Just a shell covered in skin covered in grief. He asked what she wanted. "Counseling," she said. They went the following day.

The counselor helped—at first. She showed Karen that the dead baby wasn't her fault, nor Marlon's. She helped her see that God wasn't punishing them for conceiving a child out of wedlock. She gave Karen permission to celebrate the life of the child they did have, even if it was for only a couple hours. It took some convincing, but Karen eventually let go of her belief that their child, grotesque and suffering, resulted from some unfounded punishment from God. It was a breakthrough moment. Karen sobbed and clutched Marlon and admitted that their child was the most beautiful baby she had ever seen. She needed his forgiveness for not holding it. The counselor assured them Howard knew Karen loved him. Karen became hopeful; Marlon became wishful.

That night Marlon and Karen made love. It was soft, intimate, and broke a yearlong dry spell. It was a catharsis, a cleansing of sorts, and it was punctuated with the perfect ending: another pregnancy. Karen was elated, feeling that the welcomed pregnancy further confirmed that she had been forgiven, redeemed, and rewarded. Feeling completely cured, they stopped seeing the counselor. Life was good again. They began repainting the nursery. They even engaged in a frivolous, clichéd paint "fight" where Karen ran a blue paint streak across Marlon's cheek, and he countered by running his roller over her ass. The paint went flying and the laughter grew louder and they didn't stop until they were making love on the plastic covering spread out over the carpet.

And then she miscarried. Great clots of blood spilled out into the toilet. Marlon heard the crying and rushed into the bathroom. He caught her just as she was falling off the toilet.

The following day the doctor confirmed the baby was dead. They returned to counseling. This time, Karen was unreachable. She only gave half-hearted, monosyllabic answers, never taking her glassy eyes away from the hypnotic fish tank behind the therapist's desk. If Marlon tried touching her, her skin turned cold and rigid. If the counselor asked to talk about the baby (Howard or the recent miscarriage), Karen remained silent. She didn't speak; she wouldn't move. She was a zombie, going through the motions of life simply because she knew how. She'd been doing it for twenty-five years. She dropped the façade, the fake "hellos" and artificial "how are you's" and just slept-walked through life. Marlon thought that maybe she was suicidal. She wasn't. Suicidal people have drive. Ambition. Goals. She had nothing. She was dead, and only remained alive because she didn't know how to will her body to stop functioning.

Then, on what would ultimately become their final session, a spark of life ignited. The counselor and Marlon were talking, and Karen was listening.

"When was the last time you felt truly alive, Marlon?" the therapist asked.

"When I held my son."

"Your first baby?"

"Yes. Howard."

Karen scoffed. Marlon and the therapist looked at her.

"Do you have something you'd like to say, Karen?" the therapist asked.

"Howard," she said under her breath. "The baby that wasn't a baby."

It was the most Karen had spoken in months. Marlon looked at her incredulously. Karen slowly turned her head and stared back at him. Her eyes were alive. They were no longer hypnotized orbs that stared at everything but saw nothing. They locked onto Marlon for a full minute. He studied her, trying to determine what her words meant and why she said them. And then he snapped. He dashed out of the therapist's office, slammed the door behind him, and never saw his wife again.

And now, all these years later, Marlon felt that Howard, or the other miscarried baby, had returned to him in the presence of Abigail. Howard only lived a moment, but in his brief life, Marlon took all of him in. Abigail retained his features. She was an expression of how Howard would have looked had his life extended beyond a few hours. Marlon studied the laptop photo of Abigail, and even with his broken heart, he couldn't help but smile at the manifestation of his dead son suddenly resurrected by his new daughter.

Still carrying his laptop, he got out of bed, and started down the hall. He stopped at the bedroom door but didn't go in immediately. He hadn't been in the room for five years. There was no reason to. It wasn't a nearly completed nursery; it was a mausoleum of another life with half painted walls and a lingering scent of an abandoned wife. Marlon stood for a long time staring at the door. His mind raced but no coherent thoughts formed. Finally, he clutched the doorknob, pushed open the door, and entered the musty room.

He went straight to the closet. He knew the shoebox, sitting rejected and teaming with grief, was on the top shelf. He grabbed the box and blew away the thin layer of dust covering the faded Nike logo. Marlon carried the box and his laptop to the rocking chair in the corner of the room. He sat down and five years' worth of nonuse rose from the chair's cushions and dissipated into the air. He lifted the lid from the box and dropped it to the side of the chair. On top was a wrinkled sheet of paper, faded and somewhat smeared. Marlon turned it over. It was Howard's birth certificate. Date of birth: January 21st. Date of death: January 21st.

Marlon placed the certificate on the floor and pulled a stack of photographs from the box. The first picture was of him and Karen taken at a restaurant. It was their six-month anniversary. Karen asked the waiter to take the picture. "On the count of three," the waiter said, and right after he said "two," Marlon kissed her on the cheek. She laughed, the camera clicked, and the memory was captured. Marlon smiled and filed the photo at the end of the stack. The next picture was of Karen on top of a mountain. She looked over the Utah Valley with the wind pushing back her hair. Marlon snapped the photo without her knowing. She looked like a model, without the artificial trimming and photo-shopped enhancements. The next showed Karen reading in bed, her hand resting softly on her pregnant belly. Marlon pulled all the photos that recounted their life: Karen cooking dinner, sunbathing at the beach, trying to start a fire at Island Park, running on a trail around Lake Tahoe, sleeping with her new comforter. The photos captured Karen alive, before unfortunate circumstances robbed her and Marlon of their life. The photos showed the Karen Marlon fell in love in with and still loved.

It was the Karen he knew still existed, but somehow became buried once the failed prospect of creating a new life killed her existing one.

Marlon shuffled through the various photos chronicling his and Karen's life. The bittersweet memories made him nostalgic, but Karen wasn't who he sought. He was looking for Howard. He found the picture of him at the bottom of the box, buried under the life he never experienced. Marlon took the photo shortly after the nurse brought Howard from the maternity ward. He rested Howard on his lap, pulled his camera from his pocket, and snapped the photo. Howard was smiling. Marlon looked at the photo and then looked at Abigail's picture from the laptop. It was easy to see they were siblings. How cruel for Marlon to think for eighteen years he couldn't create sustainable life. The burden of failure now lifted. He was the winner who never received his prize, the deceased artist whose genius wasn't discovered until after death. Marlon returned the contents of the box, closed the lid and then shut his laptop. He rocked silently and softly cried until he was asleep.

CHAPTER 33

Marlon started each of his class periods with fifteen minutes of silent reading. Most of his students spent this time staring absentmindedly at their books, feigning interest and waiting out the clock. They thought they were clever, pretending to do something Marlon required and scored toward their grade, when all along they fake it and received the reward nonetheless. Marlon didn't care, though. The silent reading time was as much for him as it was for his students. If they didn't use the time to their benefit, well, that was fifteen minutes of their life that they would squander and never get back. A farmer could lead a horse to water but couldn't make it drink, just as Marlon could lead his students to knowledge, but he couldn't make them think.

Marlon hadn't used his reading time for reading ever since he learned of his parenthood. Instead, he sat at his desk and stared at Abigail with awed wonderment. Often, he became so lost in his thoughts that the reading time extended to twenty or thirty minutes. Students would begin to shift in their seats and glance at the clock until Marlon broke his reverie and gave them permission to close their books.

One time Abigail, reading from the front row, stopped reading and stretched. She leaned back in her chair and audibly yawned while extending her hands above her head. Her short shirt came up to just below her rib cage, exposing her pierced belly button. She shot a glance at Marlon, who sat staring at her with bewildered eyes. He looked down at the book that sat opened on his desk when Abigail's eyes locked on his, but he didn't react quickly enough. Abigail had caught him staring. From that day forward, she would steal furtive glances in his direction, often finding him staring right back at her. There was something different in his eyes when he looked at her. It wasn't the perverted suppressed creepiness that she had witnessed so many times with past teachers, nor was it an insatiable lust often exhibited from fellow students. No, Marlon was different. There was more to his staring. He almost looked…concerned, as if his eyes were trying to find something *within* Abigail instead of just surveying what she displayed on the outside. She wasn't sure how it made her feel.

Abigail always made it a point to leave Marlon's class last. She'd shuffle to the door, pretending to read from her phone, and keep her ears opened in case Marlon said something to her. He never did, and she couldn't understand why she hoped he would anyway. Maybe she wanted him to apologize for what had happened between them, or maybe she wanted to offer her own apology. Maybe he would explain why he kept looking at her. Or maybe she just wanted him to talk to her because no one else did, and even though things were now awkward between them, she still found herself mysteriously drawn to him. It was no longer a sexual draw, just a curious one.

Marlon never stopped her, though. The bell would ring and students would quickly gather their things and file out of the class. Abigail lingered. Pretended to arrange things in her backpack until the class was nearly empty, before slowly walking to the door and into the hall. She didn't know, however, that once she exited the classroom, Marlon often walked briskly (or ran) to the door and watched as she weaved her way through the sea of students toward her next class. She also didn't know that Mr. Gibson, whose room was two doors down from Marlon's, would also stand in his doorway and wait for her to walk past.

*****

One day, as Marlon facilitated a class discussion on *Of Mice and Men,* he asked why Steinbeck didn't give Curly's wife—the sole female character in the novella—a name. The class met his question, as was the norm, with silence. Marlon had an unwritten policy that he wouldn't move on from a question until someone ventured an answer. One time he waited nearly four minutes for an answer to a question. Four minutes may not sound like a long time, but when standing in front of thirty people with a question lingering in the air, it feels like an eternity.

On this particular day, two minutes passed when Abigail's phone interrupted the silence with the chime of an incoming text message. All eyes shifted to Abigail and then back to Marlon to see how he would react to the interruption. He didn't react. He stood rigidly and waited for an answer. Finally, a student in the front row spoke up.

"She's just a stock character."

Marlon looked at the student. "What do you mean by that? A stock character?"

"She's not given a name because she doesn't have an identity. She's a cliché, a stereotype. She's a...slattern."

"Slattern, huh?" Marlon repeated. "Nice word."

The student blushed. Marlon was about to ask a follow-up question when Abigail's phone went off again.

"Abigail, turn off your phone and put it on my desk," Marlon instructed.

"It's a new phone," she argued. "I don't know how to silence it yet."

"Go put it on my desk."

"I wasn't doing anything."

"I don't want to ask again," Marlon said. "Do it now."

Abigail sighed. "Fine, dad," she sneered and then pushed her chair out from her desk and stood defiantly. Marlon froze.

"What did you say?" he asked.

"She called you 'dad,' Mr. Brown," a student said.

"I heard what she said, Marcus," Marlon said.

"Then why'd you ask?" Marcus wanted to know. Every class has one student who takes everything literally. Marcus was Marlon's student.

"Why did you call me dad?" Marlon asked Abigail.

"You treat us like children," Abigail said, walking to Marlon's desk. She tossed her phone on his desk. It slid across the surface and landed on the floor. The class laughed nervously while Abigail ran to her phone and looked it over to see if it was damaged. A thin crack lined her screen.

"Look what you made me do," she cried.

Marlon stared at her, still trying to discern if her comment meant more than she let on. The class took his silence as an appropriate affront to Abigail's behavior and laughed nervously again, feeling that Marlon would permit it since their merriment was directed at Abigail and not him.

"This was a brand new phone," Abigail said, setting it back on the desk, more gently this time. She was on the verge of tears.

"I'm…I'm sorry," Marlon said. His apology confused the class because it sounded sincere. Abigail returned to her seat and put her head down in silent protest to Marlon's lesson. He tried to collect his thoughts and continue with the lesson but couldn't. He told the class to read on their own. He went to his desk and sat staring at Abigail for the rest of the period.

When the bell rang, she didn't move. She stayed with her head on her desk until everyone had exited the classroom. When she finally sat up, Marlon saw that she was crying. She wiped her eyes and looked hard at Marlon. He couldn't tell if her tears were from cracking her phone or being embarrassed in front of her peers or both. A pang of remorse stabbed Marlon, feeling somewhat responsible for her pain since he instigated the incident.

Abigail stuffed her books in her backpack and made her way to Marlon's desk. "Can I have my phone please?" she asked.

Marlon handed her the phone. She snatched it and ran her finger over the fracture, surveying the crack. It felt smooth and indistinguishable to the touch, but the blemish was obvious to the eye.

"I'm sorry that your phone is broken," Marlon said.

Abigail pressed down on the power switch and the screen illuminated. "It still works," she mumbled, happy that she didn't break it beyond repair. She turned and started for the exit.

"How's school going?" Marlon asked. Abigail stopped and turned back to Marlon. She had waited two months for him to say something to her. Why did he choose the day she didn't want to talk to do it?

"What?"

"How's school? Do you like it here?"

"It's okay, I guess."

"Have you made any new friends?"

"Not really."

"Why?"

"The people here…they're not my kind of people."

"What are your kind of people?"

"I don't know. Everyone here is so judgmental. They don't want anything to do with you if you don't go to church on Sunday."

Marlon nodded sympathetically. It took him some time to understand the youth social dynamic of Utah. Everything was hermetically sealed and processed with a stamp of religious approval.

"What are your plans after high school?" he asked.

"I don't know."

"Are you going to go to college?"

Abigail spied Marlon, curiously. She didn't understand his sudden interest in her. "What do you care?" she asked, tersely.

Marlon shook his head and leaned back in his chair. "Why are you so angry, Abigail?"

"I'm not angry."

"You seem angry."

"You don't know me."

"Help me get to know you. Tell me something about you."

"I've already told you three things. Remember?"

"Tell me something else."

"I have a shitty English teacher."

"Tell me something I don't know."

"He's also nosey."

"Tell me something about *you*," Marlon said.

"Don't you have a class or something right now?" Abigail asked.

"No. It's my prep."

"Well, I have a class. I'm going to be late," Abigail said, but she didn't turn to leave. She wanted to keep talking with Marlon, but she wanted him to ask her to stay. She wanted to be wanted. More importantly, she wanted answers to what transpired between them in the summer. Marlon knew all this, but if she wanted answers, he would make her ask the questions.

"You don't seem to be in a hurry," Marlon said.

In an act of defiance, Abigail turned and started for the door. She waited for Marlon to stop her, but he remained silent, sitting with his arms folded. Abigail turned back around and faced him. She opened her mouth to speak, but didn't know what to say, so she quickly closed it and stared back at him.

"I thought you had to go," Marlon said, smiling.

"Why did you tell on me?" she asked.

"I had to," Marlon answered.

"No, you didn't."

"If it got back to the principal that something happened it wouldn't have looked good."

"I wouldn't have told anyone."

"I didn't know that."

"You didn't trust me?"

"I don't know you."

Abigail lowered her head. "I thought that you…liked me," Abigail said.

"I did. I do, but not like that."

"Why?"

"Abigail, you're a teenager."

"So?"

"So?" Marlon said. "That's your rebuttal?"

"Age is just a number," she argued.

"Yeah, well, to me it's a pretty important one."

"Did you get in trouble?"

"No. Did you?"

"My mom hates me," she said.

"Your mom doesn't hate you."

"You don't know her. She hates me."

"I spoke with her. She's worried about you. Raising a child is hard. You'll understand when you have your own children."

"Do your kids think you hate them?"

Abigail's question was innocent enough, but it took Marlon a long time to answer it. "I…I don't have…kids," he finally managed to say.

"What?" Abigail asked incredulously. "I thought everyone in Utah had kids."

"You know, for someone who claims to know how to see people, you keep misjudging me," Marlon said. "First you assumed I was married and now you assume I have children."

"I'll admit you throw me off sometimes. Are you…gay?"

Marlon laughed. "No."

"So…what's your deal?"

Marlon had no interest in answering her question. Instead, he asked the question that had weighed on his mind ever since he learned he was a father. "What do you know about your father?" he asked.

"What do you mean?"

"That day you were talking about your father and how you've never met him."

"I haven't. I told you, my mom got pregnant from a one-night stand. She doesn't know who he is. Doesn't even know his name."

Marlon wondered why Nichole, who appeared to have disclosed all the other pertinent information from that night, pretended not to know his name. Maybe she suspected Abigail would try and him if she had a name. With the Internet and social media, it certainly wouldn't have been hard to find someone. True, Marlon didn't have any social media accounts, but he wasn't trying to hide. A little diligence and he could have easily been found. A Google search would reveal he worked at Zion High School in Utah. Could Abigail have found him? Did Nichole ever attempt to? Or was Marlon nothing more to her than a regrettable choice made in a different life? A choice and a life that wasn't ever worth revisiting?

"How does that make you feel?" Marlon asked. "To know that you were conceived from a one-night stand?"

427

"I don't know. Kind of worthless, I guess."

"What would you say to your father if you could meet him?"

"I don't know. I've thought about it a lot, but…I don't know," she said softly.

"Do you hate him?"

"Yes. No. Kind of."

"Which is it?"

"No, I guess."

"Why?"

"He had the chance to screw someone, so he took it."

"Why did your mom do it?"

"Do what?"

"Sleep with him."

"She was drunk. She only went to the party to get back at her boyfriend."

"What do you mean?"

"My mom caught her boyfriend earlier that day with another woman, so to get back at him, she went to this bachelor party. Her best friend was a stripper, so my mom asked if she could go with her. My mom was really nervous, so she drank too much. One of the guys there took advantage of her and now here I am." Abigail paused for a moment and then added: "Her biggest mistake."

"How do you know he took advantage of her?"

"She was drunk."

"Was he?"

It had never occurred to Abigail to question the man's sobriety. She shrugged.

"You see yourself as a mistake?" Marlon asked.

"Is there any other way to see me?"

"Do you think that's why you act the way you do?"

"What do you mean?"

"I mean, look at yourself, Abigail," Marlon said. "Look at how you present yourself to the world."

"What does that mean? How do I present myself?"

"You look like you're destined for a lifetime of bad pick-up lines from guys with tribal band tattoos and too much hair gel."

Abigail scoffed. "And there's the judgmental teacher I have come to know."

Marlon realized that his words sounded harsher than he intended. He didn't mean to hurt Abigail; he just wanted her to see how others saw her. "I'm...sorry," he said, fumbling over his words. "I...I didn't mean...I think you're nice...you're not a whore or anything...I didn't mean that. Shit. I'm screwing this up, aren't I?"

"A little bit, yeah."

"I'm just worried about you for some reason."

"Why are you worried about me?" Abigail asked. "I'm no one to you. Just another generic student, right?"

"No—"

"It's okay. I get it," Abigail said. "I know you think I'm just some slutty loser." The bell suddenly rang. Abigail looked at the time. "I have to get to class." She turned and quickly walked out of the room. Marlon stood and ran to the door.

"Hey, Abigail?" he called after her. She stopped and faced him. Marlon looked at her for a long time, unable to say anything. Abigail waited a moment and then shook her head and turned back around. Marlon watched her go, understanding at that moment what it must feel like to fail as a parent.

CHAPTER 34

Marlon entered the coffee shop and looked at his usual table in the corner, and as usual, Karen wasn't sitting there. He started toward the counter when another woman, sitting at the table next to his and Karen's, caught his eye. Similar to Karen, she read a book, using it as a means to block any outside stimuli. She was beautiful. Marlon looked closer and realized it was Nichole. He looked at her for a long time, calculating the odds of running into her here of all places. He decided it really wasn't much of a coincidence since he had brought her here a few days ago. She was too engrossed in her book to realize Marlon was watching her. Marlon thought to turn and walk out of the door, but then figured he had no reason to flee Nichole. Just because they had a secret child together didn't mean they couldn't drink in the same coffee house.

Marlon stepped to the cashier, placed his order, and then stood to the side of the counter to wait for his coffee. He was in full view of Nichole, but she still didn't notice him. He wondered what book it was that had her so enthralled. A minute later the barista handed Marlon his coffee. Marlon paused for a moment. He couldn't decide whether to walk out undetected or to interrupt Nichole's reading. He decided to interrupt.

"Nichole...er...Ms. Sloan?" Marlon said, standing in front of Nichole's table.

Nichole looked up. "Marlon...ah...Mr. Brown," she laughed, realizing she stumbled at the same formality he had. "How are you?"

"I'm well. How are you?"

"I'm fine. Thanks."

"Do you come here often?" Marlon asked.

"No, this is my second time. My first time was with you last week. I had an hour to kill so...I'm sorry, is it okay that I come here?"

"Yeah, of course. The coffee is great. I've been coming here for years."

"Yeah, the coffee is great. That's why I came back. Do you live around here?"

"Yeah, I...do you mind if I sit down?"

"Sure, go ahead."

Marlon pulled the empty chair from the table and sat down. "I live about two miles down the road."

"Really? I live about five miles down the road."

Marlon shook his head and Nichole laughed, both wondering what, if anything, this absurd coincidence meant.

"Of all the gin joints in all the world, huh?" Marlon said.

"God, you must hate me," Nichole said. "Here you were living your peaceful little life in this peaceful little town drinking coffee in your peaceful little coffee house and I come along and wreck it."

"You didn't wreck it. You just…"

"Yes?"

Marlon laughed. "Renovated it."

"That's a nice way to put it."

"So what book are you reading?" Marlon asked.

"The Road."

"Cormac McCarthy?"

"Yeah."

"The feel-bad book of the decade, huh?"

"Yeah, it's bleak, but it's brilliant."

"Everything he writes is brilliant."

"Not *The Counselor.*"

Marlon smiled, impressed with the reference, and more impressed with her point. "Screenplays don't count."

Nichole smirked, impressed that Marlon knew her reference. Marlon glanced at the empty table next to them and grew somber. Nichole noticed the change in his demeanor. She thought to ask what was wrong but decided it best to stay silent. Marlon softly laughed to himself and turned back to Nichole.

"So I think I embarrassed Abigail in class," he said.

"What happened?"

"Her phone kept going off so I told her to put it on my desk. She threw it on there, it slid off and cracked her screen."

"That's a brand new phone."

"I know."

"Oh, man, "Nichole laughed. "I bet she hates your guts."

"I felt horrible."

"Don't. She shouldn't have had it on in class."

"Yeah…"

"So how's she doing?" Nichole asked.

"She has a B minus," Marlon said. He knew because he checked her grade every day.

"Good. I wish it were higher, but honestly, I'm just happy that she's passing."

"She'll pass. She's a bright girl."

"That's always nice to hear."

"What do you think she'll do after high school?"

"I don't know. I want her to go to college, but she has no interest in that. She keeps saying how she's moving back home after she graduates."

"What will she do back home?"

"I have no idea. There's nothing in Vegas for her."

Marlon opened a sugar packet and dumped it into his coffee. After a moment, he spotted his reflection in the murky beverage. "I'm sorry, Nichole," he said. She was about to ask what he meant, but when he looked up at her she understood the meaning in his eyes. She nodded sympathetically.

"It's not your fault," she said. "I was there too."

"I shouldn't have kept making you drinks."

"I shouldn't have kept asking for them."

Silence. Nichole tapped the side of her mug. Marlon looked at the table next to them.

"So…," Nichole said, "What about you?"

Marlon looked back at Nichole. "What do you mean?"

"Are you married? Do you have kids?"

"No, I'm…I'm not married. No kids."

"Well, you're kind of a rarity here, aren't you?" Nichole teased.

"I was married. I met her here actually, at that table." Marlon nodded at the table next to them. "I watched her reading at that table for two months before I finally had the nerve to go over and talk to her," he paused for a moment, lost in the memory and then added, "god, she was beautiful."

"What happened?"

"She left. About fifteen years ago."

"Why?"

"I don't want to bore you with the details."

"I'm not bored."

Marlon tried to decipher if her concern was rooted in some societal obligation or sincerity. She appeared genuinely invested. Marlon continued.

"We had a child, a little boy, but he died. He only lived for a short while. He had this rare disease. His head didn't fully develop, so his brain was exposed."

"Anencephaly?" Nichole asked, surprising Marlon once again with her knowledge of things not generally known.

"Yeah," Marlon said. "Anencephaly. Most people have never heard of it."

"How long did he live?"

"Less than seven hours."

"I'm so sorry, Marlon," Nichole said. She thought to reach across the table and take his hand but decided against it.

"It's…," Marlon began, but couldn't continue. He waved his hand away as a substitute for an explanation.

"Why did she leave?" Nichole asked.

"She thought we were cursed," Marlon explained. "About a year later she got pregnant again and miscarried. She thought together we could only produce dead babies. When she looked at me, she was reminded of the lives I couldn't give her."

"That doesn't sound fair."

"It doesn't need to be. People can leave no matter the rationale."

"Did you name him? Your child?"

"Yeah. I named him Howard."

"When I hear that name I think of *The Fountainhead.*"

"That's where it came from," Marlon said, smiling. "She was reading it when I first saw her." He looked back at the table in the corner.

"That table means a lot to you, doesn't it?" Nichole asked.

"It represents a happier time," Marlon said.

"You never remarried?"

"No."

"So you come here every day hoping to find her sitting at that table again?"

Marlon laughed softly. "That sounds desperate, doesn't it?"

"It sounds like you're not living your current life because you're waiting for your old one to return."

"I've tried moving on and I don't know how."

"Maybe you don't know how because you keep coming back."

"That's...harsh," Marlon said, smiling. "And probably accurate."

"What would you say to her? If you walked in one day and you saw her sitting there again."

"I would sit down across from her and ask her to give me an honest moment."

"What's that?"

"It's a thing she did. She hated artifice and anything that wasn't genuine. She believed that people aren't honest with each other, so if she ever felt I wasn't being authentic she would say, 'give me an honest moment,' and I'd have to come up with something real."

"An honest moment, huh?"

"Yeah," Marlon said. "I'm sure it sounds silly, but…"

"Want to give me one?" Nichole asked.

"I've already given you a few," Marlon smiled. "God, this is the most I've talked about Karen in…well…ever."

"Well, give me another one. Tell me something about you that you haven't told anyone else."

Marlon sat back in his chair and looked at Nichole. "You sure you want to go down this road?"

"Sure. It sounds fun."

Marlon nodded and then said, "I tried to find you the next day."

"What?"

"In Vegas. I tried to find you the next day."

"What? How?"

"I called the agency. They wouldn't tell me anything, though. I didn't have your name and the other girl, the one that really was a stripper, they wouldn't give me her number. They said if I wanted to see her again, I'd have to pay for her services."

"Did you?"

"Did I what?"

"Pay for her services?"

"I couldn't. You robbed me, remember?"

Nichole put her hand over her mouth. "Oh, my god. I completely forgot. It wasn't me. It was Lexi."

"Lexi?"

"Yeah, the girl I was with. She came in and woke me up. As we were sneaking out, she found your wallet."

"Is Lexi her real name or is that a stripper alias?"

"No, it's her real name. She was my best friend. She's living in Europe now. You helped pay to get her there," Nichole teased.

"Well, I'm glad I could help."

"Is that why you wanted to find me? To get your money back?"

"No. But that's what I told my friends."

"What was the real reason?"

"You."

"Me?"

"Yeah. I liked talking to you, and…I…wanted to talk to you some more," Marlon said, blushing.

Nichole smiled and tucked her hair behind her ear. "I liked talking to you too," she said. "I'm so sorry about the money. I could pay you back."

"It's not a big deal," Marlon said.

"No, really. I feel horrible about it," Nichole said, reaching for her purse. Marlon reached across the table and grabbed her hand to stop her from retrieving her checkbook.

"Please," he said. "It's okay. Think of it as…back child support." Marlon winced. He wasn't sure why he said this. It was an attempt at a joke, but the moment it escaped his lips, he wished he could take it back. Nichole's laughter alleviated some of his embarrassment.

It wasn't until her laughing subsided that they both realized he still had his hand on hers. They stared at their connected fingers, neither taking the initiative to release the other. Marlon looked at Nichole. She looked beautiful and confused. She liked feeling Marlon's hand on her own, and she hoped that whatever he did next wouldn't compel him to remove his hand from hers. But that's exactly what he did. Embarrassed, he slowly retrieved his hand and rested it in his own lap. Nichole kept her hand on the table. It sat abandoned, released so abruptly that it almost ached.

"What about you?" Marlon asked.

"What about me?"

"Want to give me an honest moment?"

Nichole thought for a moment. "How honest do you want?"

"As honest as it gets. Something about you and Abigail."

Nichole thought for a moment, ruminating through the past eighteen years, trying to find something that would fit the parameters of Marlon's request. "When I was eight months pregnant, I tried to kill Abby," Nichole said. "I found out my boyfriend, who at the time I thought was Abby's father, had poked holes in his condoms to try and get me pregnant. I was so angry I went to my friend's house—Lexi's—and got really drunk and started punching myself in the stomach. She came home and found me in a heap on her bedroom floor. I was...," Nichole had to pause a moment to collect herself. "I was so...fucking happy when Abby came out and I knew she wasn't his. I held her so close and told her that no matter what happened I would always protect her. She became my life at that moment. I swore off men, marriage, everything involving the prospect of being with another person when she came into my life. I've done the best I can with her, and yet, she hates me so much. Sometimes I think I'm being punished because of that night. Like somehow she knew that I tried to get rid of her and now she's punishing me because of it."

Nichole exhaled deeply and wiped her eyes. She wasn't sure what made her reveal something so...revealing, only that it felt nice to do so.

"She's a teenager," Marlon said. "It's in her nature to feel angry. I'm sure she'll grow out of it."

"Yeah, maybe," Nichole said. "How's that for honesty?"

"It was perfect."

"Your son that died, how old would he be if he were alive today?" Nichole asked.

"He'd be five months younger than Abigail," Marlon answered softly. Nichole could tell Marlon had recently done the math. Nichole started running her own numbers and drawing her own conclusions. She did the math, too, calculating the timeframe to put their encounter into perspective. Marlon could see the wheels turning in her head and waited for her question.

"So you and I—"

"I met her two months after I got home from Vegas," Marlon interrupted.

"Two months?"

"Yeah."

They sat quietly for a moment and processed the things recently revealed and the eighteen years that enveloped the then and now. They both felt a sorrow they didn't know they had, and they couldn't determine exactly what was causing it. It felt like regret, but it wasn't. It felt like shame, but there wasn't anything to be ashamed about. It was just…feeling. The feeling of being able to

446

feel. But what exactly? It didn't need a name; it just needed to be felt to validate it existed.

Marlon looked at his watch. "I better go," he said. "I'm going to be late."

"Yeah, okay," Nichole said. A part of her, a large part, wanted him to stay. They didn't even need to talk, she just wanted to remain in his presence, to feel...whatever it was he was helping her feel. As Marlon got to his feet, Nichole felt, for the first time since Abigail's birth, the tinge of pain that comes from the prospect of being alone. She wasn't sure what exactly had awakened the feeling, only that it had something to do with Marlon.

"It was nice talking to you," Marlon said. "Maybe I'll...see you around."

"Yeah, maybe."

Marlon stood for another minute and then nodded to Nichole and walked out the door. She stared at the closed door and wondered why she didn't dare ask him to stay. At the very least they could have finished their coffee together. In retrospect, she determined it was best she hadn't asked him to stay. After all, he was the father of her child. He was the last person she should hope to cultivate a relationship with. It would have been irresponsible on her part to reveal that she had felt more alive in the last five minutes with Marlon than she had with every date since she gave birth to Abigail. She looked back at the door. It was best he left, and as that thought solidified itself in Nichole's head, Marlon walked back into the coffee shop.

"Would you like to get a cup of coffee sometime?" he asked. "I mean, not like this, but…a meal. Can I buy you a meal?"

"A meal?"

"Shit. This is coming out all wrong."

"Why don't you try again?"

Marlon straightened and cleared his throat. "Would you like to go to dinner sometime?"

"You mean a date?"

"Yes. A date. Would you like to go on a date with me?"

Nichole stayed silent for a long time. Marlon's heart beat out of his chest. Never had another person's silence been so deafening.

"I don't know," Nichole finally managed to say. "Do you think it would be weird?"

"Probably."

"Marlon, I—"

"Tell me you didn't feel something just now."

"What?"

"Just now. As I was sitting here. When I took your hand, tell me you didn't feel something."

Nichole couldn't lie. "I may have felt...something."

"What was it?"

"I don't know."

"I don't either, but I...I would like to feel it again."

"Marlon..."

"Just one dinner."

Nichole saw the sincerity in Marlon's eyes, saw the pleading in them that wanted nothing more than to be wanted. She recognized the look because she often felt the same expression in her own disposition. She knew how many times she sat across from men on dates and looked at them with her own pleading eyes, only to dismiss them because she was after something they couldn't offer. She wanted Marlon at that moment in a way that wasn't hindered or exasperated by sex because it transcended sex. She wanted Marlon for the same reason he wanted her: to connect with another human. She felt it, and she knew he had too, but emotion always gave way to reason with Nichole. She couldn't allow herself to be vulnerable, especially with the father of her child.

"I can't have you interfering with my life," she said.

"She's my daughter too."

"Did you hear what you just said?"

"I know how it sounds, but…"

"But what?"

"Marlon, this is a horrible idea. You can't be in my life. You can't be in Abigail's life."

"Just one dinner."

"Walking away now will be easier than walking away after one dinner."

"I have to know that I at least tried. I have to know that we can't work if I'm going to walk away."

"What if we can work?"

"Then we have to try."

"And what if we don't?" Nichole asked.

"Then at least we'd know, and we wouldn't have to look back on this moment and ever wonder. Please. Just one dinner."

Marlon kneeled down and reached for Nichole's hand. She didn't pull away, and when they touched, she nearly lost her breath. "Okay," she said. "One dinner."

CHAPTER 35

As Marlon drove to work, he tried not to think about his upcoming date with Nichole, but like anything that takes effort to drive from one's mind, it became impossible to purge himself of the anticipation. He was excited, and he stopped trying to pretend otherwise. It felt good to have something to look forward to.

Upon entering his classroom, he found Abigail sitting at her desk with her head down. There was a school assembly so Abigail didn't need to be in class for another hour. Marlon said as much as he walked to his desk and turned on his computer. Abigail didn't stir. She was either ignoring him or sleeping. Under different circumstances, Marlon probably would have just let the student sleep. There were often students who asked if they could hang out in Marlon's room until assemblies were over. They were usually the outcasts of the school who spent their days on the fringes of the student body just trying to get through high school so they could move on from such trivial bullshit as homecoming dances and overhyped sporting events. Marlon often developed a kinship with those students. They didn't know how to fake being fake. If they wanted a place to hide for an hour, he would provide it. It was the least he could do.

He couldn't extend that courtesy to Abigail though. They had a history. It wouldn't look right if the principal, or any other teacher, walked in and saw Marlon alone with Abigail. He called her name again, and again she ignored him. He pulled open his door shoved a jam under the lip. (If someone were to come in it would look better if the door wasn't closed.) He went to Abigail's desk.

"Abigail," he said, a little louder than a whisper. "Wake up. You need to go to the assembly."

Abigail moaned but kept her head down.

"Abigail, you can't be in here," Marlon said. He extended his hand to shake her gently but then thought it best if he didn't touch her. "Come on. Get up. You have to go." Marlon snapped his fingers next to Abigail's ear. She whimpered, and Marlon realized she wasn't sleeping; she was crying.

"What happened?" he asked.

Abigail slowly lifted her head. Her red eyes scanned the room, looking for fellow students. When she found none, she began sobbing harder.

Shit, Marlon thought. He went to his desk, grabbed a box of tissue and returned to her.

"Can I just stay here till class begins?" she asked.

"What happened?" he asked.

"Nothing."

Marlon sighed, trying to figure out the proper protocol for this situation. Should he act in the manner of secretive father or concerned teacher? "You can stay here if you tell me what happened."

"There's nothing to tell."

"Is it a guy?"

Abigail whimpered. Marlon shook his head. It's always a guy.

"What's his name?" he asked.

"It's no one."

"What did he do?"

"Nothing."

"Did he hurt you?"

"No…he…he…just…"

"What?"

"I'm so scared."

"What happened?"

Abigail shook her head. "Nothing. Forget I said anything."

Something woke in Marlon. It was either a father's anxiety or a teacher's frustration or something more potent than both. Suddenly Marlon was shaking Abigail and demanding the boy's name. Abigail sobbed harder and Marlon shook her more forcefully. "Tell me his name," he yelled. She fell limp in his hands.

"Tell me his name! What grade is he in?"

"He's not a student," Abigail mumbled.

Marlon stopped shaking her. "He's from a different school?"

"No."

"Then what do you mean?"

Abigail's lowered her head. Marlon shook her again, violently.

"What did he do to you? What happened?"

Abigail slowly lifted her head and looked at Marlon.

"I'm pregnant," she said.

Marlon stared hard at Abigail as her words, and what they meant, sank in. He released her and then slumped down in the desk to her right. He didn't say anything for a long time. Abigail continued crying. Marlon turned over in his head what this meant.

"Who's the father?" Marlon asked after a moment.

"My mom is going to kill me," Abigail said, ignoring Marlon's question.

"She won't kill you. She'll just…," Marlon began, but then realized he had nothing to offer by way of Nichole's reaction. "Who's the father?" he asked again.

"She already thinks I'm a screw-up. This is going to kill her."

"It'll be okay," Marlon said, but even he didn't know if he believed what he said.

"They'll probably kick me out of school."

"They won't kick…," Marlon began and then looked at Abigail suspiciously. "Why would they kick you out?"

Abigail whimpered.

Marlon started to put the pieces together. "Who is the father, Abigail?"

Abigail tried to put her head down on the desk without offering an answer, but Marlon was out of his seat and had her by the shoulders again, imploring her to tell him who it was. Every unanswered inquiry solidified what he feared was true. Still, he needed to hear it from her, and he wouldn't stop the brandishing until he did.

"Who is it?" he yelled. Abigail looked into Marlon's eyes; she was terrified. He was enraged. She trembled. Marlon tightened his grip. She winced and tried helplessly to free herself. Marlon wouldn't let go; he wouldn't let up. Defeated, Abigail looked to the ceiling and said: "Mr. Gibson."

Marlon released Abigail and dropped to his knees. He looked up at her one last time, clinging to the false hope that what she said wasn't true. But he knew she was telling the truth. He knew it was Mr. Gibson before she had even uttered his name. Marlon's thoughts drifted to Nichole and how alive he'd felt with her at the coffee shop. Then he thought of Howard and Karen and the life he came so close to living. He thought of all the decisions made, consciously or unconsciously, that led him to the current moment. He was tired of life. Tired of the obstacles that kept him from the things he pursued. Suddenly, a fire flared up inside of Marlon. He rose to his feet, stole a frightening glance at Abigail, and ran out the door.

A minute later, Marlon threw open Mr. Gibson's door. Mr. Gibson sat at his desk texting on his phone. Marlon quickly surveyed the classroom; it was empty. Mr. Gibson turned and looked at Marlon. He placed his phone on his desk and asked if Marlon needed anything. Marlon's chest heaved. Mr. Gibson stood and instinctively backed away, inadvertently putting himself into a corner. Marlon advanced toward Mr. Gibson, letting his anger navigate his course. He spotted a three-hole punch on Mr. Gibson's desk. He grabbed it. Mr. Gibson raised his hands in surrender.

"Marlon, I swear to god she—"

Marlon was on him. He hit him across the face with the hole punch and Mr. Gibson fell to the floor. Marlon stood over him and rained blows down on Mr. Gibson with the hole punch. Mr. Gibson cowered and covered his head, but retracted his hands when Marlon struck him hard on his wrists. Mr. Gibson screamed, and Marlon hit him across the face, knocking out a tooth and dislodging three others. Another blow split open his eye. Another opened his cheek. Marlon hit him repeatedly with the final blow fracturing Mr. Gibson's jaw.

Marlon stopped and gasped angrily and caught his breath. He looked down at Mr. Gibson. He was unrecognizable. He coughed and spat out a line of blood. Marlon looked at the bloody three-hole punch in his hand and dropped it. It clanged to the ground next to Mr. Gibson's feet. Marlon looked back at Mr. Gibson's disfigured face. He couldn't believe he had the capacity to inflict so much pain onto another human being. The sight made him sick. He leaned over a trashcan and vomited.

A thin, raspy voice told Marlon, "She wanted it."

Marlon looked at Mr. Gibson over the rim of the trashcan. "She's just a kid," Marlon said. Mr. Gibson coughed and a line of fresh blood landed on his shirt. Marlon stood up, wiped his mouth, and left the room.

CHAPTER 36

Abigail wasn't in Marlon's class when he returned. He sat at his desk. His hands were shaking. There were specks of Mr. Gibson's blood under his fingernails and in the lines surrounding his knuckles. He tried to chip away the red fragments, but couldn't control his hands enough for the task. He rushed to the bathroom and ran his hands under the sink's warm gushing water. He scrubbed furiously until the skin was red with irritation. He scrubbed and dug out the blood remnants and then, with contrite frustration, screamed. He yelled at the top of his lungs before collapsing to the floor under the deafening echo of his own cries and the flowing water. Marlon appraised his hands again before burying his face in them.

*****

Abigail wasn't at school the following day or the day after. Marlon thought to call—Nichole had given him her number at the coffee shop—but he couldn't settle on what to say. Besides, he had Nichole's cell phone number, not Abigail's.

He wondered if she told her mom. If Nichole didn't know, did Marlon have an obligation to tell her, either as a teacher or a potential relationship partner? If he didn't tell her, and she later learned he knew, how would she react? Would she understand why he didn't tell her, or would she be upset? Would she respect him more or appreciate him less if he kept her daughter's secret, secret? He wasn't sure of his role, so he did nothing. He went about his days as if nothing happened. He would react to the situation if it presented itself. He would go on his date as scheduled, and if Nichole knew of the pregnancy and accosted him, he would try his best to explain himself, and if she didn't, he wouldn't say a word about it.

Not surprisingly, Mr. Gibson took the rest of the week off. Marlon made innocuous inquiries as to his whereabouts, feigning some made-up concern, but all anyone revealed was that he was using sick leave. Faculty members surmised he was probably somewhere exotic. Living a fairytale life that he would inevitably upload to Facebook upon his return. Marlon doubted he would return anytime soon, not with the beating he inflicted. He would be out a month, at least. When he did eventually return, Marlon felt confident not even someone as foolish as Mr. Gibson would be stupid enough to go to the principal. He would have to explain *why* Marlon beat him. Sure, Marlon could lose his job for what he did, but so would Mr. Gibson. More importantly, in most circles Marlon would be a saint, defending the honor of a student who fell under the seductive spell of a brooding Teacher. Mr. Gibson would become a pariah, ridiculed for breaking the cardinal sin of teaching: Do not sleep with your students.

Nonetheless, *if* Mr. Gibson decided to tie his own noose and accuse Marlon of beating him, Marlon didn't want to be hauled away in front of his students. So he arrived at school early and waited for the principal to knock on his door with an officer in tow. But each morning, as the minutes crept closer to the start of the school day, Marlon knew he would live to teach another day.

Three days later Abigail returned to school. She knocked softly on Marlon's door and then entered. Marlon stood at the whiteboard writing the days' vocabulary words. He looked at the door expecting to find the principal and was surprised when he saw Abigail.

She wore sweat pants and a hooded sweatshirt, and she had her hair pulled back in a fraying ponytail. Her overdone makeup was applied haphazardly and with little uniformity. She looked sick and emaciated. Marlon studied her for a beat, unsure what to say. He felt a tinge of fatherly compassion, but more than anything, when he looked at Abigail he mostly felt frustrated with her youthful ignorance. She seemed to epitomize all the generic adolescent elements Marlon despised in his students. He capped his marker and sat in the nearest desk. Abigail sat down next to him. Neither spoke for a moment. The silence was thick with questions, but neither wanted to ask them. Abigail finally broke the silence.

"Mr. Gibson wasn't at school yesterday," Abigail said. "He isn't here today either." She looked at Marlon, but since a clear question wasn't asked, he remained silent.

"Do you know why he isn't at school?" Abigail asked.

"I beat him with a three-hole punch," Marlon said matter-of-factly.

"What?"

"I beat him with a three-hole punch," Marlon repeated robotically.

"Is he hurt?"

"Probably."

"Will you get in trouble?"

"I have no idea. If he tells what happened, he would have to explain why it happened. I doubt he wants to have that conversation."

"So what's going to happen between you two?"

"I don't know. I'm just waiting for him to make the first move."

Abigail lowered her head. "Sorry. I shouldn't have told you."

"You should go to the principal."

"Why?"

"Because Mr. Gibson should lose his job."

"But won't they fire you for beating him if I tell?"

"Probably."

"I don't want you to lose your job."

"I'll find another one."

"I don't want people to know. They'll probably kick me out of school. I don't want my mom to know what happened. I don't want Mr. Gibson to know either."

Marlon turned to her. "He doesn't know you're pregnant?"

"No. Only you know."

"Jesus."

"Are you going to tell on me?" Abigail asked.

Marlon rubbed his eyes. "No. This is your problem."

Abigail nodded. "Can I ask you something?"

Marlon remained silent; Abigail took his silence to mean yes.

"Do you think abortion is wrong?" she asked

"Are you considering one?"

"It's the only way I can fix this without anyone knowing."

Marlon exhaled deeply. He looked at Abigail. "I want to ask you something, and I want you to be honest with me. I won't judge you no matter the answer, but I must know the truth."

"Okay."

"Did Mr. Gibson force you?" Marlon asked.

"Force me?"

"Yeah. If he forced you, then…well…this would look different."

"You think I should say he raped me?"

Marlon looked hard at her. "Only if he did. Only if that's the truth." Marlon waited a moment. "Did he?"

Abigail lowered her head. "No. He didn't."

"You're sure?" Marlon asked. "He didn't…seduce you or coerce you in any—"

"No," Abigail interrupted him. "I knew what I was doing."

Marlon shook his head and stood. He paced the room and then returned to the desk. "Why, Abby?" Marlon asked. The use of her shortened name felt strange to him, almost intimate. He wished he hadn't said it. Abigail noticed it, too. She thought it sounded natural. She actually felt touched with the familiarity he displayed. "Why do you do these things?" he asked, mindfully leaving her name out of the inquiry.

"I don't…," she began but trailed off.

"Your actions have consequences."

"I know, but…"

"But what?"

Abigail swallowed hard. "It's the only thing I'm good at."

"What?"

"Sex," she said. "It's the only thing I know how to do right."

"Jesus, Abby. You're seventeen years old," Marlon said incredulously.

"I know," she whispered.

"How do you know you're good at it?" he asked, and then thought better of it and said, "Don't answer that."

"So is it wrong?" Abigail asked. "Abortion?"

"It doesn't matter what I think," Marlon said.

"It does to me," Abigail said.

Marlon considered the question. "As a man, I don't feel it's my place to tell a woman what she can or cannot do with her body."

"So you're pro-choice?"

"Abigail…"

"Well, what about the life of the child?"

Marlon thought for a moment, evaluating the best approach. "Look, all women seeking an abortion have one thing in common, right? For whatever reason, they don't want the child. If a child isn't wanted, then I think the bigger sin is forcing the woman to have it."

"Do you think it's murder?"

"I can't answer that for you."

"They say the heart starts beating at five weeks. If I do it before then, it wouldn't be murder, right?"

"It depends on when you think life begins."

"When do you think it begins?"

"It doesn't matter what I think."

"Can you please just give me a straight answer?" Abigail said. "I need to know what you think."

"I think you should tell your mom," Marlon said evenly.

"I can't. I've already disappointed her enough."

"She needs to know."

"No, she doesn't. I can't put her through that."

Marlon stood and paced the room again. He stopped every few steps, turned to Abigail and opened his mouth to speak, but then thought better of it and resumed pacing.

"If I can just get an abortion," Abigail explained, "I can put this all behind me and no one gets hurt."

"The thing is," Marlon said, still pacing the room, "in the state of Utah you need parental consent to have an abortion."

"What?"

Marlon stopped in front of Abigail. "You have to tell your mom." The words drifted to Abigail, planted themselves, and she began crying.

"I'm so stupid. I'm so fucking stupid."

Marlon kneeled next to her and gingerly put his hand on her shoulder. "It's okay. We'll...we'll figure it out."

"How?" Abigail cried. "We moved out here because I messed around with a teacher in Vegas. I keep making the same stupid mistakes."

Abigail cried harder. Instinctively, Marlon hugged her. She wrapped her arms around him and sobbed into his chest. Marlon held her tight. He didn't care if someone were to walk in and see them together. On the surface, holding her may appear inappropriate, but below the superficial, he was simply a father comforting his daughter.

A thought struck Marlon. "What if I said I was your father?" he said before he could process what the suggestion entailed.

Abigail let go of Marlon and looked at him. "What?"

Marlon wished he could rescind the idea, but the sudden optimism in Abigail's face compelled him to repeat his suggestion.

"What if I said I was your father? I could give consent."

"You would do that? You would lie for me?"

Marlon weighed the absurdity of her words. "If this is what you want, I'll help you."

"I don't want it, but what other choice do I have?"

"You know your options."

"I just want it over with. I want to move on and put this behind me."

"If that's what you want, I'll give consent."

Marlon had read enough bad high school essays, and did the due diligence his students didn't, to know the laws regarding abortion. In Utah, if the pregnant person is under eighteen, one parent had to give permission. Additionally, said parent needed to know about the procedure at least twenty-four hours in advance. Sometimes, but rarely, a judge could rule that a parent need not be notified (in cases of rape, incest, of some other atrocious scenario), but that took time and, in some cases, lawyers. Time and legal fees were two things Abigail didn't have.

"I'll go to the clinic with you and tell them I'm your father," Marlon said. "Have you been to a doctor?"

"No."

"You need to see a doctor. There is a medical clinic down the road. They accept walk-ins. It will cost you thirty dollars. Do you have thirty dollars?"

"Yeah."

"A doctor needs to confirm the pregnancy and then be informed that you wish to have an abortion. He'll tell you that a parent needs to consent. Tell him you've already talked to your father. The sooner you inform a doctor, the better. There is a forty-eight hour waiting period in Utah."

"When can we do it?" Abigail asked. "It has to be soon."

Marlon thought for a moment. "In three days. Saturday afternoon. We'll meet in the parking lot. You'll follow me in your car."

Abigail nodded slowly. "Only do this if it's what you really want, Abigail," Marlon said.

"I do," she said softly. "Thanks, Mr. Brown."

Marlon looked at Abigail, unsure if he was doing the right thing.

CHAPTER 37

Abigail did as she was told. She went to the clinic, paid her thirty
dollars, and saw a doctor. He confirmed the pregnancy. She told
him she wanted an abortion, and he explained that a parent needed to
give consent.

"I already told my father," she said. "He gave me
permission. He's going with me."

"Well, then," the doctor said curtly, scribbling something on
his chart, "you can both answer for your actions in the next life." He
walked out of the room before Abigail could defend herself. She got
dressed and tried not to cry.

The nearest abortion clinic was seventeen miles from the
high school. Marlon told Abigail to follow him to a gas station just
off the freeway, and they could ride the rest of the way together.
They didn't say more than two words to one another during the
seventeen-mile drive. It wasn't an uncomfortable silence, just one
that didn't need to be filled with banal conversation. Besides, there
really isn't much to talk about on a drive to an abortion clinic.

Abigail brought a blanket and sat wrapped in it, hugging her knees to her chest. She looked like a child doing everything in her power to keep from growing up. She stared out the window and watched the city pass. Trees, pedestrians, glass office buildings all blended into one long, muted color. Everything a blur, like a life that went unappreciated because it was lived too quickly.

Marlon looked over at Abigail every so often, but his own concerns kept his mind occupied. In five hours he was meeting Nichole for dinner. He wondered how Abigail would react if she knew about Marlon's date. Would she feel betrayed? Probably not any more than Nichole if she learned that Marlon drove her daughter to an abortion clinic. Marlon believed telling Abigail was the right thing to do; he just couldn't find the right time. It seemed impossible to squeeze it in between forging parental consent forms and commutes to the abortionist. Besides, shouldn't it be Nichole's responsibility to tell her daughter that she was going out with one of her teachers? Marlon feared Nichole wanted to keep him a secret because she knew their first date would never turn into a second.

Nichole amplified this fear when Marlon offered to pick her up at home, but Nichole insisted they meet at the restaurant instead.

The one thing Marlon liked about himself and his life was its simplicity. He answered to no one. He never had to defend his actions or worry about the consequences. Ever since Abigail walked into his summer school class, the simplicity Marlon used to revere dashed. Common sense told him to leave Nichole and her promiscuous daughter alone. And yet here he was. Speeding past mile markers so his accidental daughter could terminate her pregnancy. A month ago he would have spent his Saturday going through his Netflix queue, trying to make sense of Charlie Kaufman films and the popularity of Michael Bay. Now he starred in his own Greek tragedy.

Marlon pulled into the clinic's parking lot and shut off his car. He thought he heard Abigail whimper, but he wasn't certain. He looked over at her; she clutched her blanket tighter and looked out the window.

"You okay?" Marlon asked.

"What time is the appointment?"

"Two o'clock."

"What time is it now?"

"Ten minutes to two."

There were only two other cars in the parking lot. One was a minivan. On the back window where family stickers—a father, mother, and six kids punctuated by a dog. Marlon wondered what a minivan that advertised its posterity was doing at an abortion clinic. He thought to share the insight with Abigail but figured it was in poor taste.

Abigail studied the building's entrance. It was simple. Just a plate glass door with a metal handle and the words "Utah Medical Clinic" stenciled at eye level in white, nondescript letters. Abigail spied the door and watched as a young guy and girl exited the clinic. They couldn't have been much older than Abigail. The girl wore a heavy winter coat and clutched the folds tight to her body. The boy held the door open for the girl and then struggled to keep up as she walked briskly from the clinic. She kept her head lowered, trying to stifle the brisk air that squeezed tears from her eyes. The boy raced to her and put a consoling hand on her back. Even from her distance, Abigail could see the girl's body stiffen at the man's touch. They disappeared behind a neighboring building. Marlon watched Abigail watching the couple.

"Look, Abigail, there's something I think you should know."

Abigail turned and faced Marlon, grateful for the momentary reprieve from the thoughts cluttering her mind. Marlon studied Abigail. Her eyes were red and her skin pale. She looked pure. Innocent. It was an odd realization, but as she stared back at Marlon, he realized this was the first time he had ever seen her without makeup. She looked better without it. She was naturally beautiful, just like her mother. Marlon wished he could feel proud for having a part in her creation, but he wasn't sure if he had yet earned the right. If he felt pride because of her beauty, should he feel shame for her decision-making? Parenting seemed to be a series of contradictions.

"What is it?" Abigail asked.

"I have a date with your mother tonight," Marlon said. "I feel like you have a right to know."

"What?" Abigail asked. She didn't seem shocked or surprised or angry. Her inquiry was just that: a simple question that wanted further explanation.

"A few days ago we ran into each other at a coffee shop. It was purely coincidental."

"And then what? You just asked her out?"

"Well, we talked for a minute, and…well, we got along really well and then, yeah, I asked if she would like to get dinner with me." Marlon waited for Abigail's reaction, but she seemed entirely indifferent. "I'm guessing she hasn't told you?"

"No. We don't really talk much anymore."

"Are you okay with me going out with her?"

Abigail thought for a moment, but couldn't come to a consensus. "I don't know."

"If you're not comfortable with it, I'll call and cancel." Marlon wasn't sure why he said this. No part of him wanted to cancel.

"You haven't told her about me, have you? About this?"

"No. And I won't. I swear this will always stay between us."

"How do I know I can trust you?"

"You don't."

"If she knew you helped with this, she'd probably never talk to you again."

"I know," Marlon said softly.

"So why are you doing this for me?"

"I guess I feel like…I owe you something."

"Because of what happened before?"

"Sure," Marlon said, but it had nothing to do with what happened before. Marlon spent nearly eighteen years not being a father. He figured somehow, this made up for some lost time. "I do think you should tell your mom, though," Marlon said. "I think she would be more understanding than you think."

"What do you think she would say?"

"I…don't know, but when I had coffee with her, you were all she talked about. You're everything to her. I know it's hard to see because you're so close to it, but one day you'll realize how much you mean to her and how much she has given you."

Abigail looked away and softly cried. Marlon let her cry. She needed it; it was her catharsis. After a moment, she wiped her eyes and turned back to Marlon. He reached across her, opened his glove box, and handed her some tissue.

"Wow," she said. "Isn't it going to be weird going out with my mom?" She laughed softly, finding a sliver of humor in the course her life had taken.

"It will be…different. The rational part of me thinks I should cancel."

"Is that what you want?"

Marlon thought for a moment. "No."

"Then you shouldn't cancel. I'm okay with you going out with my mom."

Marlon smiled weakly.

"What time is it?" Abigail asked.

Marlon looked at his watch. "Exactly two o'clock."

Abigail pulled her blanket tighter. "We should probably go in, huh?"

"Only if you want to."

Abigail didn't move. "Do you think she's pretty?" Abigail asked.

"Who?"

"My mom."

"Yeah, I do. I think she's beautiful."

"Most guys she goes out with don't get a second date."

"Do you think I'm like most guys?"

"I don't know. I haven't pegged you yet. When I first met you, I thought you were a prick. Then you were kind of sweet and then…," she trailed off, leaving the thought unsaid.

"And now?"

"Understanding," Abigail said. "My mom deserves to be happy. I think you could make her happy."

The compliment touched Marlon. He wanted to hug Abigail, thank her for seeing some good in him. Ever since Karen had left, he wasn't sure if there was any. For so long he had relegated himself to nothing more than just another consumer, buying things to survive so long as he maintained the capacity to keep his heart beating and his lungs filled with air. He existed, but he didn't live. Maybe now he could start.

"Can I ask you something?" Abigail asked. She stared out the window at the clinic's entrance.

"Of course."

"Do you think I'm a slut?"

Marlon thought carefully. "Describe a slut."

"Someone that sleeps around."

"Is that you?"

Abigail attempted to answer, but couldn't. Some things that are hard to say can't be said.

"I think you think too little of yourself, so you give yourself to people who don't deserve you," Marlon said.

Abigail dabbed at the corners of her eyes with the tissue. "That's just a nice way of saying I'm a slut," she said.

"No. I meant what I said exactly the way I said it."

"Mr. Gibson said such nice things to me."

Marlon's stomach tightened at the mention of Mr. Gibson. He clenched his jaw.

"I thought maybe he meant them," Abigail said.

"There are some really great men in the world, Abigail. Mr. Gibson isn't one of them. Don't mistake flattery for sincerity."

"I'm going to change," Abigail said.

"I hope you do."

"I don't like being the way that I am."

"It takes courage to admit that," Marlon said.

Abigail wiped her eyes. "What time is it?"

"Five after two."

"Will they get mad if we're late?"

"No."

"What if you and my mom fall in love and get married? How crazy would that be?"

"Let's see how the first date goes before we start talking about marriage."

"My mom has never been married. She's too picky."

"She should be. More people should be like her."

"Yeah, maybe," Abigail said. She seemed distant. "What time is it now?"

"Six after two."

"They're probably waiting for us, huh?"

"Let them wait."

Abigail kept her eyes locked on the clinic's door. She loosened her hold on her blanket, and it fell from her shoulders. She folded her arms across her stomach and breathed deeply. Her stomach growled from hunger. She quickly removed it thinking if she was hungry, the baby growing inside her must be too.

"What time is it now?"

"Seven after two."

"Is there a cancellation fee?"

"No. Do you want to cancel?"

"No. I don't know. No."

Silence.

"Okay. I think I'm ready," Abigail said. She put a trembling hand on the door handle and looked at Marlon. "Are you ready?"

"Only if you are."

Abigail willed herself to pull the door open, but couldn't bring herself to do so.

"Are you okay?" Marlon asked.

"Yeah, just give me a minute."

Another hunger pain seized her. She dropped her hand from the door and placed it back on her stomach. She pressed down hard on her abdomen, surveying it, trying to determine if the pain she was from hunger or something…else. She looked back at the clinic's entrance and once again grabbed the door handle.

"I think I may be hungry."

"Do you want to get something to eat?"

"Right now?"

"Whenever you want."

"Maybe after?"

"Whatever you want, Abigail."

"What time is it now?"

Marlon answered.

She sighed. Waited a minute. Tried to open the door. Couldn't. She turned back to Marlon. "I'm so scared," she said, her voice breaking.

"What do you need?" Marlon asked.

"I don't...I don't know," she cried.

Understanding dawned on Marlon. He nodded. He pulled his phone from his pocket, looked at Abigail, and then dialed the number. She picked up after the third ring. Marlon spoke into the phone. "Hey, it's Marlon. There's someone here that needs to talk to you." Marlon handed the phone to Abigail. She slowly took the phone, her hands shaking, and held it to her ear.

"Mommy?" she asked hopefully.

"Abby? Baby, what is it?"

Abigail broke into fresh sobs. "Mommy...mommy, I need you."